DEATH
IN A
SCOTTISH
CASTLE

BOOKS BY LYDIA TRAVERS

DEATH
IN A
SCOTTISH
CASTLE

LYDIA TRAVERS

bookouture

Published by Bookouture in 2024

An imprint of Storyfire Ltd.
Carmelite House
50 Victoria Embankment
London EC4Y 0DZ

www.bookouture.com

ISBN: 978-1-83525-775-3
eBook ISBN: 978-1-83525-774-6

To my brother-in-law, Barry

ONE

Edinburgh
September, 1912

Maud finished reading the letter, dropping the sheets written in a confident masculine hand onto the desk as she sat back in her chair. She brushed an imaginary speck of fluff from the sleeve of her white, high-necked blouse and tucked a lock of fair hair, which had escaped from its low bun, behind one ear.

'Who's the letter from?' Daisy, her assistant and friend, asked as she flicked a duster over the shelf of reference books in the agency's tiny office.

'Lord Urquhart.'

Daisy raised an auburn eyebrow. 'What guddle has his lordship got himself into now?'

Maud knew that Daisy was referring to the first time they had set eyes on Lord Urquhart. Last summer, he'd strolled into Maud's newly-established detective agency in George Street, Edinburgh, discovered it was run by two females and had promptly removed himself. Six days later, he'd returned and admitted his need of their services. They had retrieved his indiscreet letters with no harm done to anything but his pride, so she and Daisy had enjoyed the last laugh.

'He tells me he is staying at a castle near Tobermory on the Isle of Mull – as usual doing nothing, while you and I *work* for our living. It appears that a rather expensive statuette has been stolen.'

'A pilfered fancy ornament?' With her free hand, Daisy straightened the belt on her long, chestnut-brown skirt. 'It doesna sound like our sort of case.'

'What is our sort of case, Daisy? We've had everything from stolen dogs—'

'Only the one dog.'

Maud steepled her fingers. 'There was that Pekinese you kidnapped from its owner...'

'That's nae fair, Maud! Ye ken I thought the dog was wee Maximilian, the one we'd been hired to find. And I handed the pooch back as soon as I realised my mistake.'

Maud dropped her hands and laughed. 'I know, Daisy. I was only teasing.'

Mollified, Daisy put away the duster and slid into her seat at the desk they shared.

'Still, the truth is,' Maud went on, 'we've had cases ranging from a stolen dog to cold-blooded murder. I think we can accept the investigation of a missing statuette, especially since there isn't a queue of people in need of our services stretching down the stairs and into the street.'

Daisy smirked. 'I suppose it helps a wee bit that it's his handsome lordship who has asked you. Do you think the case is real, or could this be some ruse to bring you into his company again?'

Maud allowed the edge of her lips to twitch. 'That's a ridiculous suggestion, Daisy. No, stop laughing.' Maud laughed out loud herself before adding, 'Although I can't deny that it is pleasing to have Lord Urquhart request the help of the M.

McIntyre Agency. He is the first client who has come back with a new case.' Her voice held a note of satisfaction.

'But seriously, Maud, isna Mull a long way to go just to investigate a stolen knick-knack?'

'There is no other agency like ours, Daisy; remember that. Plus, it's an expensive object cast in bronze, not just some *trinket*. Naturally, Lord Urquhart will be paying our expenses to an island neither of us has ever visited; a few days out of the city will be a welcome change. And let us not forget our fee. After all, a business is built on money, Daisy.'

Daisy pulled her notebook towards her, opened it at the first clean page and uncapped her fountain pen. 'So, what do we ken about the case?'

'It's the figure of a lion,' Maud said, looking down at the letter on her desk. 'Some six inches high, on a base of approximately the same size.'

'Easy to put in a pocket?' Daisy asked as she wrote.

'It must weigh too much for that. But easy enough to carry.'

Daisy frowned and looked up. 'Why is it Lord Urquhart asking us to investigate and not the owner of the bronze beast?'

'It seems that he, Lord Urquhart, doesn't know the owner – Magnus Carmichael – terribly well. He's staying at the castle as he's interested in purchasing the statuette, which Mr Carmichael was considering selling—'

'Aha! So Mr Carmichael suspects his esteemed guest has pinched it rather than paid for it, but hasna actually said as much?'

'That's about it, my friend. His host hasn't accused him outright, but Lord Urquhart feels decidedly uncomfortable with his position there. He is still interested in the statuette, and he cannot leave now that it's gone missing, as that would appear to confirm his host's suspicion.'

'Why doesna his host' – Daisy paused to glance down at her notes – 'Magnus Carmichael get the police to investigate?'

'Accuse a man of Lord Urquhart's standing, Daisy? No gentleman would do such a thing. Better to lose the item than to cause a scandal and tarnish both of their reputations.'

'God forbid tarnishing of reputations should happen in polite society,' said Daisy with a grin, putting on her best Morningside accent.

Maud smiled, recognising a perfect rendition of her own speech pattern coming from her friend's mouth. Having left service as a maid over a year ago, Daisy would now be able to pass for a lady, Maud was sure. 'And anyway, Lord Urquhart believes one of the other guests, a Mr Neil Tremain, is the guilty party and he would like us to recover—'

'Steal back?'

'*Return* the object to its owner,' Maud said firmly. 'That way, embarrassment can be avoided all round.'

Daisy replaced the cap on her pen. 'When do we leave?'

'I thought first thing in the morning, assuming we can book accommodation for a night midway on our journey.' Maud smiled. 'Oh, and Lord Urquhart also told me that Mr Carmichael is an admirer of crime novels, so he suggests the best way to receive an invitation to the castle without raising suspicion would be if I travel as a crime novelist, with you as my secretary. What do you think?'

'It willna be much of a disguise, but,' Daisy said, her eyes shining, 'if it helps to get us inside that castle, then it's a braw idea!'

After breakfast the following morning, Maud and Daisy strapped their suitcases to the back of her motor car and climbed into the front seats, leaving the hood down the better to enjoy the views as they drove. They each tied on their hats with a motor scarf and set off.

The Napier Colonial Tourer was painted in gold, an ostentatious colour Maud would not have chosen but for two reasons. It had been the only motor car for sale in the horse and carriage repository, and the need to hasten back to Ballater where she and Daisy were working on a case.

The Tourer's paintwork flashed in the warm autumn sunshine as they left Edinburgh and began the long journey north-west to the Hebrides. The villages outside the capital gave way to forests, then to wild moorland and distant snow-topped mountains. In Dunfermline, they stopped for luncheon in a busy refreshment room in the shadow of the abbey.

'There is so much wonderful history here, Daisy,' Maud said. 'I wonder if we have time—'

'I dinna think so, Maud.'

Maud sighed and took the menu Daisy handed to her. 'I believe you're right. But many Scottish royals, including St Margaret and Robert the Bruce, are buried in Dunfermline Abbey. And it's the birthplace of Charles I.'

'That's all very interesting,' said Daisy. 'But I think I'll have the pigeon pie. What about you?'

Maud suppressed a smile. Daisy was an ardent monarchist, but history was not a topic of interest to her; food, however, was. 'Good idea. Let's order two portions.'

Their orders placed, the two friends settled themselves comfortably.

'You know, Daisy,' Maud began, 'my fictional detective will need a name, and I will need a nom de plume, a pen name.' Maud sipped her water.

'Och, let me think.' Daisy toyed with her cutlery. 'What about Gridley Quayle for your detective?'

'Gridley Quayle!' Maud almost choked. 'Whatever made you think of such a name?'

'Nae idea, it just came to me.'

'It's a good one.' Maud patted her lips with her linen napkin. 'But I would prefer a female detective, so I will call her

Gertrude Quayle. And I'll be Maisie Smart. Maisie because it is an amalgamation of Maud and Daisy...'

'And Smart because she is!' Daisy beamed.

'Exactly.' Maud smiled. 'You will also need a cover name, Daisy.'

'That's easy. I've always fancied myself as a Lucy. And Graham, as that was my mither's maiden name.'

Maud nodded. 'Miss Maisie Smart will be on Mull seeking inspiration for her next novel, with her trusted secretary and confidant Miss Lucy Graham.'

Daisy smiled as the waitress appeared, set down their portions of pigeon pie and departed. 'How many books has Miss Smart written?' Daisy asked, picking up her knife and fork.

'Only two,' Maud said, 'and they have been only moderately successful, otherwise Mr Carmichael might wonder why he hasn't heard of Gertrude Quayle, detective extraordinaire.'

As they ate, Maud gave her attention to the titles Maisie Smart had written. *Mischief in Midlothian* had had a certain ring to it. And perhaps *Havoc in the Highlands*. For her current book, she had in mind *Trouble in Tobermory*. Yes, that would do well.

Luncheon finished, they climbed into the motor car and continued their journey, stopping only to buy a can of petrol from the display of goods outside a chemist shop.

The landscape gradually changed from green to autumn gold and brown. After a while, the mist came down on the narrow winding roads, making the blind summits even more precarious. It was with some relief they finally reached the bustling little village of Pitlochry, basking in the early evening sunshine. Maud admired the many handsome Victorian build-ings on the main street and the unusual cast-iron canopy over one side of the pavement.

'There's the place you asked me to book us in for the night.'

Daisy pointed to a substantial building on the corner of the road.

Maud drew the Napier to a halt in front of Fisher's Hotel, parked and untied the silk scarf securing her hat. Daisy paled a little as she stared up at the grand entrance to the hotel.

Maud alighted. 'Modest evening gowns to be worn at dinner this evening, Daisy. And we shouldn't be late to bed. It's some sixty miles to the Corran Ferry, so we'll meet in the dining room tomorrow morning at eight o'clock sharp, if that is agreeable to you.'

Daisy reached up and untied her motoring scarf. 'Seven would be better. We might come across a hold-up or two.'

'Seven it is, then.'

The following morning, after a few *pliés, dégagés* and a *rond de jambe* to maintain her fitness, plus a respectable number of Indian club swings, Maud had dressed, taking her cue from the novelist Miss Taft. She and Daisy had met the woman at Duddingston House when investigating a jewel robbery and murder. Miss Taft, admittedly a romance novelist and therefore given to flights of fancy, had worn costumes of particularly eye-catching colours and styles. Maud had kept that in mind when hastily shopping in Jenners for her outfit.

She now sat in the driver's seat of her Napier, wearing a pale yellow dress, its tunic with a fluted hem at hip length, and a matching cloak of yellow silk with black lining. On her fair hair, swept up into a full pompadour, she had pinned an eye-catching hat. Black and excessively large with a single black feather, it was an import from France by a new designer named Gabrielle Chanel.

Daisy came out of the hotel. As befitting her status as secretary, she wore a high-necked cream blouse and plain brown skirt, her red hair in single side swirl under a small felt toque.

She slid into the passenger seat and smiled at her friend. 'Stylish that hat may be, Maud, but you need to tie it down or we'll be forever stopping to chase after it.'

Before long, the pair were on their way, passing deep blue lochs and ancient forests, gurgling burns and snow-capped mountains. Nature at its finest, Maud thought with a soft sigh. Before mid-morning, some ten miles beyond Fort William, they reached the Corran Ferry at Nether Lochaber. Maud positioned her motor car on the slipway and waited for the boat to heave into sight. Rising from the smokestack into the blue sky, a plume blown sideways by the wind signalled its approach and, before long, the small ferry appeared round the headland. It reached the slipway, docked, and the handful of foot passengers disembarked.

The weather-beaten skipper strode down the gangway. 'All aboard, ladies!' he called.

Maud took a breath. 'Here goes, Daisy.' She drove cautiously on to the deck, relieved that they were the only passengers.

Within minutes, the skipper and his elderly crewman had secured the Tourer with straps, and Maud paid their fare. She and Daisy remained seated in the motor car as the boat chugged across the loch, the sun on the rippling water, Maud enjoying the breeze on her face.

Daisy looked pale and grim. 'I think I'm going to boke.' She held tight to the side of the motor car as it bobbed from side to side on the deck.

'It's a short crossing, miss,' said the crewman, taking pity on her. 'Just keep your eye on the lighthouse on the other side. That's where we're heading.'

Within a few minutes, to Daisy's obvious relief, they arrived at Ardgour on the opposite bank. The crewman cranked up Maud's motor car with the starting handle, handed it to her and she drove off the ferry.

'Next stop in thirty miles,' Maud announced, putting her foot down on the pedal.

'Then we'll be on Mull?' asked Daisy, holding on to her hat at the sudden acceleration.

'Not quite... From Lochaline we need to take a second ferry.'

Daisy groaned. 'I'm nae sure my stomach can manage another loch crossing...'

'Sorry, Daisy, but the next stretch of water is part of the Atlantic Ocean, which means it will possibly roll a little more.' Maud glanced over at Daisy. Seeing her friend's horrified face, she added quickly, 'But it does mean we'll have reached Tobermory.'

TWO

The Lochaline to Tobermory ferry approached the island's capital. Fishing smacks with their sails furled and a small tramp steamer lay at anchor in the sheltered bay. A row of houses painted in ochre yellow, vivid blue and rose pink lined the main street, curving round the harbour and rising into the hillside.

Before Maud could look for Lord Urquhart and his host on the sea wall as arranged, the cheeky-faced young crewman cried, 'Hold on to your hats, ladies!'

They didn't need to be told twice. Maud checked the silk scarf securing Maisie Smart's elaborate hat, while Daisy gripped the side of the motor car, her hat be damned. With a grin, the man set to pushing the handle on the deck's turntable and the Tourer began to turn.

'Crivvens!' Daisy exclaimed. 'First we're tossed up and down and from side to side, and now we're being spun round.'

The ferry slowed, turning with a churn of water to enter the harbour. The turntable came to a halt, leaving their motor car facing forward, as the skipper brought the ferry to rest, dipping and rising with the slight swell, beside the quay. The crewman cranked up the Napier, then took hold of the thick rope, jumped lightly onto the pier and threw it around a bollard. He stood back, and as Maud bumped off the gangplank, spots of sea spray tickling her cheek and herring gulls wheeling and shrieking a welcome, he gave them a grin and a salute.

Daisy waved back as they drove away. 'The wee hempie,' she said, with a grin of her own, her face returning to its normal healthy colour.

'Daisy, look!' Maud drew her attention to two gentlemen on the sunlit seawall. 'There is Lord Urquhart.' Looking as impossibly handsome as ever, she thought. Her pulse jumped and her cheeks grew warm.

The last time they had met was when she and Daisy, with the members of the Fort William choir, had dined with the King and Queen at Holyrood Palace. Lord Urquhart had also been invited and he'd been amiable, amusing, attentive even... Maud pushed the memory away. She was here on a case and must not be distracted by the frivolous Lord Urquhart.

'I suspect that older man is Magnus Carmichael,' Maud went on. 'Remember, Daisy, that Lord Urquhart is unknown to Maisie Smart and Lucy Graham. We'll pull over near them and pretend we are in need of directions.'

Maud drove round crab pots, parked and climbed out of the Tourer. She took the map Daisy handed to her and opened it, spreading it out on the bonnet, the paper flapping in the breeze. Out of the corner of her eye she saw the two gentlemen walk towards her as she twisted the map around the right way and looked for a street sign.

She resolved to ignore the fluttering in her stomach at the sight of Lord Urquhart's impressive frame in his tweed suit. He had the dark hair and eyes of many Highlanders, but he would never blend in with the men who were working or idling at the harbour. For a start, he was easily the tallest there. Secondly, his manner and easy grace proclaimed him a man of some authority and social standing.

'Good morning, madam.'

Maud turned towards the voice. 'Good morning.' She addressed the elderly gentleman who had spoken. Lord Urquhart's companion had long white hair with a matching beard. He wore a tweed jacket and the blue and green – now faded – tartan of the Carmichael clan.

She glanced at Lord Urquhart to include him in her reply and observed again his finely chiselled features. He raised his tweed cap, the sun glinting on his dark hair, before quirking an appreciative eyebrow at Maud's outrageous costume, and smiled.

'We were taking a stroll before luncheon,' the elderly man continued, 'when we observed your delightful Napier Tourer arriving on the ferry. I do hope you will forgive us, but both the motor car and the turntable are such fascinating mechanisms, we could not resist. But, there, I go on about nothing you ladies would be interested in.'

Maud smiled. Both she and Daisy had been under the bonnet of the Napier more than once to check the oil and top up the radiator, and knew how to change a tyre if need be.

'You ladies appear to be lost,' he went on with a smile. 'Can we help in any way?'

Then Lord Urquhart spoke, his deep voice sending a thrill down Maud's spine. 'Perhaps we should introduce ourselves, Magnus.'

'Of course, of course. I am Magnus Carmichael and this gentleman is Lord Hamish Urquhart, my house guest.'

Maud inclined her head. 'I am Miss Maisie Smart and this lady is my secretary Miss Lucy Graham.'

Lord Urquhart frowned in a credible manner. 'Miss Smart? I feel I know that name...'

Maud gave a demure smile.

'Miss Smart writes books,' chimed in Daisy, climbing out of the car.

'Miss Maisie Smart... Yes, that's it! I read a feature on you in *Tatler*.'

How convincingly Lord Urquhart lies, Maud thought.

'Good heavens, Magnus,' Lord Urquhart went on, turning to his host, 'this lady is a crime novelist.'

'A writer of crime novels!' A beam spread across Mr Carmichael's thin face. 'Tell me, who is your detective? I must have heard of him, for mystery stories are my favourite reading.'

'My private investigator is a *lady*, Mr Carmichael. Gertrude Quayle. Perhaps you have read one of my books. *Mischief in Midlothian*?' suggested Maud. 'Or *Havoc in the Highlands*?'

The older man hesitated, clearly too embarrassed to admit he had not. 'No, but now we have met, I must correct that oversight.'

'Magnus,' Lord Urquhart intervened, to Maud's relief, 'we cannot leave these ladies standing about.' He nodded at the map and addressed them. 'Where are you bound?'

'We need somewhere to stay for the next few days while Miss Smart conducts research for her new novel,' Daisy said in her business voice, making a small adjustment to her hat. 'I was assured there was such a place but was unable to track down a telephone number to make a booking.'

'I regret that the telephone service has not yet reached the Hebrides,' Magnus told her.

'Then it would be most helpful if you could direct us to a hotel suitable for young ladies.'

Lord Urquhart considered. 'It's still the holiday season, so I'm not sure...'

'Wait! I have the very thing!' Mr Carmichael exclaimed. 'You must allow me to provide hospitality.'

Daisy smiled demurely. 'We couldn't possibly take advantage.'

'I must insist. I have a small number of friends staying at the castle at present and my sister is acting as hostess, so you need have no fear about propriety. Do please say you will join us. A real-life authoress in the castle, eh, Hamish?'

'It would certainly make us a lively group, Magnus.'

'Och, well, thanks very much,' said Daisy.

Maud gave a little cough to distract from Daisy's slip out of character and smiled at her host.

'Clachan Castle.' Magnus Carmichael, seated beside Maud in the Tourer, gestured to the tower rising above the conifers and a flagpole with the Carmichael colours flying. 'Clachan means stone. It's been home to generations of my family.' He gave a contented sigh.

Daisy leaned forward from the back seat as Maud turned between the lichen-covered pillars and drove down the winding avenue. As the trees thinned, smooth lawns appeared before the castle, which basked in the autumn sunshine. Maud came to a halt in front of the stone tower house and Lord Urquhart parked his cream Sunbeam beside her.

Magnus Carmichael bid the ladies leave their cases and escorted Maud through the open front door and into the lobby, with Daisy and Lord Urquhart bringing up the rear. Magnus tossed his bonnet onto the table as he walked by and led them up a short flight of stairs into the great hall, calling for Finlay and Grace as he went. Maud let her gaze wander over the vaulted ceiling, the high, narrow windows of stained glass and the blaze in the hearth. No matter how warm it was outside, it was chilly inside the thick stone walls of a castle.

The manservant, Finlay, appeared and was despatched to fetch their luggage. The housekeeper, Grace, a small round woman with rosy cheeks and quick steps, speaking in the soft accent of the Highlands, showed Maud and Daisy to guest bedrooms on the second floor.

'I'm afraid the rooms aren't quite ready as we weren't expecting visitors, but Isobel will light the fires and bring up hot water for washing.'

'I'm sorry we are putting you to so much trouble,' Maud said.

'Not at all!' The housekeeper smiled. 'It's a pleasure to have you both staying.'

A flustered young maid, perhaps fifteen, scurried up the stone spiral staircase behind them and hastened into Maud's room. She knelt in front of the hearth and began to lay the fire.

'I hope you'll be finding everything you require, Miss Smart,' Grace went on.

Maud glanced around. With its four-poster, nightstand, chest of drawers with a small looking glass, two easy chairs, dressing stand with jug and bowl, wardrobe, numerous pictures and three Armenian rugs with geometric designs, the room was decidedly crowded.

'It looks very comfortable, Grace. Thank you.'

There was a light tap on the door, and it opened to reveal the manservant with their two suitcases. He wore a kilt and a green jumper that had seen better days.

'This is my husband, Finlay,' Grace said with a modicum of pride. 'He is Mr Carmichael's butler, valet and, just as important, his piper.'

Finlay nodded politely. 'Which will be your luggage, Miss Smart?'

Maud indicated her own case, and Finlay set it down. Like his wife, he was short, of middle years and had apple-red cheeks, but he was as thin as she was round. Maud thanked him, and he withdrew with Daisy's suitcase.

'Luncheon is served in the great hall at one o'clock, miss,'

Grace said, and she left the room to show Daisy to her bedroom along the corridor. The fire having come to life, Isobel got to her feet, bobbed a quick curtsy to Maud and hurried after them.

Maud crossed to the window. The deep blue waters of the Sound of Mull, part of the Atlantic Ocean separating the island from the mainland, glittered in the sunshine. In the distance rose the mountains of the Ardnamurchan peninsular. She turned the handle and opened the casement, standing and breathing in the fresh air deeply.

Daisy entered the room and crossed to stand beside her. 'My view's the same. I hope it gives you inspiration for your next novel.' She grinned at Maud.

'Undoubtedly it will.' Maud lowered her voice. 'Remember that a secretary should be quiet and helpful, not buoyant and excited.'

'Right you are, Maud. You can rely on me.'

'We have thirty minutes to wash and change before luncheon. In case it is a while before we have the opportunity to speak again in private, and as we can't both search for the missing statuette without drawing attention to ourselves—'

'We should decide now who is going first?'

Maud nodded. 'If you have no objection, I will search Mr Tremain's room this afternoon. We will reconvene before bed to discuss what steps it might be necessary to take tonight.'

A little later, Maud and Daisy entered the great hall. Lord Urquhart stood by the fireplace, resting his elbow on the mantelpiece. Maud was admiring his tall, slim yet muscular build when a severe-looking woman in her fifties, wearing a tweed jacket and skirt, stepped forward. Her tall, thin frame, white hair and prominent nose suggested she was their host's sister.

'Miss Smart and Miss Graham, I'm delighted you could join

us.' She smiled, her severe features softening as she extended a hand to each in turn. 'I am Ailsa Carmichael. My brother Magnus tells me you're a crime novelist, Miss Smart.'

'Miss Smart.' Lord Urquhart smiled and pushed himself away from the hearth. 'I am looking forward to making your acquaintance over luncheon. Miss Graham, I'm sure you must have some tales to tell, working for such a well-known authoress.'

'Aye,' Daisy said. 'There's never a dull moment in this job.'

Ailsa turned slightly and indicated, rather unwillingly Maud thought, a short, grumpy-looking fellow with a tuft of grey hair on either side of a bald head, seated in a high-backed carved wooden chair. 'This is Mr Neil Tremain, an old friend of my brother's.'

Mr Tremain, the possible statuette thief, Maud thought, as he half rose, a cigar still clamped between his teeth. He nodded at them before sitting heavily again. From his waistcoat pocket, he pulled out a small tin and withdrew a white lozenge. He removed the cigar, put the tablet in his mouth, replaced the cigar and grunted. Glancing round the room, he scowled, his thick grey eyebrows meeting. 'Where is that confounded daughter of mine?'

'Here I am, Papa.'

All eyes turned towards the door. A petite young woman in an elegant pink gown stood poised in the doorway. If it were not for her height, thought Maud, she would be the perfect Gibson Girl. Miss Tremain had a voluptuous figure, emphasised by her tightly-corseted slim waist. Her glossy dark brown hair was drawn into a high pompadour. A waterfall of small curls framed her pale oval face, highlighting a pair of wide, brown eyes.

Maud knew that she could never be a fashionable Gibson Girl. Maud was tall and slim, certainly, had a certain physical grace and self-confidence, perhaps, but lacked that crucial element of both fragility and voluptuousness. And her hair was pale, her wide eyes grey.

'Oh.' Miss Tremain reached up an elegant hand to touch the flowers on her large hat. 'Am I late?'

'You know you are, my girl,' growled her father. 'You always like to make an entrance.'

She gave a light laugh, and Maud watched as she glided – there was no other word for it – into the room. 'I see we have been joined by two new ladies.' There was the briefest of pauses as she lifted one eyebrow. 'How charming.'

'Jane.' Ailsa bent down to press her cheek briefly to the young woman. 'Now that we are all here, let us eat.' She gestured for them to take seats at the long oak table in the centre.

Jane Tremain's face and name seemed familiar, Maud thought, but before she had time to think about it further, Magnus pulled out a chair for her at his right hand. Maud observed Jane slipping into the chair next to Lord Urquhart, smiling prettily at him as she did so. Maud flushed; no doubt, she thought, because she was seated in the direct blaze of the fire.

Finlay, still wearing the kilt but now with a smart blue jumper, entered the great hall, bearing a large covered dish, followed by a short, stocky man in his late-thirties in footman's livery, carrying a sauce boat. Finlay went first to Ailsa, removing the cover and holding the dish for her to help herself.

'Ah, rabbit in mustard sauce.' Neil Tremain, seated opposite Maud, peered down the length of the table and rubbed his hands together. 'With extra mustard sauce.'

Finlay, followed by the footman, moved round the table with the dishes. Tremain's gaze followed the food as Lord Urquhart, seated at Ailsa's right hand, helped himself.

'Is this your first time here, Mr Tremain?' Maud needed to begin her investigation.

'I visit Magnus on occasion.' Tremain turned to Maud. 'I stay on Ulva. Do you know it?' She shook her head in response. 'It's a small island off the west coast of Mull.'

Maud looked over at Jane. 'And do you live with your father, Miss Tremain?'

'Goodness no.' The young woman gave a shudder. 'There's absolutely *nothing* to do there.' She took a tiny portion of rabbit and waved away the sauce boat. 'I'm at present visiting my father. I stay in Edinburgh.' She glanced at Lord Urquhart from under her lashes.

Maud remembered where she had come across the woman's name. In the society pages. *Lord Urquhart seen again in the company of Jane Tremain.* Well, if he wanted to be involved with such a silly woman that was his affair. *She* had a case to solve.

Tremain was helping himself to a generous amount of rabbit and sauce. 'This I *can* eat.'

'Neil suffers with his digestion,' Magnus explained, as Finlay moved round to him, 'but mustard apparently helps.'

'Do tell us about your writing, Miss Smart,' put in Ailsa.

'I believe you write penny dreadfuls,' Jane said. 'I've never read any myself.'

Daisy, after glancing around at the splendour of the great hall, had been quiet during the meal. Now she visibly bristled and enunciated in her best Morningside accent, 'Actually, Miss Smart writes mystery novels for *educated* folk.'

'We have a treat lined up for this afternoon,' Ailsa said hastily. 'The Repertory Players are to put on a performance of a couple of scenes from *A Midsummer Night's Dream*. Lord Urquhart has kindly agreed to join me in playing Mendelssohn's opening duet.'

Maud paused as she helped herself from the offered dishes and gazed at him. Was there no end to the man's talents? He

winked at her, but she thought again of his being seen with Miss
Tremain, and looked hastily away.

'The actors travel round villages and small towns that have
no theatres of their own,' Ailsa went on. 'They come to Tobermory every year, and we've invited the local folk as usual.'

Maud shot Daisy a glance and saw that her friend understood. This would provide the perfect distraction for Maud's
search of Neil Tremain's room.

THREE

The servants had been bustling around since luncheon, and now the large drawing room was filled with a collection of chairs from around the castle for the performance, with red curtains at one end to hide the area marked as the stage for the occasion.

It was due to begin at three thirty, and a few minutes before time, the large room was almost full. Maud and Daisy slipped in and took seats at the back. Scanning the group to be sure all the house guests were present, Maud saw Tremain and his daughter seated at the front. Her gaze went round the room. Lord Urquhart and Ailsa were seated together at the grand piano, ready to perform the duet.

As the keys to the 'Overture to A Midsummer Night's Dream' were struck, the curtains jerked slowly apart, revealing a tree made from wooden planks. Beside it, a large notice on a pole read *A Wood near Athens*. On the other side of the stage, a bank covered with green cloth was sprinkled with paper flowers. Upon the bank lay the sleeping Titania, Queen of the Fairies, white-robed, her black hair spread about her shoulders. Maud waited until Bottom and the other comic characters had got into their stride, before she touched Daisy's arm to indicate she was about to slip away.

She mounted the spiral stairs, its curved walls decorated here and there with two-handed claymores, long-bladed dirks and other murderous weapons. Maud could almost see the fearsome Highlanders, hear the yells and clash of iron as they defended their stronghold.

On the second floor all was still; the laughter of the appreciative audience below came faintly to Maud's ears. She glanced about her. Yes, she was alone.

Cautiously she moved towards the room, by a process of elimination, she was certain was Tremain's. With a glance over her shoulder, she placed a hand on the brass knob. To her horror, the door was slightly ajar and the sound of someone moving about drifted out of the room. Maud silently cursed herself for not noticing Tremain leaving the play. She backed away, one step, then a second one, and bumped into a large masculine body. Before she could let out a shriek, a hand closed gently over her mouth.

'Don't be alarmed,' Lord Urquhart murmured in her ear, his deep velvety tones doing nothing to still the rapid beating of her heart.

She turned and looked up at him. 'What are you doing here?' she whispered. He was standing far too close for comfort.

'We should move away from the scene of the crime.' He drew her around the corner.

'The *crime*?' she hissed as he pulled her into a narrow alcove. 'What have you done?'

'I was under the impression it was *you* who might have done something.'

'You asked me to retrieve an item. I was attempting to do so.' A thought struck her. 'Do you not trust me to do the job you have engaged me to do?' Her voice rose. 'Of all the—'

They turned to the sound of heavy footsteps. Lord Urquhart moved her back against the wall and loomed over her.

'Who's there?' Tremain's voice demanded from some feet away.

Maud was squeezed tight into the alcove; the space was so shallow that Lord Urquhart's hard torso pressed alarmingly against her. She held her breath, trying to ignore the heat she felt at every point of contact. They waited in silence. His heart beat strong and steady. Her own heart thumped – purely from the fraught situation, she knew.

Tremain's footsteps retreated into his room, and they heard the door being closed. After a few moments had passed, Maud decided it was safe to leave. 'Excuse me,' she said politely to Lord Urquhart. 'Shall we return to the play? Separately,' she added.

He stepped aside and smiled. 'It's been a pleasure, Miss Smart.'

Maud drew in a sharp breath and turned, striding along the corridor and down the staircase with undisguised annoyance until she reached the door to the drawing room. Steadying her breathing, she slipped into the room and back into her seat.

Daisy sent her a questioning look. Maud shook her head and turned to watch the performance. Now the actors were performing the Pyramus and Thisbe scene. The audience were so engaged that she doubted anyone had noticed her absence. Finally, the players took their bows to a burst of applause, and Magnus made a speech thanking all who had made the afternoon so enjoyable. Then everyone clapped again, and they finished with singing 'God Save the King'.

Maud discreetly dabbed at her brow with her handkerchief.

That evening at dinner, Magnus smiled as he lifted a forkful of curried lobster to his mouth. 'I think this afternoon was a success, don't you?'

The great hall at dinner was lit by thick candles in a huge iron ring suspended by a chain from the centre beam of the ceiling, casting deep shadows around the walls.

It wasn't a success from my point of view, Maud thought, smoothing her skirt of blue taffeta, but she agreed with everyone round the table that it had indeed been most enjoyable.

Lord Urquhart sat there, in a dark suit, white shirt, cravat and pin, playing with the stem of a wine glass and looking far too handsome for his own good.

'I'm sorry you weren't able to come to the performance, Roderick.' Magnus was addressing the solid-looking gentleman in his mid-thirties with bright blue eyes who'd been introduced to them as the local doctor and a family friend.

The doctor gave a rueful smile. 'My patients must always come first, Magnus.'

'Of course.'

'You have a useful and interesting profession, Dr Munro,' Maud said.

'You too, I think, Miss Smart.'

'Not useful, surely.' She smiled.

'I'm not so sure. Your novels must tell us something about the human condition.'

'That covers a rather large area.'

'Tell us, then, is there any quality which all murderers have in common?' Dr Munro resumed eating.

'Human beings are not so different from one another,' Maud told him, thinking of those she had met in her investigations. 'In real life, almost anyone might do almost anything.'

Magnus frowned. 'Do you mean that ordinary people whom one meets every day are capable of murder?'

'It depends on the circumstances.'

'So, a person may kill and otherwise be perfectly decent?' asked Tremain.

Ailsa gave a harsh laugh. 'Nonsense!'

'It's *you* who is talking nonsense,' snapped Tremain.

Maud caught her breath at the sudden, violent exchange. She sent a glance towards Daisy, in a puff-sleeved ivory blouse and still a little subdued by her surroundings.

'Neil, please!' Magnus remonstrated.

'I believe you used to live in Glasgow, Dr Munro,' Lord Urquhart put in smoothly. 'Do you find life rather quiet on Mull, after the bustle of the Empire's second city?'

'I prefer a quieter pace of life,' he replied. 'And you, sir, do you favour town or country?'

'Each has its charms,' Lord Urquhart said, his eyes on Maud.

'I've thought of writing a novel,' put in Jane.

'Then why do you not?' Maud dabbed her mouth with her napkin.

'Oh, I will when I have nothing better to do. Although it could never be for publication.'

'Indeed,' Maud murmured.

When the last person at table had set down their cutlery, Finlay and the footman stepped forward to clear the dishes. On the oak sideboard, two large apple pies waited to be served.

Jane waved away the pudding. 'It is not *de rigueur* in my set to overindulge.'

'Oh, *your set*,' Tremain said, mimicking his daughter's voice. She sent him a sullen look.

'For all the apparent opportunity in Edinburgh' – Tremain glared at his daughter, before pouring a generous helping of cream over his pudding – 'Jane hasn't managed to find a husband for herself. It's costing me a small fortune.'

'Really, Papa.' Jane glared back at him.

Tremain shovelled a laden spoon into his mouth. 'By the

way, Magnus, you need to have a word with your servants. There was some disturbance outside my room this afternoon.' He rubbed his chest with the flat of his palm. 'Damned indigestion. I had it this afternoon and I've got it again now. And I've run out of lozenges.'

'It's your own fault for being so bad-tempered,' Jane muttered.

'I can give you something for heartburn, if you wish,' Dr Munro offered. 'I carry my medical bag with me at all times. One never knows when it will be needed.'

'Thank you,' Tremain spoke grudgingly. With a deep sigh, he pushed away his unfinished dish of apple pie topped with cream. 'I'm going to my room.'

Dr Munro excused himself to retrieve the bag from his pony and trap. Not long afterwards, Ailsa rose from the table. 'We are small enough to dispense with the separation of the sexes.'

Ushering them into the small drawing room, she crossed to the sideboard. She was dispensing the drinks, which had been set out on a silver tray, when the door opened and Dr Munro entered. 'A whisky for you, Roderick?'

He nodded his assent. 'I've given Mr Tremain bicarbonate of soda. That should settle him for tonight.' He put his brown leather bag on the floor by the side of the sofa and accepted the glass. 'I see that your footman is acting as his valet, Magnus.'

'Neil doesn't bring one, so Andrew is helping him. Now, how about a game of whist?'

Maud partnered Dr Munro, and Lord Urquhart partnered Magnus. Daisy read a magazine. Ailsa went briefly to the kitchen to speak to the cook about breakfast in the morning. Jane wandered about the room, picking up items and putting them down, before going upstairs for a handkerchief. All in all, Maud thought, the evening was proving to be uneventful.

The evening was drawing to a close when they heard the sound of the heavy knocker on the front door and shortly after

Finlay entered the room and approached the doctor. 'A boy came with a message for yourself, Dr Munro. It's the widow Hardie, in need of some relief from her suffering.'

'Thank you.' The doctor took his watch from his waistcoat pocket and glanced at it. 'Getting on for half past ten. I'll go straightaway. I can let myself out, Finlay.' Replacing his watch, he turned to his host. 'Magnus, please excuse me. I'll return first thing in the morning to check on Mr Tremain.'

'Of course, Roderick.' Magnus put down his cards.

Dr Munro rose. Bidding everyone good night, he picked up his bag and left.

The little party chatted on for a while before Ailsa announced she was retiring for the night and everyone followed suit. All took a candle from the hall and went to their respective bedrooms. Apart from Daisy, who joined Maud in her chamber.

'What now?' Daisy hissed. 'I can hardly search the room of a man who isna well.'

'Take your turn tomorrow, Daisy, as soon as he's up and about.'

Maud was woken the following morning by the sound of commotion along the corridor. Hastily she pulled on her dressing gown and came out of her room to an astonishing scene.

Magnus, wearing a dressing robe and nightcap, was pounding on Tremain's door, with Lord Urquhart in dark trousers and rolled-up shirt sleeves attempting to restrain him. Andrew, along with what appeared to be the rest of the servants, hovered in the passage.

'Neil!' Magnus was calling through the door. 'Are you all right, man? Open up!'

Maud approached the little gathering. 'What is the trouble?' she asked Finlay.

Daisy joined them, tying the belt on her dressing gown.

'When Andrew came to wake Mr Tremain and help him dress, the door was locked, miss, and there was no reply from within,' said Finlay. 'He left the gentleman for another twenty minutes or so, thinking he was still asleep. But when Andrew returned and knocked harder, there was still no reply. It was then that he informed the laird and myself.'

'Step aside, gentlemen,' Daisy said.

The murmuring of the servants quietened and everyone stared at her. Magnus stepped back from the door, followed by Lord Urquhart. Daisy lifted her dressing gown a little above her ankles and knelt. She put her eye to the keyhole.

'Can you see anything?' Maud asked.

'Nothing.' Daisy got to her feet. 'It's too dark.'

'Do you have a spare key?' Maud asked Magnus. 'It would save any of you gentlemen from possibly breaking a bone as you batter down the door.' And would be preferable to Daisy openly picking the lock, thought Maud, sure that she intended to do just that.

Finlay shook his head. 'It was lost years ago and never replaced.'

'We have to get in,' said Daisy. 'It sounds like something has happened to Mr Tremain.'

FOUR

Dr Munro came hastening along the corridor, carrying his medical bag. 'I let myself in and heard all the noise. What on earth is going on?' He reached the group outside Neil Tremain's door. 'Has Tremain been taken ill again?'

'I don't know.' Magnus shook his head. 'We've knocked and called, but he's not answering.'

The doctor looked relieved. 'Oh, he'll merely be asleep.'

'No, sir,' Finlay said respectfully. 'It must be more than that.'

Maud and Daisy stood back as Ailsa came hurrying towards them, her brown candlewick dressing gown flapping about her legs, her white hair tightly plaited about her head. Jane stepped out of her room on the opposite side of the corridor, tying the belt of her rose-pink silk dressing robe. 'What is it? Is my father all right?'

'We don't know yet,' Maud told her gently.

'Papa?' Jane called, moving towards his door.

Maud caught hold of her as Dr Munro stepped forward, knocked on the door and called in a deep voice, 'Tremain!'

Still there was no sound from the room. He turned the handle, but the door was fast.

'We've tried that, Roderick,' Magnus said.

Dr Munro dropped his bag to the floor and crouched down to peer through the keyhole. 'It's no use.' He straightened. 'The door curtain is pulled across.'

'There's no alternative but to force the door, Magnus,' Lord Urquhart said. 'Would you like me to do so?'

'Allow me.' Dr Munro put his shoulder to the door and pushed hard. The door creaked but didn't move. He repeated the movement a few times, putting all his weight behind it, but still nothing.

'Here,' said Lord Urquhart. 'Let me try.'

'No, it's alright. I think it'll go this time.' The doctor threw his shoulder at the door once more. There was a splintering of wood as the brass lock and bolt finally came free and the ancient wooden door flew open. He stumbled forward, landing on his hands and knees on the rug. He hastily scrambled to his feet and strode over to the bed, gesturing to the others to stay back.

'Tremain?' he said as he approached the bed. 'Neil?'

Tremain did not move.

Maud stepped forward to peer into the large room, gloomy with the shutters closed over the window. Andrew staggered past her, coming to an abrupt halt. In the huge four-poster, its head against the right-hand wall, lay an unmoving shape.

From where she was standing and with some natural light leaking in from the passage, Maud could see Neil Tremain curled on his side facing the door.

Dr Munro put his bag on the floor beside the bed and laid his hand on the man's shoulder. He rolled him gently onto his back and drew down the sheet. Moving his bag to the night-stand, the doctor ordered Andrew to open the shutters. The valet stood visibly shaking, too distressed to move.

'The shutters, man!' Dr Munro repeated gruffly, not looking up from his examination. 'I need some light to see the patient.'

Lord Urquhart stepped into the room and moved quickly to unlatch the pair of wooden shutters at the window and fold them back. The casement window was already ajar, and he threw it wide.

Sunlight poured into the room as the doctor placed his hand in front of the man's mouth to feel for breath. He moved his hand to touch behind Tremain's ear, searching for a pulse. He shook his head and straightened. As he did so, Maud noticed Tremain's contorted face and a small patch of blood on the front of the man's white nightshirt. The doctor drew the sheet back up and over the man's head.

'I'm sorry to tell you this, Magnus,' Dr Munro said, 'but I'm afraid Tremain is dead.'

'He can't be,' said Magnus in a faltering voice, coming into the room.

'Follow me,' Maud whispered to Daisy.

'I'm right behind you,' Daisy replied.

They slipped into the bedchamber behind their host.

'*Papa!*' Jane wailed as she rushed towards the bed, Ailsa close behind. The girl stopped just short and crumpled to the floor.

Dr Munro glanced round. 'What do you all think you are doing? A dead man's chamber is no place for ladies.'

Jane began to sob. Ailsa put her arm around the young woman's shoulders and helped her to her feet.

'We are—' Maud paused. She was on the point of saying private detectives, but that would not do. It might be useful to maintain for a little longer their cover as novelist and secretary. She was saved from finishing her sentence by the good doctor.

'I must insist that you leave.'

'He's right, you know,' Lord Urquhart said. 'The police and

the Procurator Fiscal must be informed as it's a sudden death. It's better that no one disturbs the room.'

He was correct: the evidence must not be disturbed. Unless she was very much mistaken, thought Maud, this was a case of murder. Mixed with her natural concern for Tremain's daughter and for his host and friend Magnus Carmichael, Maud felt a tingling of anticipation as her detective faculties sprang to the fore.

Lord Urquhart was ushering Jane and Ailsa, Maud and Daisy, and the quivering valet out into the corridor.

'We should go too.' Dr Munro placed a hand on Magnus's shoulder, and they joined everyone else huddled in the corridor.

'One moment,' the doctor added. 'I need to make certain notes...' He sent an apologetic glance towards Ailsa, her arm still around Tremain's distraught daughter.

Ailsa took the hint and led away the sobbing Jane, muttering comforting words about a heart attack and how quick the end must have been.

'Do you think you could arrange for the police officer and the Procurator Fiscal to be informed, my lord?' Dr Munro asked Lord Urquhart. 'I suspect Magnus would be grateful for your assistance. And would you mind ensuring the servants return to below-stairs? I will remain here to make notes on the precise position and condition of the body before it is disturbed.'

'Certainly.' Lord Urquhart encouraged Magnus to return to his chamber and dress, then he began to shepherd the servants towards the stairs.

'Andrew,' Maud said quickly, calling him back, 'you had better stay. The policeman will want to speak to you.'

The valet, white-faced, stood a little away in the corridor, clearly ill at ease. The doctor re-entered Tremain's bedroom.

'This is frustrating,' murmured Maud to Daisy as they stood on the threshold once more.

Daisy agreed. 'Aye, standing and watching from the doorway is nae our style.'

The doctor looked unhappy as they followed his movements. He removed a notebook from his bag, stood again with his back to the door and peeled back the bed sheet. He began to write.

'Tremain is in his nightshirt,' Maud observed, keeping her voice low, 'so whatever his cause of death he had time to finish his preparations for bed and to climb in. And his bedside candle has not burned down but been extinguished, suggesting all was as normal when he first got into bed.'

'It's strange that he locked his door,' put in Daisy. 'I didna think that was done in these country houses.'

'It is indeed most unusual, for it suggests Neil Tremain did not trust his host or his host's guests.'

'Maybe he had reason not to. Neil and Ailsa had that wee stramash last night over dinner.'

Dr Munro was now feeling around the dead man's neck and jaw.

'What's he doing?' Daisy whispered.

'I imagine checking for rigor mortis.'

He returned to making notes.

'You'll notice how orderly Tremain's bedroom is and the money on his dressing table, which suggests there was no struggle,' Maud went on.

'So his death might have been a heart attack?'

'I doubt it. I caught a glimpse of blood on the man's chest before the doctor replaced the sheet.'

Daisy drew in a sharp breath. 'Then someone entered a locked room to murder him?'

'And exited the room, still leaving it locked? Yes.'

Maud tried hard not to let her excitement show. A murder was not something to be celebrated. But she could hardly believe they had their own locked-room mystery to solve. Joseph

Rouletabille was working on such a case in *The Mystery of the Yellow Room*, but that was in the novel she was currently reading and this was real life.

'I wonder why someone might want Neil Tremain dead,' Maud murmured.

'Aye. That's what we'll have to find out.'

Dr Munro had returned the cover over Tremain and was now examining the floor around the bed.

'Hmm,' said Maud, watching him.

'You know, Maud,' Daisy said carefully, 'when the doctor first pulled the bed sheet over the deid man's heid, I thought I saw it flutter a wee bit.'

'The window is open.'

'But there's nae a breath of wind.'

It was true; the air was humid and heavy. Maud's interest quickened. What could have caused the sheet to move? She gazed around the dead man's bedroom. The panelled wall...

'Perhaps there is a secret panel which hasn't quite closed after the killer's hasty exit. Shall we? Time is of the essence.'

Maud marched back into the room, Daisy at her heels. The startled doctor looked up from where he knelt on the floor.

'Don't mind us,' Maud said. 'We're just going to inspect the panelling.'

'Miss... Smart!' Lord Urquhart caught the slip in time. 'What are you doing?'

'My lord,' said Dr Munro, getting to his feet and coming towards the door, 'thank goodness you've returned. Perhaps you can persuade the ladies to leave, for I cannot. And I'm not sure what they are about.'

Maud turned from tapping the panel to the side of the fireplace. 'Examining for a secret panel, as you see.'

'I think, Miss Smart, your detective... novels have got the better of you,' said Lord Urquhart. 'The constabulary and the

Fiscal are on their way. Until then, Dr Munro needs to be allowed to work unhindered.'

Daisy gave several defiant taps on the wall.

'I see,' Maud said, tightening the belt on her dressing gown. 'Come along, Miss Graham.'

They sailed from the room, only to stand again in the doorway. In a few moments, they were joined by Magnus. Lord Urquhart crossed to the doorway to speak to him.

'How is Jane?' His tone was so soft that it drew Maud's attention.

Jane? She shot a look at him. *No longer Miss Tremain, then?* She breathed deeply.

'Ailsa is with her,' Magnus replied.

Dr Munro closed his notebook and slipped it into his jacket pocket. 'I'll make arrangements for the body to be taken to the dead house. There's nothing more I can do here, I'm afraid.' He lifted his bag from the nightstand and walked towards the doorway.

'You'd better take this, Magnus.' He bent to pick up the key from the rug by the door. 'It must have fallen when I forced open the door.' He handed it to Magnus and followed everyone out into the corridor.

Magnus put the key in his trouser pocket and closed the bedroom door behind him. 'I'll get Finlay to repair the door as best he can once the Procurator Fiscal and Sergeant McNeish have done what they have to.'

Maud couldn't help herself. 'Dr Munro, what did your examination of Mr Tremain's neck and jaw tell you?'

'Well, I suppose there is no harm in telling you. Rigor mortis is not yet apparent, suggesting that he died less than three hours ago.'

'So he's still warm?' asked Daisy.

The doctor inclined his head.

'Do you mind my asking how long before a body is cold?' Maud thought it would be a useful thing to know.

'Generally, a body feels cold to the touch within eight hours of death. But that is a generalisation, you understand. There are many variables.'

'Such as?' Daisy asked.

'Ladies, these questions are most unusual.' Dr Munro shifted his bag to his other hand.

'Not for a crime writer, they aren't,' said Daisy, a sweet smile on her face.

'I suppose so. Well, room temperature, changes in the weather and the amount of clothing on the body all contribute to the conclusion. As does the deceased's weight, his muscle bulk...'

Then they were startled by a noise down the corridor.

FIVE

'Ah, there you are, Magnus!'

Mr Greig, the Procurator Fiscal, tall and thin, and dressed in a grey suit, came striding along the corridor. He was clean-shaven and wore a pair of wire-rimmed spectacles on his nose. Behind him hastened a burly young policeman with ginger hair, his ruddy face partially covered by a short beard and scrubby red eyebrows. They reached the little assembly outside Tremain's bedroom door.

'So' – Mr Greig rubbed his hands together as if he were setting out for a stroll round the harbour – 'what do we have?' He paused as his gaze fell on Maud and Daisy. 'And you two ladies are...?'

'Miss Smart.' Oh dear, Maud thought, is it an offence to give false information to a prosecutor? 'And this is my secretary, Miss Graham.'

'I see,' he said, in a voice that showed he clearly did not. 'And what is your status in the castle?' His frown went over her dressing gown and her long night plait, before turning to Daisy, who was similarly attired.

'They are guests of mine, William,' put in Magnus.

Mr Greig gave a curt nod and strode into the room, followed by the sergeant, Dr Munro, Magnus and Lord Urquhart, with Maud and Daisy bringing up the rear.

'It's Neil Tremain, another guest of mine,' Magnus told him, as the small group circled the bed. 'Andrew was acting as his valet, and when he came upstairs with Tremain's hot water before breakfast, he found the door locked. When there was no answer to his knocking, Andrew fetched me. Lord Urquhart and I were trying to gain entry when Dr Munro arrived. He forced the door open and... well, we found poor Neil like this.' He gestured to the body in the bed.

'He'd had an attack of heartburn last night,' added Daisy.

The doctor stared at Daisy. 'Quite so, Miss Graham, but this outcome is unaccountable.'

The Procurator fiscal folded back the sheet and placed his hand on the dead man's neck. 'Still warm and no sign of rigor yet. Any idea what time he died?'

'I arrived about nine o'clock,' said Dr Munro, 'and I would estimate that death must have occurred relatively recently.'

'Can you be more specific?'

'Perhaps within the hour; two at most.'

'Which means death occurred somewhere between seven and nine o'clock this morning.'

'Earlier than nine,' the doctor replied. 'As I understand it, the valet had been trying to rouse him for some time before I arrived.'

'Half past eight, sir,' came Andrew's nervous voice from the doorway. 'I'd been trying to wake him since half past eight.'

'Ah, Andrew, come in,' said Dr Munro. 'I was just going to suggest we call for you.'

The Procurator Fiscal pulled the sheet back a little further. His eyes widened. 'Have you seen the blood on his nightshirt, doctor?'

'Yes.' Dr Munro drew open the neck of the garment to reveal a grey-haired section of chest.

The Fiscal peered down at the body. 'I see a small wound, with some blood, in the region of the heart.' He straightened.

'A puncture wound,' the doctor said carefully. 'Penetration of the precordium into the heart itself would explain why there is little blood; it would have leaked into the chest cavity.'

'Which means that death...?' Mr Greig trailed off, looking at the doctor over the top of his spectacles.

'Would have been instantaneous.'

'Any suggestion as to what implement was used?'

'The incision is clean, so I would guess at something thin, smooth and sharp.'

The Fiscal took hold of each of Neil Tremain's hands in turn and examined them. 'No defence wounds – the palms and fingers are unmarked.' He looked at Dr Munro. 'Could this have been self-inflicted?'

'Impossible to say from the wound. But—'

'I agree with Dr Munro.' Maud could remain silent no longer. She stepped forward. 'There is no apparent sign of a weapon on the floor.' She crouched down to be certain. 'Not that I can see with a cursory examination.' She stood and met the astonished gaze of the Fiscal. 'I believe the doctor came to the same conclusion,' she added helpfully. 'And there is nothing on the deceased's nightstand' – her eye moved to the table at the side of the bed, which held only a candle in its stick, a watch and a wallet – 'that could be considered a suitable weapon. I imagine it would have been impossible for the victim to have inflicted such a wound on himself, then have the strength and willpower to hide the instrument and remove every trace of his having left the bed for that purpose. Wouldn't you agree, Dr Munro?'

Before the bemused doctor could reply, Daisy spoke. 'There

might be something in his bed...' She put out a hand to feel in the sheets around the corpse.

'Stop!' The Fiscal narrowed his eyes first at Daisy and then Maud. 'What exactly are you two ladies doing in this room?' He turned and addressed Magnus. 'Have you known them long?'

Excuse me, thought Maud, *we are standing here. You do not need to discuss Daisy or me in the third person.* She opened her mouth to say so.

'About a day,' said Magnus, looking a little uncomfortable.

'Take their details, Sandy,' the Fiscal ordered the sergeant. 'This death looks very much like foul play.'

'Foul play?' Magnus's hand went to his chest. '*Murder?*'

The sergeant hastily pulled his notebook and pencil from the top pocket of his uniform.

'Carry out a thorough investigation and report back to me,' concluded the Fiscal.

Magnus gave a disbelieving shake of his head. 'Perhaps you'd like to use the unoccupied bedroom at the end of the corridor as your office while you're here, Sandy,' he added.

The sergeant's natural hue deepened. 'Thanks very much, Mr Carmichael.'

'A wee dram before you go, William?' Magnus asked Mr Greig.

'Don't mind if I do.' The Fiscal rubbed his hands together.

'Hamish, will you join us?'

'It's a little early for me, thanks, Magnus. I'd prefer to get some fresh air.'

Magnus nodded towards the doctor. 'Roderick?'

'Not for me.' The doctor shifted his medical bag from one hand to the other. 'I have other patients to attend to.'

'Another time, then.' Magnus and William Greig took their leave.

Pencil poised, the sergeant addressed Lord Urquhart. 'Can I have your name and address, please, sir?'

'Urquhart, Strathbogle, Inverness-shire.'

Sergeant McNeish blinked. 'That's it?'

'Hamish Alexander Jonathan Edward Maurice Urquhart. Baron. Strathbogle, Inverness-shire,' Lord Urquhart qualified.

Why have one Christian name when you can have five, thought Maud. No wonder life was a game to him. The man had no real depth of character and yet he doubtless thought that every woman who glanced his way was pining for him. Maud avoided looking at him. *She* would never sacrifice anything for him.

'Thank you, your lordship.' The police officer wrote laboriously in his notebook.

'May I go now?'

'Certainly, your lordship.'

Lord Urquhart shot Maud a *behave yourself* look and left the room.

'You know my name and address, McNeish,' said Dr Munro, 'so I'll be on my way.'

'You ken me too,' put in Andrew, making to leave.

The sergeant nodded at the two men and turned to Maud. 'Can I have your address, miss?'

'Certainly, officer. But before I provide it, could I suggest you ask the two people who were first to enter the room to turn out their pockets?'

'I beg your pardon,' Dr Munro spluttered.

'I mean nothing by that, Dr Munro,' Maud said. 'Merely that it seems – I am sure that it is – good practice.'

'Aye, it is.' Then, seeing the angry flush on the doctor's face, the sergeant added, 'I'll start with Andrew.'

The valet gave a nervous laugh and pulled out his trouser pockets. 'It's like being back at school.' In one pocket was a clean white handkerchief, neatly folded; the other was empty. There were no pockets in his jacket.

'Thanks, Andrew.' As Sergeant McNeish turned to face the

doctor, he caught Maud's warning glance. 'Dr Munro, if you would come with me to my temporary office, we can do the necessary there.'

A little mollified, the doctor accompanied the policeman along the corridor to the bedroom at the end. Maud and Daisy followed. The sergeant opened the door and he and Dr Munro entered. Maud and Daisy didn't wait to be invited in.

'It's useful to have a witness or two, don't you think, Dr Munro?' Maud moved casually over to the writing table. She looked at the policeman and gave a pointed glance in the direction of the doctor's bag.

The sergeant understood. 'Would you mind putting your medical bag on the table, Dr Munro? I'll just have a wee look in there as well after I've seen what's in your pockets.'

With a sigh, the doctor did as he was bid. He emptied his pockets, which contained his notebook and pencil, handkerchief, some coins, a bar of chocolate and a tobacco tin which proved to contain a few hand-rolled cigarettes.

Turning to the leather bag, he undid the brass clasp and opened it. Sergeant McNeish, Maud and Daisy peered in.

'Can you tell me what these are all for, Dr Munro?' asked the puzzled sergeant.

The doctor removed each item in turn from his medical bag. 'The spirit lamp and chemicals are for detection of proteinuria – a high level of protein, which can be a sign of kidney damage. Stethoscope; well, you know the purpose of that. Dover's Powder for colds and fever, Sydenham's Laudanum for pain and various other complaints. Haemoglobinometer to detect anaemia.' The doctor opened a small black box to reveal the meter. 'Urinometer,' he went on, taking out a glass cylinder with a mercury bulb, 'to indicate renal function.' A delicate-looking hammer came next. 'Percussion hammer to examine the reflexes of the deep tendon and to check for any abnormalities of the nervous system. Ophthalmoscope' – he opened a dark purple velvet-lined case to reveal a number of small metal objects – 'to look into the back of the eye. Thermometer, tongue depressor...'

By the time the doctor had finished, the table was covered with a fearsome array of instruments.

'Much obliged, Dr Munro,' said the sergeant.

'May I now visit my next patient?'

'Certainly, sir.' Sandy McNeish began to help the doctor return the items to the bag.

Dr Munro stopped him. 'It's best if I do this, Sergeant, as everything needs to go in its particular place to fit in.'

'Aye, of course.' The police officer attempted an air of nonchalance as he stepped away. 'Though I'll need to interview you later, doctor, about the body and so on.'

'Come to my house after surgery is closed for the day,' Dr Munro told him while repacking the leather bag. When it had been completed to his satisfaction, he took it up, nodded to the sergeant, said, 'Ladies,' to Maud and Daisy, and left the room.

Sandy McNeish looked at Maud and Daisy. 'I have to get on with the investigation, so you ladies had best go to your rooms. I'll let you know when I'm ready to interview you.'

'It's a wee bit strange, don't you think,' said Daisy, 'that Neil Tremain was found dead in his room with the door locked? I mean, how could the killer have got in – and out – again?'

The policeman frowned.

Maud waited for him to say or do something, but he continued to stand there, looking unsure of his next move. There clearly was little crime on Mull, thought Maud. She decided to help point him in the right direction.

'I've only had a cursory glance, of course, Sergeant, but these rooms are on the second floor, which makes it unlikely anyone entered via the window. The room is tidy, which suggests no struggle took place, and there is cash on the dressing table, which makes me think the intruder's motive wasn't theft.' The sergeant's mouth had fallen open. 'Another point of inter-

est,' Maud went on, 'is that Mr Tremain had locked his door.
Why?'

'Last night over dinner there'd been a wee stushie between
Neil Tremain and Ailsa Carmichael,' put in Daisy. 'I wonder if
that's significant?'

The sergeant swallowed before speaking again. 'You ladies
seem to know a lot about detective work.'

Maud turned to Daisy. 'Shall we tell him?'

'Why not?'

They turned towards him and he took a step back. 'What?
Tell me what?'

'We are,' said Maud, her forefinger moving between Daisy
and herself, 'the M. McIntyre Agency of Edinburgh.'

'We investigate crimes,' Daisy added.

He started. '*Lady* detectives?'

'Yes,' Maud said.

'The lady detectives from the M. McIntyre Agency?'

'Aye,' said Daisy.

'The two ladies who find stolen jewellery, reveal art fraud
and unmask murderers?' His scrubby red eyebrows rose. 'I
never thought I'd meet such a thing.'

'We are hardly *things,* Sergeant McNeish,' Maud pointed
out severely.

The burly young officer pulled himself up. 'No, you have
me wrong. I'm honoured to meet you both. I'm impressed with
what you've done, even though everybody else in the constabulary thinks you both should be at home raising babies.'

Maud drew in a sharp breath.

He hurried on. 'I'm pleased to make your acquaintance.'

Daisy gave him a charming smile. 'Would you like us to take
a look at the scene of the crime? We're aye used to doing that.
Then we can give you the benefit of our thoughts.'

Maud wasn't sure – she'd never seen Daisy do such a thing
before – but it looked as though her assistant had batted her

eyelashes at Sergeant Sandy McNeish. He certainly thought so, for he coloured.

'If you wouldn't mind,' he mumbled.

Daisy's smile widened. 'Och, we'd be delighted.'

'And perhaps in return you could maintain our cover with the other guests, for the time being,' Maud stated.

Maud and Daisy hastened to their respective rooms to dress as quickly as they could. It was difficult to be businesslike while wearing a dressing gown.

When Maud had dispensed with Daisy's services as her lady's maid last summer and had instead appointed her as assistant to her new role as detective, she had forsworn those clothes and other matters that required a considerable amount of attention. She knew of more than one lady who still expected her personal maid to do everything from dressing hair to pulling up her mistress's drawers. That sort of attention had never been for Maud, even before she'd set up the detective agency. Life was too short to spend an hour or more simply preparing to greet the day.

Maud pinned her hair into a chignon at the base of her neck, washed and dressed in a simple but pleasing sky-blue linen dress with an embroidered back and a belt in a darker shade of blue. It wasn't appropriate to wear an outrageous costume today as favoured by Miss Maisie Smart. She clipped on a pair of sapphire earrings and hurried along the corridor towards Daisy's room, just as her assistant came out. Neatly dressed in finely pleated pale green blouse and skirt with a wide belt at the waist, Daisy was pushing her small notebook into her skirt pocket.

'I wonder if that Sandy McNeish has found anything,' Daisy said as they made their way back to Neil Tremain's room. 'I hope he hasna beaten us to it.'

They reached the bedroom and, in deference to the sergeant's official position, waited outside. Sergeant McNeish gave them a nod and continued looking diligently for clues.

'Were you flirting with the sergeant before, Daisy?' Maud whispered, watching as he lifted the candlestick on the nightstand.

'I'm going to sook up to all policemen in the future. They'd be so handy, dinna you think, if I were taken up for dog-napping or something?'

Maud suppressed a smile.

The officer moved on to examining the chest of drawers, and then the shutters. Satisfied the wooden lock worked as it should and that it was intact, he looked behind the thick curtains which hung to the side of the window and had not been drawn the previous night. He peered up the chimney, then opened the door of the oak wardrobe and gazed inside. Next, he turned to a narrow cupboard set into the wall at waist height and opened the door.

'That could be where your draught came from,' Maud murmured.

She held her breath as Sergeant McNeish peered inside the space.

SIX

The sergeant shut the cupboard door.

'Perhaps not,' Maud said, letting out her breath.

As the policeman's search came to an end, the undertakers arrived. The two men had removed their hats and held them in their hands. They nodded respectfully at Maud and Daisy as they passed into the room. Their hats now rolled and pushed into their jacket pockets, the undertakers strapped Tremain's feet together and wrapped his body firmly in the top sheet of the bed.

The larger of the men took hold of the strap around Tremain's feet and looked at the other fellow. The much younger man was braced to lift the body's torso. 'Ready?'

The younger man nodded and together they hefted the corpse off the bed.

'Remember, I'm to go first,' the older man said. 'We wouldn't want the deceased gentleman to look back and call yon Sandy to join him.'

The policeman paled under his ruddy hue.

'But Neil might call back to *us*.' Daisy shivered as the undertakers started to move towards the door.

'It's just a superstition,' Maud said.

'I ken that. But it doesna mean it isna *true*.' Daisy crossed herself as Tremain's swaddled corpse passed by. 'I'm nae a Catholic,' she added, seeing Maud surprised look, 'but there's nae harm in covering myself.'

Sergeant McNeish looked around one last time, then tramped over to Maud and Daisy. 'I'm away to interview the servants now. The room is yours, ladies – that is, detectives.'

'Thank you, officer.' Daisy smiled prettily at him.

He flushed and hastened away. Daisy grinned.

They stepped quietly into the bedroom, and Maud closed the door behind them. The air felt heavy, and she found herself speaking in a hushed voice. 'Time to get to work. You start at the fireplace end, Daisy. I'll begin with the bed.'

She moved to the last place poor Neil Tremain had drawn breath and studied the indentation in the pillow where his head had lain. Her eyes travelled down to the sheet covering the mattress. There was no blood, which didn't surprise her given there had been only a little on Tremain's chest. As Dr Munro had said to the Procurator Fiscal, the wound must have been caused by a thin implement.

Maud lifted the pillow. No weapon of any description there. She replaced the pillow and turned to the nightstand. On it lay the candlestick, a gold watch with gold chain and a small leather wallet. The wallet was a strip of brown leather folded over to form two inner pockets. She opened it. Inside were a few visiting cards with the deceased's address on Ulva, two five-pound notes, eight one-pound notes and two ten-shilling notes. Perhaps the two lower-value notes were tips for Finlay and Andrew for looking after him, when he left the castle. Five shillings would be considered an unacceptable amount, ten shillings generous.

Maud glanced across to see how Daisy was getting on. She had moved to the fireplace. A quick look up the narrow chimney was enough to show that it could not have provided an escape route or a hiding place. Further, the grey embers in the hearth, where one or two red sparks still glowed, showed no recent fall of soot to indicate any disturbance up the chimney, whether by weapon or killer.

'Naething up the lum,' Daisy said. 'But look at the fancy carving on either side of the mantelpiece. It's ayeways here in novels that secret passages are found.'

'Catherine Morland looked for one in the fireplace surround,' Maud admitted, crossing the polished wooden floor to stand next to Daisy.

'Who's Catherine Morland? Is she a wifie in one of your Sherlock Holmes stories?' Daisy's fingers were tracing the intricate carving.

'Miss Morland is a character in *Northanger Abbey*.'

'Oh,' Daisy said, continuing to press all the likely-looking bumps in the woodwork. 'There *must* be something here.'

Maud didn't add that Jane Austen's heroine had been unsuccessful in her search. Daisy bent to examine the carvings more closely. 'Here's one with an interesting shape. An acorn – and it's worn. It looks like lots of fingers have pressed it before.' She pushed down with her thumb, and it twisted round.

They caught their breath, waiting for an opening in the panelled wall to reveal a dark passage beyond.

Nothing.

'That's nae supposed to happen.' Annoyed, Daisy poked the carving again. 'It's just a wobbly piece of fancy carving.'

There was a soft tap on wood. For a moment, they stared at each other. Was there a passage, after all?

'Undertakers again, ladies,' a man called from the corridor.

Maud gave a wry smile. 'Come in,' she said a little curtly, still disappointed with the lack of a secret stairway. The bedroom door opened.

'We'll just close the curtains and cover the looking glass,' said the older man, carrying a length of dark crêpe cloth.

'We'll do that,' she told them, 'once we have finished in the room.'

'Very good, miss.' He nodded at her and Daisy.

'What a foolish notion,' she said, when the men had gone. 'As if a mirror could suck in the deceased's soul and trap his image.'

Daisy looked dubious. 'It certainly canna once he's safely buried. Did you notice Lord Urquhart opened the window as wide as it would go? Do you think he was giving Neil's spirit a chance to leave the room?'

Maud shook her head. 'I think it was more to do with possible smell. Daisy, if we find out nothing else today, we can at least get the answer as to whether or not the lion statuette is in the room. Let us examine that press.' She marched to the wardrobe and flung open the doors.

Tremain's jackets and trousers hung tidily there. In the little brass cups in the back of one door sat his collars, collar studs and cuff links. His ties were looped over their own small brass rail behind the other wardrobe door. Maud felt amongst the pockets of the garments, while Daisy lifted out each boot one by one and tipped it out. All pockets and boots were empty. On the top shelf was a folded blanket and together they removed it and shook it out. Nothing. Maud let out a sigh of frustration as she bundled up the blanket and replaced it. Daisy shoved the footwear into the wardrobe and shut the door.

Maud moved over to the chest of drawers. On top lay a leather-covered whisky flask, a cigar case containing three cigars, a match box, a few loose coins and ivory-backed hair brushes and hat brush. All the items looked expensive. Clearly Neil Tremain hadn't been poor, so why had Lord Urquhart thought he would steal a valuable item like the bronze?

Daisy joined her and pulled open the top drawer. 'I ken the

killer canna be hiding in here, but I might find the murder weapon.' She gingerly moved around the handkerchiefs and underclothes.

'Do you think it's probable, Daisy,' asked Maud in exasperation, 'that Tremain stabbed himself, staggered across the room to this piece of furniture, buried the implement under his intimate garments and staggered back to bed, leaving no trace of blood on the floor?'

'It's nae probable, but it might be possible.' As Daisy moved on to the second drawer, which proved to be empty, there was a touch of triumph in her voice. 'You taught me that, Maud. When you have eliminated the impossible, whatever remains, however improbable, must be the truth.'

'It's not my quote, but one by Sherlock Holmes.'

'Then it must be true. That Conan Doyle fellow knew a thing or two about investigating.' Daisy finished her search and closed the last drawer. 'There's naething of interest in there, so where now?' She looked around. 'Under the mattress? Come on, give me a hand.'

Daisy took one side of the mattress and Maud the other. Together they lifted it to reveal only the metal springs. They dropped the mattress back onto the bed frame with a gesture of annoyance.

'Under the bed?' suggested Daisy, getting down on all fours. She peered at the floorboards under the bed frame. 'There's something here, Maud.' Her voice was muffled as she crawled under. 'Let me see if I can get it.'

'Is it the murder weapon?' Maud couldn't keep the excitement out of her voice.

'Dinna ken. I'm just trying to avoid the chamber pot which hasna been emptied yet.' Daisy backed out from under the bed, stood and held up a single long white hair.

'You have exceptionally keen eyesight, Daisy.'

'I got it from my mither. This hair isna the murder weapon,

but do you think it could be Magnus's? It canna be Neil Tremain's, as he's almost as bald as a coot.'

Maud's hopes had been dashed again. 'I suppose it wouldn't be strange if it was Magnus's hair, given he owns the castle. He might reasonably be expected to visit his friend in this room.'

'Or it could be a hair of the wifie Ailsa. But I canna see her coming to his room.' Daisy frowned. 'Maybe she came here after everyone else had gone to bed, to continue the stushie they had over dinner. But I dinna ken why her hair would be *under* the bed.'

'Or indeed why would Magnus's? But it might be a clue. Start a fresh page in your notebook, Daisy. Everything of interest should be written down, no matter how seemingly irrelevant.'

Daisy dusted down her hands and skirts and took the cloth-bound notepad and pencil from her pocket. 'I'll keep this.' She folded the single white strand into the book and turned to a new page. 'Nae that we're suggesting Neil was stabbed with a strand of hair, nae matter how coarse.'

'But it could provide us with a clue as to opportunity. Perhaps the villain got into the room last night and waited in hiding under the bed, then killed Tremain and somehow escaped when the door was opened this morning.'

'What?' Daisy scoffed. 'In front of all of us gathered in the corridor?' She caught Maud's eye. 'I'll add it, anyway.' She sat on the chair at the desk. '*Clues.*'

'Note, too, that the spare key to the room is missing and has been for a while. We need to find out exactly when the house-keeper noticed it had gone.'

'Aye.' Daisy jotted down a note to speak to Grace. 'I'll also put valuables left untouched, so the motive wasna robbery.'

Maud nodded her agreement. 'And no sign of a struggle, so Tremain must have either known his killer, or been fast asleep when the killer crept into his bedroom.'

Daisy continued to write. 'But how did the murderer get in?'

'The bedrooms are on the second floor, which must be some fifty feet from the ground. I wonder if there's any ivy or such like to help a person climb?'

Maud went to the window. It was still wide open as Lord Urquhart had left it. Daisy joined her, stood on tiptoes and tried to lean out. 'I'm nae tall enough,' she muttered.

Maud, being taller, had a better view. This bedroom, unlike her own and Daisy's, looked out over the back of the castle grounds. It had no view of the Sound of Mull, but overlooked the gardens with their wide green lawns and gnarled oak trees. In the distance, a loch glistened in the sunlight. In its centre, a small island with a wooded area of silver birch interrupted the blue of the water.

Maud looked down onto the ground directly below. 'There's a narrow path abutting the castle, with shrubs lining it on the other side.' She leaned out a little further to examine the castle wall. The stone finish was rough, but it didn't lend itself to any hand- or toe-holds. 'Nothing useful on the wall.'

Maud drew her head back in. 'Also, of course, the shutters were closed and Sergeant McNeish found no damage. It *might* be possible to exit by the window and lock the shutters after you, but I can't see how in the circumstances.' Maud checked the shutters for herself. 'All intact.'

'Window ajar on account of the warm night,' Daisy wrote again in her notebook, 'but entry nae made that way.'

'We'll have a look outside shortly just to be certain, but we'll finish in here first.' Maud's eyes lighted on the cupboard set into the wall.

It was fastened with a small piece of wood that swivelled on a nail. 'No doubt meant for the occupant's use in the days when people travelled with their belongings in chests.' Maud turned the simple latch. 'With wardrobes and chests of drawers, these cupboards are no longer necessary.' She opened the door and was disappointed but not surprised to find only an empty, shallow cavity. 'Odd that it's panelled inside,' she murmured.

'There may not be a secret panel in the wall, Maud,' came Daisy's voice, 'but maybe there's one in the floor or the ceiling.'

Maud turned. 'Did you notice a trap door when you were under the bed?'

'I canna say I did.' Daisy's face fell. 'Just a minute, I'll have another wee keek.' She disappeared again under the bed frame.

Maud heard a twang as something hit the bed springs.

'Ouch!' cried Daisy.

'Are you all right?' Maud called, pausing in her own search for any concealed opening, footprints or blood on the rest of the floorboards.

'Aye, just dunted my heid. Nae harm done.'

Daisy emerged from under the bed, rubbing the back of her head. 'Naething. But that draught must have come from somewhere.'

She looked up hopefully at the panelled ceiling.

Maud followed Daisy's gaze. 'The ceiling is too high to reach.' Looking around the room, her eye lit upon the nightstand. 'If I stand on that and use, say, the handle of a sweeping brush, that should work.'

'I'll borrow one from the kitchens.' Daisy pushed her notebook and pencil back into her pocket and dashed from the room.

Maud moved the objects off the top of the nightstand, put them on the bed and dragged the nightstand towards the corner of the room. She needed to be methodical; to start in one corner and work her way round. Sitting on the small table, Maud gathered up her skirts with one hand and tentatively climbed to her feet.

Yes, she thought, looking up at the ceiling, it was certainly too high for a person to reach. Even if an intruder could jump down from a concealed panel in the ceiling, he would not be able to climb back that way.

Maud's thoughts strayed to the current crime novel she was reading, *The Mystery of the Yellow Room*. What other methods did the investigator Joseph Rouletabille consider when Mademoiselle Stangerson was attacked in a locked room? Surely Maud had thought of all of them.

There was one other possibility. In Conan Doyle's *The Sign of the Four*, Bartholomew Sholto had been killed by a poisonous dart pricking him just above his ear. How likely was it that someone in the castle had a blowpipe or a poisoned dart? It would be easy to conceal a blowpipe – a thin sliver of wood, sharp-tipped, less than three inches long – and even more so a tiny thorn-like dart. Maud had not examined Tremain's chest, and neither the doctor nor the Procurator Fiscal had found such a thing, but perhaps a small thorn could be buried in the man's wound. If that was the case, then the post-mortem would reveal it, but meanwhile Maud would continue with her investigation.

Assuming the killer had the necessary equipment, there would need to be an entrance for him to fire the dart. If there was a hidden panel in the ceiling, the killer need only open it, blow the poisoned projectile at the sleeping Tremain and then replace the panel.

Daisy burst into the room. 'Maud! What are you doing up there?' she scolded. 'You should have waited for me to get back before you climbed up.' She handed up the broom.

'I've realised a secret panel can't explain how the murderer got into the room, but it might have allowed him to kill Neil Tremain.' Maud explained her thinking on a poisoned dart to her friend.

'Aye, it's a possibility. Try the sweeping brush.'

Maud agreed. Holding the broom by its head, she tested the ceiling carefully with the handle. It wouldn't do to bring down pieces of centuries-old painted wood. 'Nothing moving in this section.'

She climbed down, then together they moved the night-stand and Maud repeated the process until all the ceiling had been examined.

Daisy sighed. 'There must be something else we can try.'

Once more Maud ran through her mental catalogue of detective stories. 'Detective McLevy, one of Edinburgh's first real detectives, who is said to have inspired Mr Conan Doyle's character, Sherlock Holmes...'

'Aye,' Daisy said impatiently. 'What about Detective McLevy?'

'I'm trying to remember.' Maud's face cleared. 'I've got it. A certain Jean Brash used to entice men to her house. In the corner of a door panel of every bedroom was a small hole closed up with a wooden button and the lower panels had been made to slide. At night, she would unblock the hole and peep through to see when the candle was extinguished and, while her victim slept, she'd creep on all fours through the opened panel and steal the watch off the side table or money from their pockets.'

'Michty me,' Daisy murmured, impressed in spite of herself.

Maud was already striding towards the bedroom door. 'We need to examine the panels.'

She and Daisy tapped on the wooden panels, trying to slide them and looking for peepholes, all to no avail.

'I'll make a note of that, anyway.' Daisy once again took out her notebook and pencil. 'We've got nae robbery, nae struggle, nae secret panel in the floor, ceiling, wall or door and nae ivy outside the window. Nae matter – even something ruled out is a step forward.'

'Indeed.'

But, Maud thought, it had been impossible to enter that room. So, how had the killer done it?

SEVEN

Maud went down the stairs, with Daisy behind her carrying the broom, and through a low doorway to the kitchens to look for Sergeant McNeish. A cooked joint of meat sat on the scrubbed pine table, a basket of apples rested on a chair and two female servants were preparing food.

'You've just missed the sergeant, Miss Smart. He's been down here asking questions about poor Mr Tremain,' said the cook, wiping her hands on her apron.

'Did you know the gentleman?' Maud asked, without any real hope.

'No, miss. He never came down to the kitchens. I'm Mrs Baillie. My daughter is Isobel, the housemaid you met yesterday. She's upstairs at present, cleaning the bedrooms. Perhaps you remember her?'

Maud remembered the flustered young woman on their arrival at the castle. 'I do indeed. Isobel is a delightful girl. You must be proud of her.'

The cook, a plump and placid woman with frizzled hair, beamed. 'That I am, miss.'

'And this is...' Maud smiled at the kitchen maid. She was a

short girl of an indeterminate build, with brown hair, not particularly attractive but with large dark eyes that held intelligence.
Maud thought she would be good-looking when she smiled.

'I can speak for myself,' said the girl, at present scowling.
'I'm Kirsty. And I willna be a kitchen maid scrubbing greasy
pots for ever.'

'That's no way to speak to the ladies.' Mrs Baillie made to
hit Kirsty on the side of the head with the wooden spoon she'd
been using to stir the broth, but the young woman was too quick
for her. She ducked.

'I might have to work for a living, but I'm just as good as
they are.' Kirsty glared at the cook.

'Miss Graham and I also work for a living,' Maud said.

'Do you ken where we can find the policeman?' put in
Daisy, propping the broom against the wall.

'He went upstairs, miss.' The cook turned to frown at
Kirsty. 'I'll speak to you later, my lass. Now get on with
preparing our dinner.'

Kirsty shrugged and turned away to put the plates in the
warming oven.

'Thank you, ladies,' said Maud. 'We'll see if we can find the
officer.' She wanted to interview Mrs Baillie and Kirsty, and the
other servants, to find out anything they might know about Neil
Tremain, but this wasn't the right time.

They mounted the stairs to the ground floor. In the great
hall they found the sergeant, looking lost.

'Miss McIntyre and Miss Cameron,' he said, relieved. 'I was
looking for the laird. I have a few questions for him.'

I can think of more than a few, Maud thought.

'Magnus could be anywhere,' Daisy said. 'It might take a
wee while to find him in this place. Why don't we go outside
and see if the murderer could have got in that way?' She gave
him her sweetest smile. 'Us gingers have to stick together.'

The unfortunate man blushed to the roots of his sandy hair, swallowed hard and nodded.

Daisy sashayed across the flagged floor, under the gaze of the portraits and heavy antlers of mountain stags ornamenting the walls. She turned back and smiled at Sergeant McNeish, before leading him through the lobby. The large front door stood open as it had done the previous day, sunlight flooding in. Maud made a mental note to find out at what time it was closed and bolted for the night, and when it was opened again in the morning.

They followed the wall of the castle round to the back and came to a halt on the path. Maud, feeling sorry for the sergeant, took charge.

Shielding her eyes with one hand, she gestured with the other up to the second-floor window. 'That is Mr Tremain's chamber. I wonder what that room is below?'

'You think the killer climbed out of that window and up into Neil's bedroom?' Daisy asked, peering up at the windows.

Sandy McNeish looked with admiration at her. She turned and smiled at him.

'I'm considering every possibility, my friend.' Maud continued to stare up at the building. 'Although I can't see how the murderer could have managed that feat with no purchase in the stone.' She turned her gaze to the path. 'We need to ascertain if there is any soil on the path, or any footprints or other marks in the soft ground or damage to the shrubs lining the path. Don't you agree, Sergeant McNeish?'

'That's right, Miss McIntyre.' Bending to hide his obvious embarrassment at not suggesting this himself, he studied the flagstone path. 'It's clean, so the intruder couldn't have come this way.'

'Not necessarily, Sergeant,' Maud said gently. 'The gardener or his boy might have swept here this morning.'

'That is true, of course.' Sergeant McNeish's ears went pink. 'And something I'd better ask him.'

Daisy was examining the shrubbery. 'I can't see any damage to the plants.' She parted the leaves of azaleas and hydrangeas to consider the soil underneath. 'Nor are there any marks where a ladder might have stood.'

She set off along the path, Maud and the sergeant following, walking slowly to study the path and greenery.

Daisy came to a halt. 'The shrubbery's a wee bit damaged here.' She pointed to where a small bush had been slightly flattened. 'Do you think a ladder could have done that?'

Maud and Sergeant McNeish took turns examining the spot.

'Perhaps,' Maud said, straightening.

'Then again, it might have been made by the castle cat,' put in the sergeant. 'I've seen it lying in a sunny patch along here on more than one occasion.'

'You've been called to the castle a number of times in the past?' Maud asked quickly.

'No, miss. I meant when I come to the annual play and for a wee dram at Hogmanay with the other local folk. That's what we Highlanders call New Year's Eve,' he added.

'We may be Lowland Scots, Sergeant,' Maud said a little sharply, 'but we do know the term Hogmanay.'

He shot Maud and Daisy an embarrassed look.

Maud realised her disappointment was making her brusque. The policeman did not deserve that. She swallowed her impatience. 'We must find the gardener and his boy. After you, Sergeant McNeish.'

They followed the sound of wood being chopped. Through a gate that led into the kitchen garden, they spotted an elderly man brushing soil from potatoes and loading them into his handcart. He wore an old jacket with its buttons missing and his trousers were tied round the waist with a length of garden twine. Clearly the gardener. Sergeant McNeish pushed open the gate to the vegetable garden and stepped over the threshold to hold it aside for the ladies. With a nod of thanks to the sergeant, Maud strode straight over to the old man.

'Good morning,' she said to him with a smile.

He straightened his back as much as it was possible and removed his cloth cap, a worried frown wrinkling his brow. 'Morning, miss... and to you, miss, and you, Sergeant.'

Maud gave him a reassuring smile. 'May I ask you and your boy a few questions?'

He turned and called loudly over his shoulder. 'Peddie!'

The chopping ceased and a boy wearing a hessian sack as an apron came running from round the corner of the vegetable garden. Peddie turned out to be a chubby boy with a choirboy expression and a head of sandy curls.

'Aye, Mr Dalgleish?'

'The sergeant and these two ladies want to ask us a few questions. Mind you answer truthfully.'

'Of course, Mr Dalgleish.' He fixed them all with a solemn expression.

'Thank you,' Maud said. 'I expect you will have already heard of the sad death of Mr Tremain?'

Both gardener and garden boy nodded.

Sergeant McNeish stepped forward. 'I should be asking the questions, miss,' he said, his tone just a little defensive.

Maud thought she saw a smirk pass over the boy's beatific features.

'Did either of you notice anything strange earlier this morning, between seven and half past eight?' the sergeant went on.

'What sort of strange, Sandy?' asked Peddie.

'Sergeant McNeish,' corrected the officer firmly, before addressing Maud out of the side of his mouth. 'What sort of strange, Miss McIntyre?'

Peddie's smirk appeared again briefly.

'Did you see anyone in or around the castle grounds who had no cause to be here?' Maud asked. 'I imagine you must both start work early.'

'Aye, we do, miss. I must have passed the back of the castle around that time, but I can't say I was noticing anybody going in or out. What about you, Peddie?'

'Do you mean we might have seen a bad 'un?' Peddie's eyes grew wide.

'Did you?' demanded Daisy.

The boy shook his head of curls.

'Can you show us where the ladder is kept, Mr Dalgleish?' Maud said. 'I would like to examine the legs for signs of soil.'

'We keep our equipment in tip-top condition, miss.'

'That's as may be, Dalgleish,' the sergeant said, straightening his back, 'but I'd be remiss in my duty as an officer of the law if I didn't at least take a look.'

'Are the ladies coming?'

'That we are,' said Daisy.

The three investigators followed the gardener and his boy round to where stood a large potting shed, its door open.

'Does the door have a snib?' Daisy asked.

The gardener looked surprised. 'No, miss. There's no need to be locking things round here.'

If that also applied to the door of the castle, Maud thought, and she was beginning to feel that it did, then anyone could walk in at any time.

The ladder hung horizontally on a wall inside the shed. Maud walked up to it and examined the feet.

'They look clean to me,' Daisy said, joining her.

'That's what I was telling ye, Sandy.' The gardener was politely indignant. 'If you left damp soil on them, the wood would rot. And the last thing you want is a ladder with rotting feet. It wouldn't be safe.'

Maud nodded. 'When did you last use it?'

'A day or two ago, when the laird asked me to clear out the guttering on an outbuilding.'

'It must be heavy for one person to lift,' put in Daisy.

'I have wee Peddie to help me these days, but I can manage the ladder on my own if needs be.'

'What length would you say it is, Mr Dalgleish?'

'I know its exact length, miss. It's thirty feet.'

Thirty feet, Maud thought. Surely this wouldn't reach the windows on the first floor, much less the second floor where the guest bedrooms were?

Daisy was clearly following Maud's train of thought. 'How far up the castle walls would it reach?' she asked.

'Not far,' the gardener admitted. 'For work on the castle, the laird has to get someone in to do it.'

'Is this your only ladder?' Maud said.

'It is, miss.'

Her eye travelled down to the stone floor of the potting shed. No soil lay there.

'You keep this shed very clean and tidy, Mr Dalgleish.'

The gardener beamed. 'Aye, I do that, miss.'

'Do you sweep the floor often – and the path round the castle?' the sergeant asked before Maud could.

'Every evening, regular as clockwork, before I finish for the day.'

'And what time would that be?' the sergeant went on.

'At this time of year, it'll be about six o'clock.' He touched the pocket of his old waistcoat, proud to show that he owned a watch.

'Thank you, Mr Dalgleish,' Maud said. 'You've been very helpful. We will leave you both to get on with your work.'

As she turned away, she caught a glimpse of the gardener's boy sticking out his tongue at the policeman's back. That child is either foolish or intelligent, she thought. Perhaps intelligent enough to keep a piece of useful information to himself unless some sort of payment was offered. She'd discuss with Daisy how they could contrive a way to speak to him without Mr Dalgleish or the sergeant present.

'It must be time for luncheon, dinna you think, Maud?' Daisy asked hopefully, as they walked back along the path. 'My insides tell me it is.'

On cue, the sergeant's stomach rumbled. 'Sorry, Miss McIntyre. I'd like to thank you both for your assistance.'

'Miss Cameron and I have found that people reveal more to a woman than they ever would to a man, or to the police, and that's where we have an advantage.'

Sergeant McNeish nodded. 'It makes sense. Perhaps we should be employing women.'

'You should,' stated Daisy.

'It'll never happen.' He smiled apologetically. 'The chief constable wouldn't stand for it. There's already resentment throughout the force towards the M. McIntyre Agency. Your success rate has got the whole constabulary reeling.'

'That's rather good to hear,' replied Maud with a small smile, 'but unsettling all the same. I think you're wrong, though, Sergeant, about women joining the force. It will take time, but things have to change. Women's emancipation is sure to happen within the next ten years, and I can see women filling half the constabulary positions after that.'

'Sandy.' Daisy took hold of his arm and brought him to a stop. He turned and looked down into her eyes. 'We need enlightened men like you,' she said.

The sergeant coughed. 'Perhaps we can meet again later this afternoon to discuss the case?'

'Och, why not. By then Miss McIntyre and I are sure to have discovered something of interest,' she told him with a grin.

EIGHT

Luncheon was understandably a desultory affair. Jane Tremain had chosen to have a tray taken to her room, Magnus was silent and ate without raising his head and Ailsa was stony-faced – what was she thinking, Maud wondered, given the woman's apparent dislike of the dead man? Lord Urquhart sought to keep up everyone's spirits by instigating conversations that avoided the topic of Neil Tremain's murder. Dr Munro had been invited to stay for the meal and he had accepted.

'Dr Munro,' Maud began in an undertone, 'what is your impression of Mr Tremain's death?'

The doctor took a slow sip of his wine and put down the glass. 'It's a very sad affair, of course.'

'Of course. But what other observations have you to make?'

He blinked. 'You are most direct, Miss Smart.'

'I find it best to be so, Dr Munro, when one wants answers to one's questions.'

'What specifically would you like to know?'

'How it is decided whether a sudden and unexplained death is suicide, an accident... or murder?'

Her voice had risen a little. Finlay, in the act of pouring

more wine for Magnus, knocked the bottle against the glass. Maud turned to see shock in his face.

'What makes you think that Mr Tremain might have been murdered?' asked Dr Munro with a note of surprise in his voice.

'Miss Graham and I couldn't help but hear what the Procurator Fiscal said,' Maud pointed out. 'A fatal wound to the heart, which looks like foul play.'

'Will what I say appear in one of your novels?'

'I can assure you that it won't.' Maud glanced around the table. 'Would you prefer we had this conversation in a different room?'

'Actually, Munro,' said Lord Urquhart, 'I should also be interested in the answer to Miss Smart's question.'

'Yes, stay,' stated Magnus.

'But Miss Carmichael?'

'Ailsa has a tougher stomach than me.' Magnus gave his sister a fond look. 'Don't you, old girl?'

'I suppose if propriety is to be cast aside so blithely,' she remarked, 'we may as well discuss the details over lunch, so long as Miss Graham doesn't object.'

'I don't,' said Daisy quickly. 'Deadly details are essential to Miss Smart's creative process as a crime writer, so I'm privy to them when I type out her manuscripts, if not before, since we discuss plots. I'm more of an assistant than a secretary.'

'There you go, Roderick,' Magnus replied. 'Permission all round.'

'Very well.' Dr Munro placed his knife and fork on the plate containing his unfinished lunch and returned his attention to Maud. 'I believe you wish to know about the puncture wound to Tremain's heart. It was small, but lethal.'

'Would death have been immediate, as you told the Procurator Fiscal?'

'Immediate or as good as,' he confirmed.

'Would Mr Tremain been able to stab himself, hide the weapon and get back to his bed before expiring?' Daisy asked.

The doctor frowned. 'Why ever might he want to do that?'

'To hide the fact that he'd killed himself?'

Magnus looked up. 'There's no reason to suppose Neil's spirits were so low. The heartburn got him down, of course, but not to that extent.'

'Some years ago,' Ailsa put in, 'he suffered from a severe bout of melancholy.'

'When was that?' Maud said.

'It was when he lived in Glasgow, before he moved away to Ulva.'

Magnus shook his head. 'That's old history.'

'I'm not sure that self-murder is a criminal offence in Scotland,' put in Lord Urquhart. 'I believe there's a split in the thinking on the subject. In any event, it is clearly impossible to prosecute anyone who commits suicide, and forfeiture of the dead person's goods is not legal in Scots law.'

Maud sent him a look of surprise.

He inclined his head. 'I read widely.'

'So,' Daisy said a little impatiently, 'could Neil Tremain have taken his own life, Dr Munro?'

'Stabbed himself and hidden the weapon? No, there wouldn't have been time before death.'

'We – that is, Sergeant McNeish – couldn't find a weapon. What do you think it might have looked like?'

'Something of a reasonable length, sharp and thin.' Dr Munro picked up his cutlery again.

'Like a sword or dagger?' Maud suddenly thought of the weapons arranged on the staircase walls.

'No, such a blade would be too broad.'

'A hat pin?' Daisy asked. 'Or a knitting needle?'

'Possibly,' the doctor said slowly.

'Or a... I don't know... a meat skewer?'

'Those are all implements a female might reasonably be expected to own or have access to, Miss Graham,' he remarked. 'Are you suggesting Tremain's assailant is a member of your own fair sex?'

'No, I'm not.'

'Well, it's unlikely to have been a meat skewer,' Dr Munro continued. 'The metal would be a little too thick, not to mention twisted. The post-mortem will give us a better idea.'

Maud could see they would have to be content with that for the time being. Meanwhile, there were other questions to ask. They had a murder without a weapon, taking place inside a locked room.

'Mr Carmichael, are the doors to the castle secured at night?'

He looked up. 'Sorry, what did you say?'

Maud repeated her question.

He thought for a moment. 'I see what you mean. Yes, my man Finlay bolts the doors last thing at night and unbolts them first thing in the morning.'

'What time is considered last thing?'

'That depends on whether we have guests or not. Last night, it would have been after Dr Munro left. What time was that, Roderick?'

'I looked at my watch when the message came about Mrs Hardie. It was a little after half past ten. You'll remember I left immediately and let myself out of the front door.'

'Finlay will be able to confirm that,' put in Magnus. 'He keeps an ear out for who comes in and goes out.'

'And what time would the bolt have been drawn back this morning?'

Ailsa frowned. 'You are beginning to sound like Sergeant McNeish, Miss Smart.'

With a start, Maud remembered she was supposed to be posing as a crime novelist.

Daisy saved the day. 'It helps in her line of business to have a naturally enquiring mind.'

'Why, yes, of course,' Ailsa said.

'And this morning,' went on Daisy, 'Finlay would have unbolted the door as the servants were going about their business.' She turned to the butler, now standing at the side of the room. 'What time was that, Finlay?'

'About half past six, miss.'

'So,' Maud observed, 'there were two full hours, between half past six and half past eight when Andrew raised the alarm, in which an intruder could have entered the castle.'

'I suppose so.' Magnus took a gulp from his glass of wine. 'But, as I've said, Finlay would have known if anyone had come in through the front door. And I'm told the other servants are always in and out of the kitchens, so one of them would have noticed an intruder entering through the rear door.'

Maud sighed. With the problem of Tremain's door being locked, she couldn't see how anyone could gain entry into the man's room, whether they had come from outside or inside the castle. There was also the matter of why someone wanted him dead. She decided against probing any further, at least not until the right time presented itself to reveal their true identities.

'It must be very hard for you, Mr Carmichael, and you, Miss Carmichael, to lose a dear friend.' In your own house too, Maud thought. 'Had you known Mr Tremain long?'

'We were at school together – Fettes, you know,' Magnus said, his voice dull. 'There's nothing like boarding to make life-long friends.'

And perhaps lifelong enemies, Maud wanted to add. She had been fortunate at her school in Switzerland, where she had made no bosom pals but no enemies either. Boys' boarding schools, she was assured by her brothers, brought out the inner animal.

'I'm also an Old Fettesian.' Lord Urquhart looked at her over the top of his wine glass.

As soon as the meal was over, Ailsa went to her bedroom to rest, promising to drop in on Jane to see if there was anything she required, and the three gentlemen walked down to the stables to admire Magnus's new chestnut mare, leaving Maud and Daisy free to hurry along to Tremain's room.

'To recap,' Maud said to Daisy, as she pushed open the bedroom door, 'there was no one hiding in the room when the doctor broke open the door, no weapon found, and although the window was ajar, the shutters remained secured. What are we missing, apart from the whereabouts of the bronze lion we're here to retrieve?'

'We're missing a secret panel, a trapdoor in the floor and a removable door panel.' Daisy sighed.

'And outside,' Maud continued, 'no stranger was seen this morning by the gardener or his boy, there are no marks on the path, in the soil or on the ladder, which is too short, anyway, and no significant damage to the shrubbery.'

'There's still the missing spare key to Neil's room,' Daisy said doubtfully.

'A slim chance, but it's the only lead we've got. We need to find out how long ago it went missing.' Maud crossed the floor to the cupboard set into the wall. 'First, though, this cupboard is bothering me.' She peered inside to inspect the panelling once more. She was disappointed. 'We were right the first time, Daisy. It's nothing but an empty cupboard.'

'Let me try.' Daisy nudged her friend aside. Putting her hand inside the cavity, she felt for a hidden catch. 'Maud!' Her eyes lit up. 'There's some sort of knob in the wood. I have a better feeling about this one. I'm going to see if it'll move.'

Maud's heart began to race. Surely the investigation was turning in their favour at last. She held her breath as a creaking sound began, and the back of the cupboard slid slowly to one side.

Maud darted forward. 'It's a priest hole!' The panel had opened to reveal a second small chamber.

Daisy grimaced. 'I hope there's nae a pile of old bones.'

They peered inside. On the floor of the hidden space stood a bronze statuette in the form of a lion.

'Michty me!' Daisy's words came out in a startled squeak. 'The statuette!' She reached in and drew the object out.

In silence they looked at it. Maud cleared her throat and smiled. 'Well, that's one mystery cleared up.'

'Aye,' said Daisy, frowning, 'but who stole it? I mean, can we be certain it was Neil?'

'That's a good point, Daisy. It would be reasonable to assume that Tremain was the thief, unless...' – Maud hesitated as she thought – 'it was stolen by someone else who had access to this bedroom.'

'Like Andrew, you mean?'

'Exactly like Andrew. In fact, is it likely that a guest would have known about the priest hole? Our host, I imagine, would know, and presumably his sister.'

'And we have that clue of a white hair. Although' – Daisy tapped her chin with a dusty finger – 'why would Magnus pinch his own statuette and then as good as accuse Lord Urquhart?'

'The plot thickens, Daisy.' Maud felt rather pleased. 'This must be as complicated as any crime Sherlock Holmes had to solve.'

Daisy glanced down at the statuette in her hands. 'How long has Andrew worked at the castle? And we mustna forget to interrogate Isobel. She must come into the bedroom every day to clean it and make up the fire.'

'Now I think of it, Daisy, I'm not sure that Andrew or Isobel would have known of the priest hole. When these secret spaces were constructed, their existence would have been known only to the laird, his heir apparent and the unfortunate priest who needed to hide in it.' Maud knew such chambers were places to hide Roman Catholics after the failure of the risings of the House of Stuart.

'Maybe Tremain found it by accident.'

'You mean fiddling around inside the cupboard, having heard of such things as priest holes?'

'Aye.'

'It's possible...'

'You ken, Maud,' Daisy said after a pause, 'we havena considered whether Neil Tremain could have been killed by someone looking for the statuette. Or if our finding it shows that if the murderer had hidden in the secret cupboard, then he left the lion behind because it was of nae interest to him.'

'So, what are you saying?'

'I'm nae sure, but it sounded good.'

Maud and Daisy stared into the chamber. It was no more than five feet in height and less than that in width. 'They were built into thick walls,' Maud explained, 'behind fireplaces or bookcases, between floors and ceiling. I'm sure I read of one, scooped out of a foundation wall, that was large enough to hold fifty or sixty people. But this one...' She shuddered. 'Imagine hiding in such a confined space.'

'There's nae need to imagine it,' said Daisy, setting the statuette on the floor. 'That was getting heavy. Now, give me a hand up. One of us needs to try it and it canna be you – you're too tall.'

Maud helped her to climb into the cupboard. Daisy drew up her knees and gathered her skirts around her legs. Even with her diminutive stature, she had to bend her head at an uncomfortable-looking angle in order to fit into the cupboard.

'Pooh!' She wrinkled her nose. 'It's mingin in here.'

'It probably smells of must.'

'As long as it's nae a deid body. Pass me that lion, Maud.'

Maud did so. Daisy placed it in her lap. 'It's awfa cramped, but it's possible.' She clambered out, the statuette under one arm.

'Well done, Daisy. You've proved that a person could hide in there if they are small enough.'

Daisy wiggled her shoulders, like a hen puffing up her feathers after a night squashed in a coop. 'Who lives in the castle and is the same size as me?'

'I don't know, Daisy, but that is something we can find out.'

NINE

'We should return to my room to discuss the case,' Maud said.

'I'll nip downstairs first,' Daisy told her, as they left Tremain's bedroom, 'and put this troublesome wee object back on the table in the great hall.' She gestured to the statuette.

'Thank you, Daisy. Lord Urquhart told us our host didn't want to draw attention to its disappearance, so he'll be pleased to see it returned to its rightful position.'

'Nae to mention surprised!'

Maud smiled. 'We will discreetly inform Magnus of our find this afternoon. I heard him and his sister say at luncheon that he was going to rest for a couple of hours, so we need not be concerned that he'll see the bronze before tea time. Tremain's death has been a shock to him. Now off you go before the servants start moving about upstairs again.'

'I willna be long.' Daisy set off along the corridor towards the spiral staircase, the bronze lion tucked under her arm.

Maud crossed the corridor to her chamber diagonally opposite Tremain's room and left the door ajar for Daisy, before settling herself in one of the two deep armchairs.

'That was quick,' Maud said when Daisy entered the room, closing the door behind her and dropping into the other chair.

'Because I didna want to get caught.' Daisy pulled out her notebook and pencil from the pocket of her skirt.

'Who have we got,' Maud began, leaning forward in the chair, 'who could fit into the secret chamber? Let's call it *Suitable-Sized Suspects*. I've been thinking about it, and amongst those of us upstairs, only Jane Tremain would be petite enough.'

Daisy gave her a sharp glance. 'Do you honestly think Jane would murder her faither?'

'Not really,' Maud admitted. 'Magnus and his sister are both thin enough to fit into the hidden space, but they are too tall.'

'As to the downstairs folk,' observed Daisy, scribbling in her book, 'Andrew is stocky, and Grace the housekeeper is too plump, but her husband Finlay could probably squeeze in.' Daisy continued to write. 'Mrs Baillie the cook also wouldna fit in, nor I reckon would Kirsty the kitchen maid. Isobel the housemaid might manage at a pinch. But what would be the motive for Jane, Finlay or Isobel?'

'Let's consider Jane first, as I can think of a motive for her. If Jane is her father's only child – that is something we need to find out – then she must be in line to inherit his fortune. I know he complained at dinner yesterday about the cost of keeping her, but that could simply have been bluster.'

'Maybe it wasna normal expenses – maybe Jane needed the money for something else?'

'Yes, but I'm not sure what.'

Daisy shrugged. 'Blackmail?'

'Write that thought down; it's something we should keep in mind. We can dismiss Dr Munro as Tremain was dead before the doctor arrived,' Maud went on. 'There are the outdoor servants to consider, I suppose. We've not set eyes on the groom yet, but the gardener isn't the right build to fit into that space. What about his boy, Peddie?'

'The laddie is wee enough, but I canna see him hiding in the cupboard.'

'Because he looks so angelic?'

Daisy laughed. 'Maybe. But bairns of his age dinna sit still for long. He'd fidget so much that he'd give himself away.'

Daisy would know, Maud thought, as she was the eldest of a large family. 'So we have Jane Tremain, Finlay and perhaps Isobel as possible suspects inside the castle, or an unknown person outside. And, apart perhaps for Jane, no obvious motive.' Maud sighed. 'Not much to go on...'

'We can solve this, Maud.' Daisy looked up from writing in her book, with a determined look on her face. 'Just as we've solved all our other cases.'

Maud still felt dispirited. It was their most difficult case yet. 'You do realise that we've not been employed to investigate this, Daisy?'

'Aye, I ken. But Sergeant McNeish isna up to it, and we should do our civic duty and give him a hand.'

'Civic duty, is it?'

'Of course, Maud.'

'Very well.' Maud smiled and straightened her back. 'Note down *Motive* against Jane's name and put *Inheritance* next to it.'

'To murder her own faither, the motive would need to be strong.' Daisy finished writing.

'Money *is* a strong motive: not having it and fed up with being attached to her father's apron strings.'

'Or in need of money because she's being blackmailed?'

'I don't know, Daisy. Revenge? Hate? Love?'

'Aye, love,' Daisy said thoughtfully. 'Maybe she was in love with some mannie that her faither didna approve of.'

'Then it can't be Lord Urquhart,' Maud said sharply.

Daisy sent her a quick glance. 'I never said it was.'

'I meant,' Maud went on quickly, 'that surely Tremain would approve of *him* as a son-in-law.'

'Nae if he reads the society magazines. Our handsome lordship seems to go through debutantes like nobody's business.'

'Daisy!'

'I'm nae saying Lord Urquhart's a womaniser, but Neil Tremain might have thought so. And then there's the lion. Magnus could have confided in Neil that he thought Lord U had stolen the statuette.'

'No, that won't do, Daisy. If Tremain was the thief, he'd know the accusation was false.'

Daisy flopped back in the armchair. 'This case is making us go round in circles.'

'We need to go back to basics,' Maud said firmly.

'I'm going to start a new list: *Questions to Be Answered.*' Daisy turned to a fresh page in her notebook. 'One. Why would someone want Neil Tremain deid?'

'Two. Who knew of the priest hole? Three. Which room is above Tremain's and which one below?'

Daisy wrote furiously. 'Four. Is the key to Neil's bedroom door still missing? Five. Has anyone lost a hair?'

Maud laughed. 'Perhaps rephrase that last question.' Daisy grinned.

'Six,' Maud went on. 'Where was everyone at approximately half past seven this morning when Tremain was murdered?'

'And if the murderer didna sneak into the bedroom earlier to hide in the secret chamber, how did he get into the room through a locked door? That's number seven. Question eight will be: if the killer had used the hidden cupboard and came out to stab Tremain, how did he escape from the room?'

'You know, Daisy, the more I think of it, the less likely it seems that number eight could have happened. The killer would have had to hide in the priest hole—'

'Or in the wardrobe or behind the curtains or under the bed,' put in Daisy helpfully.

'Yes, any of those, and he'd have to have been hidden before Tremain went to bed.'

Daisy looked pleased. 'That would narrow down our suspect list a lot.'

'It would, but why would the killer wait all through the night and only stab his victim about an hour before Tremain would normally wake? It doesn't make any sense.'

'It could be that he didna fancy spending the night in the same room as a deid body.'

'Rather late to suffer such sensibility. And by staying in that cupboard – that very *cramped* cupboard – the killer ran the risk of being caught. And surely,' Maud added, thinking of Daisy's recent comments, 'Andrew would have spotted a villain in the wardrobe or under the bed.'

'Aye.' Daisy sighed. She brightened. 'But maybe not behind the curtains and definitely not in the secret cupboard. And not if Andrew was in on the murder. Or if he is the murderer.'

'Hmm, yes, that's true. There's still the question, though, of why wait all those hours to do the deed?'

'I'm going to leave in number eight about how did the killer escape from the room, and add nine: why did the murderer wait until morning to stab Neil?' Daisy looked up from her notebook. 'Is there anything else?'

Maud thought for a moment. 'Ten. Why did Tremain lock his bedroom door last night? Magnus said it was most unusual for him to do so.'

'Aye, what had happened to make Neil feart?' said Daisy, still writing. 'Eleven,' she went on. 'Why did Ailsa dislike Neil?'

'We need one more question to bring the list to a round dozen. I like to keep things tidy. Of course! Twelve. Who inherits Tremain's estate? That brings us nicely back to Jane Tremain.'

Daisy nodded and continued to scribble.

'Daisy!' Maud suddenly whispered. 'Can you hear something outside the door?'

They both listened. There came the faint but unmistakable sound of a creaking floorboard. Then silence.

'Someone's listening,' Daisy hissed.

Maud cleared her throat and raised her voice. 'Now, where was I, Miss Graham?' She sent Daisy a meaningful look and began striding up and down the bedroom.

'Gertrude Quayle is stumped, Miss Smart. She can't find anything in the dead woman's bedroom that points them towards a probable motive for stabbing Lady Marchpane.' Daisy sent Maud a grin.

'Oh, yes.' Maud cleared her throat. '*Gertrude paused in the act of pulling back the bed sheet to reveal the extent of the damage to Lady Marchpane's throat. Her heart thudding—*'

'Not thudding,' said Daisy.

Maud stopped pacing. 'Why not?'

'Just now you said' – Daisy pretended to flip a couple of pages of her notebook – '*Gertrude sprang towards the four-poster, eager to—*'

'All right. *With a light step, she hastened towards the bed, her tweed skirt and coat—*'

'Not a tweed skirt and coat.'

'Why not?' Goodness, who was writing this novel? Maud wondered.

'She's wearing a nightgown.'

Maud drew in a sharp breath. 'Oh, *is* she?'

'Shall I read back what you dictated earlier, Miss Smart?'

'Yes, why don't you,' Maud said, a touch of exasperation in her voice.

'*The cupboard door burst open and a bearded man jumped out, a dagger in his hand. "Put that knife down," cried Gertrude*

in a steely voice. "Scream all you want, you little fool," he
snarled, his features twisted viciously.'

Really, thought Maud, Daisy was doing an excellent job,
but can features twist viciously?

'"There's no one to hear you",' Daisy continued, mimicking
a male voice.

She changed to that of a female. '"I should warn you that
I'm trained in unarmed combat." He gave a contemptuous
laugh. "Do your worst." Gertrude sprang forward and knocked
the blade from his hand. "I don't need to scream for help. I don't
need any help, you swine," she hissed, "and certainly not when
dealing with the likes of you." He cringed as the dirk spun across
the floor. "You're too quick for me, Miss Quayle." "One down
and three to go," Gertrude drawled.'

Daisy paused and looked at the door, Maud's gaze
following.

Maud nodded and trod softly towards it. She turned the
handle, snatched the door open and looked out. The corridor
was empty.

Maud closed the door and came back to her seat. 'Whoever was
there has gone.' She beamed at her friend. 'That was a remarkable
piece of invention, Daisy. I think you should be the crime novelist.'

Daisy laughed. 'I'll keep that in mind if I ever need a new
job.'

Maud glanced at her wristwatch. 'It's just after three
o'clock. We need to carry out some interviews below-stairs and
this will be a good time. Their tasks should be finished for the
present, and with luck, they will all be in the kitchen.'

As Daisy rose, she glanced at the window. 'Look at the
colour of that sky!'

Maud turned. It was the shade of an angry bruise. 'It looks
like the warm weather is going to break soon.'

'Whatever the weather is doing, I'm going to keep my

bedroom window shut tonight in case anyone tries to get in and murder me in my sleep.'

'I'm sure Mr Tremain was specially chosen by the killer, Daisy.'

They descended the stairs to the semi-basement, and Maud pushed open the door to the servants' hall. They were all seated round the long pine table, half-drunk cups of tea in front of them and two large brown teapots in the centre. The cook had her hands in a large mixing bowl and the kitchen maid was slicing a mound of runner beans.

'... murder,' Finlay was saying.

Six pairs of eyes turned towards Maud and Daisy. They all got to their feet respectfully, Mrs Baillie hastily wiping her hands on her white apron.

Finlay recovered himself quickly. 'Good afternoon, Miss Smart, Miss Graham. Is there something you require?'

'Only a few moments of everyone's time, if that is convenient?' said Maud.

'Certainly.'

Grace hurried to plump up the cushion on a rocking chair. 'Miss Smart, if you would like to take this seat and Miss Graham...' The housekeeper looked around the room as if to find another rocking chair.

'Please do not trouble yourself, Grace. If everyone could take their seats again, Miss Cameron and I will be happy to join you round the table.'

'Miss *Cameron*?' The cook cocked her head to one side and stared at Daisy.

Finlay hastened to move two chairs standing against the wall and place them at the table. As Maud and Daisy slid onto the seats, the cook returned to her chair at the table and motioned the rest of the servants to follow suit.

'Aye, Mrs Baillie, I'm Miss Daisy Cameron. And this is Miss

Maud McIntyre. She's nae a novelist and I'm nae her secretary. We're private detectives from Edinburgh.'

'*Detectives!*' Isobel gasped. 'So it really is murder?'

'It can't be,' stated the cook. 'We've never had a murder in this house.'

'There's a first time for a'thing, Mrs B,' said Kirsty.

Grace put up her hand in rebuke. 'If Mr Tremain was murdered, the laird will be informing us in his own good time. Perhaps the poor gentleman was after doing it himself.'

Kirsty finished slicing the runner beans, threw down the knife and leaned back in her chair. 'What, stabbed himself in the chest as a cure for indigestion?'

'There's no need for your cheek, my girl,' admonished the cook.

'So you have been informed of the details?' Maud asked.

'Not officially, no, but Andrew and I were not ordered to keep the information to ourselves,' said Finlay. 'It is strange, though, his locking the bedroom door like that. It's not the usual practice for guests, and that includes Mr Tremain on the rare occasions he comes.'

'Aye, he'd no call to do that,' put in Mrs Baillie, gathering the dough in her bowl into a ball.

Andrew finished his tea and put the cup back in the saucer. 'He told me—'

'Heavens!' cried Grace, her chins wobbling as she climbed to her feet. 'I'm forgetting my manners. Would you ladies like a cup of tea? Kirsty can easily make a fresh pot.'

Kirsty looked less than enthusiastic at the prospect.

'No, thank you, Grace. We've had a delicious and satisfying luncheon.' She turned to Andrew. 'You were saying that Mr Tremain had told you...?'

'He said he was upset by a noise he'd heard outside his room in the afternoon. He was definitely nervous about something. I think he'd got it into his head that a thief might be on the prowl.

He told me that he was going to lock the door as soon as I had left.'

Maud groaned inwardly. Was the brief incident between her and Lord Urquhart the reason Neil Tremain had locked his door? It hardly seemed sufficient to justify that action. She sent Daisy a glance and saw that her assistant was thinking the same.

'He's probably read too many detective stories, like the laird,' added Andrew.

The mention of detective stories caused the servants to remember why Maud and Daisy were there. They all stared at the duo.

'Rest assured,' said Maud, 'we'll find the murderer.'

TEN

'All this is most interesting,' Maud went on. 'Can you tell us who took up the bicarbonate of soda to Mr Tremain's room last night?'

'That was me, miss.' Isobel spoke quietly. 'Dr Munro asked for the drum of bicarbonate and a glass of water.'

'And how did he convey this message to you?'

Isobel frowned. 'In the usual way we receive messages from upstairs, miss. He rang the bell for me.'

So neither Andrew nor the doctor had been left alone in the room with Tremain. Maud made a mental note.

'And you were in the room when Mr Tremain took the mixture?' Daisy asked Isobel.

Isobel shook her head.

'I was, miss,' Andrew said. 'Isobel left, the doctor mixed the powder and the water, waited for Mr Tremain to drink it and then he went back downstairs. Not long after, I finished my valeting duties and came down to help clear the dining room.'

'And you are certain that Mr Tremain did lock the door?' Maud asked.

'I didn't hear him do so, miss, but I assume he left his bed to do it himself. As I came out of the room, I noticed that the key was in the lock.'

'Very well. I think that's everything for now concerning yesterday evening. Just one more question if I may: the second key to Mr Tremain's bedroom door – when did it go missing?'

Grace wrinkled her brow. 'That's a difficult one to answer. It could have been last year, or perhaps the year before. What do you think, Finlay?'

'It was May 1910,' he told his wife. 'I remember the old king had died and the Prince of Wales proclaimed George V. The guest we had at the time – Mr Smith, the kirk minister from the mainland – was full of apologies for having mislaid it. He blamed it on distress at the old king's passing and we've not seen the key since.'

Another disappointing answer, Maud thought. How helpful it would have been to find the missing key amongst someone's belongings!

Daisy spoke again. 'We'd like to know where everyone was between seven and half past eight this morning.'

'That's what the sergeant asked us earlier.' Mrs Baillie threw the dough on to the floured end of the table. 'Imagine – the silly man asking us questions and be expecting us to answer when the kitchen was hoatching. Everyone was in and out. Upstairs luncheon to be got ready and the breakfast washing-up needing to be done, and our own crockery, and everything put away, fires to be checked and all sorts.' She began to roll out the dough.

'If you want my opinion, the daughter did it,' stated Kirsty firmly.

Maud's pulse quickened. 'Why do you say that?'

'You mustn't mind Kirsty, Miss McIntyre,' said Grace quickly, sending a fierce look at the kitchen maid. 'She's one of those new *socialist* types.'

Kirsty sat up in her chair. 'The idea of everyone being equal isna new,' she retorted. 'And it's about time it happened. Anyway, I think it's Miss Tremain because when someone has been murdered a member of the family is always the obvious suspect.'

'Why would she wait 'til they were away?' asked the cook, cutting out scones with a metal cutter. 'Why not do it at home?'

'And be even more the obvious suspect?' Kirsty scoffed. 'Besides she may have been driven over the edge by his nagging about her finding herself a husband.'

Maud was reminded how servants hear everything and discuss it amongst themselves below-stairs. She remained silent.

'No self-respecting young woman wants to marry just to keep a roof over her head,' Kirsty retorted. 'Then there's the laird and Miss Ailsa.'

'Kirsty!' Finlay spoke sharply. 'We all know the laird and his sister would never think of doing such a thing.'

There was a brief moment of silence before the cook spoke again. 'There's Lord Urquhart, but I think we're all agreed about him.'

'A nice gentleman,' said Grace. 'Always courteous, never demanding.'

'Which makes him suspicious, if you go by detective stories,' added Kirsty.

'I think he's a lovely gentleman!' whispered Isobel and blushed.

'Och, he is!' added the cook.

Finlay shook his head. 'I suppose all this enthusiasm has nothing to do with the fact that's he's a good-looking man?'

'Everything,' said Kirsty. 'Though he wasn't looking half his usual self when I saw him coming down the stairs yesterday afternoon, when he was supposed to be watching that stupid play. I'd like to ken what he was up to, because he looked awfa flushed in the face.'

Maud felt a slight flush to her own cheeks and hoped no

one noticed. She must have just missed the girl by seconds. As to why Lord Urquhart looked heated, could it be anything to do with their being so physically close in that small alcove...

'It could be any reason,' Grace snapped. 'A gentleman can go to his own bedroom if he wishes.'

'*If* that's where he was going,' the kitchen maid muttered darkly.

'What were you doing, Kirsty, to have observed Lord Urquhart on the stairs?' Maud tried to keep an accusatory note out of her tone.

It was the girl's turn to colour. 'I thought I heard a noise and I was worried someone was upstairs who shouldna be.'

Was she telling the truth? Maud couldn't be sure.

'That's it, then,' Finlay said. 'There's no one else staying in the house.'

'Does anyone ken why Mr Tremain has been here only a few times before?' asked Daisy. 'I thought he and the laird were old friends.'

'The laird told me once that Mr Tremain was something of a recluse. He doesn't travel much and doesn't have his own valet,' Finlay explained. 'He gave up his job and moved to Ulva about ten years ago and hardly ever leaves the island.'

'Do you know what his job was before then?' asked Maud.

'I believe he was quite high up in the ship-building industry,' Finlay told her.

I wonder what happened to bring about that change, Maud thought. Of course, he may just have grown tired of the work and wanted a peaceful life. But Ailsa had said – what? – that Tremain had been severely depressed before he'd moved to Ulva. She wondered what had occurred to cause such a thing. Jane would have been young then, perhaps about twelve. Had the girl's mother died ten years ago? With a start, Maud realised she didn't know if the woman *was* dead. There had been no mention of Tremain's wife, and so she and Daisy had assumed Jane was Tremain's next of kin.

'Can you tell me where you all were between seven and half past eight this morning?' Daisy was repeating her earlier question in her best detective voice.

'Kirsty here is up at six o'clock every morning, Miss Cameron,' explained Finlay. 'It is her job to get the kitchen range hot enough to boil the water. The rest of us rise at half past six to ready the rooms on the ground floor and light the fires. And the breakfasts have to be made for below- and above-stairs. We eat at eight o'clock...' He paused. 'Do you require to know what we have for breakfast?'

'That won't be necessary,' Daisy told him.

Finlay continued. 'As soon as our breakfast is finished, Isobel takes tea and toast up to Miss Ailsa in her bedroom. She likes a breakfast tray in her room.'

'Miss Ailsa has no lady's maid?' Maud asked. Now she thought of it, there wasn't one seated at the table.

'Her maid, Lizzie, retired last year and lives in a cottage in the grounds. Shieling Beag. It's Gaelic for small dwelling. Miss Ailsa didn't feel the need for another lady's maid. She is uncon-ventional in that way. With Mr Tremain bringing no valet of his own,' Finlay went on, 'Andrew took the can of hot water for washing and shaving up to the gentleman.'

'And you, Finlay?' Maud said. 'Where were you at this time?'

'I was preparing to carry out my morning role as valet and barber to the laird. I was about to go upstairs to the laird's bedroom when Andrew came back into the kitchen with Mr Tremain's hot water, saying he couldn't wake the gentleman and that the door was locked.'

'And this was at...?'

'Shortly after half past eight. I said I thought the gentleman was likely still sleeping and that Andrew should wait another twenty minutes or so.'

'Which you did, Andrew?'

'Yes, miss. I went up about five minutes before nine with fresh hot water, but there was still no reply. I knocked harder, turned the handle and again tried to open the door, but it remained locked. I ran down the stairs to the laird's room on the first floor to tell him and Finlay, and they came up and the laird started shouting and banging on Mr Tremain's door, fit to raise the dead.'

Kirsty snorted back a laugh.

'My apologies, ladies.' Andrew hung his head.

'Go on,' said Daisy, seeing the cook glare at Kirsty.

'I reckon it would have been about nine o'clock by then and the doctor arrived shortly after.'

The servants would have been rushing about hither and yon with their usual tasks, Maud thought, but with all the coming and going, could any of them really give each other an alibi for the hours around Neil Tremain's murder? Although from eight o'clock to half past they were all eating their breakfast and any absence would have been noted.

'So you all rose from the table about half past eight?'

'That's correct.'

'Not quite, Finlay,' Grace said. 'You left about ten minutes before that, don't you remember? You said you'd forgotten to clean and polish the laird's boots.'

'You are right,' he told his wife. 'I had forgotten. I nipped off into the boot room next door.'

Oh, had he? thought Maud. Had he really forgotten? The boot room had access onto the corridor which ran past the rest of the kitchens, which meant that Finlay could have crept past the hall where the other servants were still taking their breakfast. It seemed that all the servants appeared to have an alibi for the time of Tremain's murder, bar Finlay.

'We'll let you all get on.' Maud rose, followed by Daisy.

'Those scones look like they're going to be bonnie,' Daisy added with a grin to the cook.

Mrs Baillie smiled. 'You'll be getting them with your tea this afternoon, miss.'

Maud thanked them all for their time, then she and Daisy made their way back upstairs.

'So,' Daisy observed, 'we can cross the missing key off our list of questions to be answered.'

'It looks like it.'

'One down and eleven questions to go.'

'Now we should find the sergeant and see if he has learned anything of interest,' Maud said.

They reached the second floor and hurried towards the policeman's room at the far end of the passage, on the other side of the corridor to Daisy's room. Maud knocked on Sandy McNeish's door. He opened it, and when he saw Daisy next to Maud, his frown turned into an anxious smile.

'Hello, Sergeant.' Daisy gave him a warm smile.

'Miss Cameron. Miss McIntyre. Please come into my bedroom.' He coloured at the realisation of what he'd just said and hastened on. 'I meant to say come into my office where we can discuss the case.' He stepped aside to let them enter.

'Exactly what we were going to suggest, Sergeant,' Maud said as she stepped over the threshold. 'What a delightful room for an office,' she told him as they entered. It was in fact a smaller version of her own chamber but no less crowded with furniture. The room was rather chilly as the fire had not yet been made up.

He gestured to the two armchairs, which Maud and Daisy took, and perched himself on the edge of the bed. 'Have you ladies learned anything?'

'You first, Sergeant,' Daisy said. 'What have you got jotted down in your pocketbook?'

He drew his notebook from his uniform pocket and leafed through a few pages until he came to the one he wanted. He cleared his throat and began to read.

'*At about half past nine on the morning of Saturday, 14th September 1912, I went to Clachan Castle and there found the dead body of a man identified to me as Mr Neil Tremain, lying in bed with a stab wound to his chest. The door of the room had been broken open to gain access. The room was tidy, with a sum of money, and there were no signs that a struggle had taken place. The window was open, but the shutters securely fastened across it. The deceased's room was about forty feet from the ground with no way of climbing up. I searched the room and found nowhere a person could be concealed. No man could have got out of the room and then fastened the shutters or locked the door behind him. The door key was found inside the room and there was no spare. I was unable to find any weapon in the room.*'

'Most thorough,' Maud said graciously.

'Nothing gets past you, Sergeant McNeish,' said Daisy in her best admiring voice. 'And have you learned anything from below-stairs?'

'One of the servants is of the opinion that the guilty person is Lord Urquhart.'

This didn't come as a complete surprise to Maud, but to hear it from a police officer was concerning. 'What is the evidence for such a belief?' she asked.

'It seems that the girl caught sight of him acting suspiciously yesterday afternoon, when everyone else was watching the play.'

Not quite everyone else, thought Maud. 'In what way acting suspiciously?'

'He was coming down the stairs and looked mighty flushed.'

'That's suspicious behaviour?' Daisy asked. 'It doesna sound very suspicious to me.'

'He was *creeping* down the staircase, the girl said.'

'Creeping? Haivers! I canna imagine how such a big man would be able to *creep*. But he would be going quietly, wouldn't he, if the play was on? He wouldna want to disturb those watching it.'

Sergeant McNeish squirmed uncomfortably, perched on the bed. 'The kitchen maid seemed to think that he should have been watching it with the others.'

'Well, what was the kitchen maid doing there?' demanded Daisy.

Sergeant McNeish looked embarrassed. He had clearly not asked Kirsty that question.

Maud felt she should intervene at this point. 'We have some news of our own, Sergeant.'

'Aye?' He gazed at her with relief.

'Miss Cameron and I have discovered a secret cupboard, a cupboard within a cupboard, in short a priest hole, in Mr Tremain's chamber.' Maud decided not to say anything about the stolen statuette. She needed to maintain client confidentiality and the theft wasn't necessarily relevant to the murder case.

'And we think a person could have hidden inside it, before or after murdering Mr T,' Daisy said. 'It would have to be a dainty wee person like myself.' She smiled at him from under her lashes.

Maud gave an inward smile. Daisy was again pursuing her plan of ingratiating herself with the policeman.

'Miss Cameron, would you show me the secret cupboard, please?' A hopeful look had appeared on his face.

'Certainly. Are you coming, Maud?'

'The task doesn't need both of us, Daisy. I'll wait here, if that is permitted, Sergeant?'

Daisy and Sergeant McNeish left the room. Maud wrapped her arms around herself and stared at the empty hearth. She closed her eyes to think about Lord Urquhart yesterday afternoon. What had the man been doing in the corridor? Hadn't he engaged the M. McIntyre Agency to investigate the theft? Not that being squeezed in the alcove with him hadn't been an... enjoyable experience. One part of her mind understood the necessity of being concealed there by his body. But the other part of her brain didn't seem to be functioning properly. She mused on the problem.

'A very exciting discovery.' Sandy McNeish pushed open the door and held it ajar for Daisy to enter, his face flushed with pleasure. 'This takes the investigation a step closer to finding the culprit.' He took out his police notebook again and began to write.

Maud looked up as the door opened for a second time. Magnus, Lord Urquhart and Dr Munro entered without knocking. Daisy slipped her notebook and pencil down the side of her armchair. She, like Maud, had remembered that Magnus and Dr Munro were still unaware they were private detectives.

'Ah, ladies,' exclaimed Magnus, seeing Maud and Daisy seated there. He turned to address the officer. 'We thought we'd come along to see how the case is progressing, Sandy, but I can see you're chatting to the ladies. Perhaps Miss Smart can give you a few pointers, eh? Keep you on the right track, so to speak.' He gave Maud a stage wink.

'The sergeant has made a most interesting discovery, Mr Carmichael. Perhaps he would like to tell you about it?'

Sergeant McNeish, his ears red, told the three men about the priest hole. 'So it looks like a small fellow might have hidden there and committed the murder,' he concluded.

Magnus stared. 'The only *small fellow* in the castle is my man Finlay – and I can assure you he would do no such thing. He came to me as a young man, and I'd trust him with my life.'

But what about with Tremain's life? That was a question Maud would like to have asked.

The policeman was stuttering his apologies, clutching his

notebook and pencil nervously. 'It's only a remote possibility, sir, just one of a number of avenues to be investigated. In fact, I'm seriously considering another suspect.'

'Who is it, man? Out with it!'

'It'd be more than my job's worth, sir.'

'It should be more than your job's worth to cast aspersions against a good man.' Magnus humphed and left the room.

The police officer looked at Maud, sweat beading on his brow.

Ever the diplomat, Lord Urquhart was the one to break the awkward silence. 'It might be useful to consider why anyone would want Neil Tremain dead. To consider who hated him enough to kill him?'

Dr Munro shook his head. 'Surely that's not what happened here.'

'What makes you say that?'

'Well, it's obvious, my lord. Tremain visited the castle only occasionally. He doesn't really know anyone other than Magnus on the island.'

The clock over the stables struck four.

When the last strike had died away, Dr Munro spoke again. 'Almost tea time. Can we gentlemen escort you ladies down to the drawing room?'

Maud and Daisy rose. 'Sergeant,' said Maud, 'are you joining us?'

The policeman had struck a match from a box he'd removed from his pocket and was lighting the oil lamp on the writing table. Heavy banks of cloud gathered in the sky outside the window and the room was growing gloomy.

Sergeant McNeish turned to face them. 'I've got some notes to write up, but it's not my place to take tea above-stairs. I'll go down to the kitchens.' The policeman looked more embarrassed than ever. He raised one hand to his throat as if about to undo the top buttons on his uniform jacket, before realising how unacceptable that would be in the company of ladies.

'Shall we?' Dr Munro gestured to the door. He followed everyone with the exception of the sergeant out of the room, closing the door behind him. The little group had just reached the top of the staircase, when Daisy exclaimed, 'Och, I've left something behind in Sergeant McNeish's room. I'll just nip back for it.'

'Don't be long,' said Maud. She set off down the spiral stairs with the two gentlemen, as Daisy retraced her steps along the corridor.

The trio had just reached the first floor when they heard Daisy scream.

ELEVEN

'Maud!' Daisy's voice was distraught. '*Maud!*'

Maud set off at a run back up the stairs and towards the policeman's room, Lord Urquhart and the doctor close on her heels.

In the flickering light of the lamp flame, Sandy McNeish lay on his back in the middle of the floor, staring wide-eyed up at the ceiling, Daisy kneeling beside him in horror. One of the man's arms was crooked above his head, and his jacket hung partially open, revealing a small red stain on his white shirt.

Dr Munro brushed past Maud and fell to his knees beside the policeman on the floor, trying to find a pulse. He raised worried eyes to Lord Urquhart. His voice shook when he spoke. 'He's... dead.'

Maud dragged her gaze from Daisy and stared at the doctor, her heart speeding up. 'Dead! But how can that be? We've only just left the room.'

'Miss Smart,' Lord Urquhart murmured, putting his arm around her shoulders.

'No.' She shook him off. Her heart thudded as she glanced

frantically around the room. But apart from the four of them still alive, there was no one there.

Lord Urquhart joined the others around McNeish, knelt and touched the stain on the man's chest. He looked at his bloodied fingers. 'Miss Smart is right. How is this possible?' he murmured.

Think! drummed Maud's brain. *Think!* She forced herself back into detective mode. 'Daisy!'

Daisy looked up at her, eyes wide in her ashen face.

'When you arrived was the door to the room shut?'

'Yes,' she whispered.

Picking up the poker, Maud advanced to the window and prodded the heavy curtains viciously. If the killer was hiding, she'd find him. She strode over to the wardrobe and flung the door open. Her thoughts raced as she stared into an empty space. How could the murderer have escaped?

Away in the distance came the first grumbling of the storm.

'We met nobody in the corridor,' she said. 'But there are other rooms in which a person could hide.'

Lord Urquhart jumped to his feet and ran from the room, calling over his shoulder, 'Doctor, you stay here to look after the ladies.'

Maud returned the poker to the hearth, moved back to the window and opened it wide. She looked down at the castle wall. 'Nobody has come this way.'

Dr Munro got to his feet and stared down, white-faced, at Sergeant McNeish's body.

'Are you sure?' the doctor asked Maud in a hoarse voice. 'There is no ladder or rope?'

Maud shook her head. 'Two deaths carried out the same way. And on the face of it, it's impossible that murder can have been committed in either case.'

Daisy pulled herself together and gazed around the bedroom. 'There's no sign of a struggle.'

The doctor frowned. 'You heard no cry?' he asked Daisy.

'No.'

'How long do you suppose since we left McNeish in the room?'

'Perhaps a minute,' Maud said.

Dr Munro stepped out into the corridor. As he looked from left to right, Maud joined him. About a yard away to the left the passage ended with a window set in the wall. To the right were the other bedrooms on each side of the corridor.

'The oil lamp in the corridor has not yet been lit,' said the doctor, 'and the passage is shadowy.'

'I ken that!' shouted Daisy, anger replacing distress as she held Sergeant McNeish's large hand.

'Miss Graham, I'm only trying to establish how you could have missed seeing someone running away from the door.'

'I wasn't looking for a murderer. I was coming back for my...' Daisy began to search the policeman's body.

'What are you looking for?' asked Maud, stepping back into the room.

'His notebook.'

'Have you found anybody?' called the doctor along the passageway.

'Not yet,' came Lord Urquhart's deep voice.

Where was Jane? Maud wondered. The young woman's room was next door to Maud's and obviously empty given Lord Urquhart's response.

The doctor turned back into the room and shut the door. 'If we leave the door open, the killer may get away.'

'But there's nobody here.' Maud gestured about her.

'He must have hidden somewhere!' The doctor sounded uneasy.

'It's a case of making a thorough search.' Daisy got to her feet and threw open the wardrobe door. 'We must have over-looked something.'

Dr Munro began to prowl around the room, clearly agitated. 'Does anyone else have the feeling that we're not alone?'

'No.' Daisy closed the wardrobe door. 'That's empty.'

Maud searched under the bed. She looked around the room. Where else could an assassin hide? There was no cupboard set into the wall here. She pulled open the drawers of the dressing table, while Daisy did the same at the writing desk.

'Nae weapon,' Daisy groaned.

Maud now noticed a smallish, flat, dark object lying half concealed under one of the armchairs near the sergeant's body. 'Look, Daisy – there's his notebook. That may provide a clue.'

'I don't understand—' Maud's use of a different name for her secretary now registered with doctor. He sent them both a curious look.

Their true identities must be disclosed soon, Maud thought as she picked up the book. 'He must have been writing in it when the murderer entered the room.' She opened it and hastily flicked through it until she came to the last entry the sergeant had made, which he'd read out to them. She turned to the next page. '*Oh!*'

'What is it, Maud?' Daisy came to stand beside her.

'A page has been torn out.' Maud showed her the jagged edges of what would have been the following page.

They looked up as the door opened. Lord Urquhart entered. His eyes met Maud's and he shook his head.

'No one here either,' she said, 'but we've found the sergeant's notebook. A page has been ripped out.'

'Sergeant McNeish must have been close to working out who was the killer. Or the killer thought so,' said Lord Urquhart. 'Is it clear how he was murdered, doctor?'

Dr Munro returned to the dead man, crouched down and examined the blood stain again. 'The same as last time. A puncture wound to the heart.'

'But this time with a little more blood,' Maud pointed out. 'What does that mean, Dr Munro?'

'The man wasn't lying down asleep, or it could be that the killer wasn't quite as accurate as before.'

'Presumably because he had less time?'

'Presumably.'

'Could it be the same implement as was used on Tremain?' asked Lord Urquhart.

'It's certainly possible.' The doctor rose.

'What's happened to Sandy?' Magnus stood in the doorway.

'I'm afraid he's dead, Magnus,' Lord Urquhart told him. 'He's been murdered in the same way as Tremain.'

Magnus staggered backwards in shock.

'Mr Carmichael,' Maud said, 'we've examined the room and now we need to look outside the castle.'

'Oh... of course,' Magnus said faintly, his face drained of colour.

Maud placed the policeman's notebook on the writing table. Lord Urquhart took the key out of the door and motioned to the others to vacate the room. They left the room, Daisy giving one last look back at the red-haired man lying dead on the floor. The doctor shut the door behind them, still peering along the corridor for the assailant, and Lord Urquhart locked it.

They passed the closed door to Tremain's room, then the slight bend in the passage, the alcove where Maud and Lord Urquhart had briefly hidden. Maud cast a glance at the alcove. She would have noticed if someone had been hiding there when they'd walked past on their way to the stairs only a very short time ago.

Magnus led the way out of the front door. The sky was overcast and there wasn't a breath of wind. They could hear the sharp cries of gulls, in from the sea to escape the coming storm.

'I can smell thunder,' Magnus muttered as they rounded the castle wall. 'That doesn't bode well.'

It didn't need thunder to tell them things weren't well, Maud thought bitterly.

Magnus stopped under McNeish's window at the back of the castle, still faintly illuminated by the lamp the man had lit. There was no sign of any attempt to climb the wall; all was as it should be.

'We will now examine the path and shrubbery,' Maud said.

She and Daisy did so. There was no mark to indicate a ladder had been placed there. Only the slight indentation remained in the greenery they had observed along the path that morning.

'I understand the castle cat likes to lie there in the sun,' Maud said to Magnus, pointing to the small, flattened area.

'He does, yes.'

'We examined the ground under Neil's window too,' Daisy put in. 'There was no footprint or mark from a ladder there either.'

'Whose room is that under the sergeant's?' Maud asked, pointing to the unlit window immediately below.

'Another bedroom, unoccupied at present,' Magnus replied.

'And above Sergeant McNeish's window?'

All the third floor windows were also in darkness.

'The two small, barred windows immediately above Sandy's are the nursery,' Magnus told her. 'It's not been used since Ailsa and I were children.'

Maud glanced up at the window between Neil Tremain's and Sergeant McNeish's respective rooms. It was Lord Urquhart's bedchamber. A shiver slid down her back as she realised the occupants on either side of him had been murdered in their rooms.

She pointed further along the stone wall of the building. 'And above and below Mr Tremain's room?'

Magnus thought for a moment. 'Apart from the nursery and the servants' rooms, the third floor is taken up with the long gallery, built to allow the ladies to exercise on days when the weather was inclement. Below Tremain's chamber is my sister's sitting room.'

Could the killer have gained access by climbing out of a window on one floor and climbing in through the window on another? It would be difficult. And how the murderer could have got in and out of Tremain's bedroom without disturbing the locked shutters, she had no idea. Nor could she fathom how he could have got in and out of Sergeant McNeish's room in less than a minute.

'It doesna seem possible than anybody *could* have entered the sergeant's room without me seeing him.' Daisy gazed up at his window.

'Impossible,' agreed Dr Munro. 'We all would have seen them leave, at the very least.'

After some deliberation, the group made their way back to the main door and passed through into the lobby. Two outdoor coats now hung on pegs, one a severe dark brown tweed and the other red with a squirrel collar.

'I see my sister and Jane have returned from the stables,' muttered Magnus. 'The new mare might be skittish when she senses a storm approaching.'

That explained their absence just now, Maud thought, and they weren't in the castle to hear the commotion.

They entered the great hall where oil lamps placed around the large room glowed softly. Magnus turned to face Maud and Daisy.

'What is going on?' he demanded, his face red. 'You two ladies seem too well informed for my liking. You've positively taken over the investigation.'

'Let me explain.' Maud glanced at Daisy, who nodded.

'Miss Cameron and I comprise the M. McIntyre agency. I am Miss Maud McIntyre.'

'And I'm Daisy Cameron.'

'And we are private detectives,' Maud added.

'Ah,' said Dr Munro, the truth dawning. 'That explains your use of different Christian names just now in the sergeant's room.'

Magnus's face had gone from red to purple, and looked quite startling in the lamp light. '*Detectives*? What is the meaning of this? You claimed to be Miss Smart and Miss Graham, a novelist and her secretary.' His voice grew louder. 'This is your doing, Hamish. You've deliberately deceived me and brought these two *unmarried* women here. What have you to say for yourself, man!'

Oh dear, thought Maud, we have gone from ladies to women of ill repute in just a few seconds.

'There was a very good reason for my subterfuge,' Lord Urquhart said.

Magnus folded his arms across his chest. 'Well, what is it? I'm waiting.'

'When your bronze lion went missing—'

Magnus dropped his hands. 'I knew it was you behind the theft!'

'And yet it wasn't,' Lord Urquhart went on smoothly. 'I had my own suspicions, but I felt it best that an outside agency dealt with the case. I asked these two brave *ladies* to find the statuette with minimum disturbance to the household.'

'They've hardly done that.'

'We have actually found it—' Maud began, realising Mr Carmichael had yet to be told.

'And replaced it on the table in the great hall, as per Lord Urquhart's wishes not to make a fuss,' finished Daisy.

Magnus huffed impatiently. 'Where did you find it?'

'In Neil Tremain's room,' Daisy told him.

'Are you saying my old friend stole the bronze? I don't believe it.'

'We're not saying any such thing.' Maud's voice was soothing. 'Merely stating the fact that we found the statuette in his room, and it is now back in its rightful place.'

Magnus frowned. 'Thank you.' He sounded only slightly pleased with their endeavours. 'Where exactly was it in his room? There was no sign of the lion when Sandy McNeish searched in there this morning.'

'It was in the priest hole.'

Magnus's frown deepened. 'What priest hole?'

'It's behind the cupboard in the wall,' Daisy explained. 'There's a second wee cupboard hidden behind the obvious one.'

'Well...' Magnus was at a loss for words.

'The theft of the bronze is a different matter to murder. That kind of investigation must be left to the professionals,' said Dr Munro. 'I think you should send for the Fiscal straight away, Magnus. I can break the news to Ailsa, if you would like me to. She'll be in her room, I take it?'

'Have a care with her, Roderick.' Magnus was visibly deflated. 'I fear she will take the news hard and may need a sedative.'

'You can rely on me.'

Once Magnus and the doctor had gone, Lord Urquhart addressed Maud and Daisy. 'You must allow me to protect you both. We can wait in the small drawing room until the Procurator Fiscal arrives.'

Maud cast a glance at Daisy, to check she had her assistant's agreement. Daisy nodded.

'Thank you, Lord Urquhart, but we must decline. You and I, and Daisy and the doctor have provided each other with an alibi. Magnus, his sister and Jane will all need to be questioned.

But first, we will interview the servants to ascertain if they heard or saw anything.'

'Then let me come with you.'

'They'll likely be more willing to talk to us without your lordship present,' Daisy commented.

'There's a killer on the loose. Do neither of you fear for your own safety?'

Maud arched an eyebrow. 'If you are looking for something to do, why don't you go and check on Miss Tremain? I'm sure she would welcome your ministrations.' Maud could have bitten her lip as soon as the words were out. She understood that what she felt was simple jealousy, but she had been unable to stop herself.

Lord Urquhart took a small step backwards, looking surprised. 'If that is your wish.'

She thought of the police sergeant lying dead on the floor. What did it matter whom Lord Urquhart was interested in when a second man's life had come to such an abrupt end?

'It *is* my wish.' Maud felt wretched for saying such a thing, but it was too late to back out now. 'I'm sure she will appreciate being looked after.'

'Very well.' He drew himself up to his full height and tugged at his waistcoat, but a flicker of hurt flashed across his eyes. 'I'll do as you ask, but take care, please.' He turned on his heel and went out of the room. Her legs began to tremble as soon as he had closed the door. Why had she treated him like that? She didn't know. Yes, she did, she thought. Jane was the type of young woman who got what she wanted, and Maud didn't want to do anything as undignified as compete with Jane for him.

Daisy was staring at Maud, a bemused look on her face. Maud told herself she was an absolute fool; Lord Urquhart was only being kind. And, after all, he was right – there *was* a killer on the loose. One who must be living in this very castle.

TWELVE

'The two murders must surely be the work of one person,' Maud said to Daisy, as they once again descended the narrow stone stairs to the kitchens.

'The same method and the same weapon. It's too much of a coincidence if it isna.'

'And we don't believe in coincidence.' Maud's voice was firm. 'We should hurry these interviews along, Daisy. Something tells me that very soon we will discover our host not to be as hospitable as before.'

'Aye, and we dinna want a third murder on our hands.'

'Why would there be another murder?'

'If Sandy was killed because of what he might have kent, what's to stop the murderer coming for one of us?'

'Perhaps because we still know so little?' Maud immediately flushed at her flippant remark. She caught her friend's eye. 'Sorry, Daisy; you are right, of course.'

The pair hastened into the servants' hall, where they found everyone busy.

'Och, ladies,' the cook exclaimed, barely looking up as she placed a variety of small cakes on three-tiered cake stands. 'I'm very sorry, but we have no time to speak to you at the moment. We need to get the tea up to the drawing room for half past four. Kirsty,' she added, addressing the girl, 'hurry up with buttering those scones.'

'I think, Mrs Baillie, that the normal routine won't apply this afternoon.' The solemn tone of Maud's voice brought all to a sudden halt.

'Why? What's happened?' asked Finlay, pausing as he rolled down the sleeves of his smart afternoon jumper.

'I'm afraid there's been another death,' Daisy told them gently.

Grace sank into a chair. 'Another one?' she whispered. 'You mean another ... murder?'

'Aye.'

'*A Dhia m' anam!*' Grace put a hand to her cheek. 'God preserve us.'

Isobel's wild-eyed look went between Maud and Daisy. 'Do you think one of us is going to be the next victim?'

'Don't be ridiculous,' Kirsty told her, licking butter off her fingers. 'It's just those above-stairs.'

'The police sergeant was not an above-stairs,' Maud pointed out.

'Sandy?' Andrew, in the act of putting his playing cards back in their packet, went pale. 'It's Sandy McNeish who's been killed?'

'He might nae be an above-stairs,' Kirsty conceded, 'but he's nae a below-stairs either. Why would Miss Tremain kill him? Do you think he'd found her out? Or maybe he was her lover and she'd had enough of him?'

'That'll be enough from you, my lass.' The housekeeper was white with shock. 'You'll show respect for those upstairs—'

'Whether the sergeant's an above- or below-stairs,' Daisy said, bringing the focus back to the investigation, 'is not important. What is important is that we catch this fiend and to do that we need you to answer a few questions. Now, did anyone hear or see anything unusual between the time we left you after luncheon and shortly after four o'clock this afternoon?'

'Nothing.' Finlay glanced round the room at the other servants. 'We've all been here in the kitchen.'

There were murmurings of agreement, and Andrew blurted, 'I'm glad I didn't find him. If it had been me again, I'd be a prime suspect.'

'Never mind about yourself, laddie.' Finlay turned back to Maud and Daisy. 'Who did find him?'

'I did.' Daisy's tone wasn't as chirpy as usual, Maud noticed. But how could it be, coming across a still-warm body when you'd seen the man alive only a minute before? With a sinking feeling, she had to acknowledge it was now looking worse for Daisy than the footman.

Maud and Daisy entered the drawing room as the clock over the stables struck half past four. Jane was already seated in an armchair by the fireplace, with Lord Urquhart standing by her side. With her gaze on Maud, Jane reached up a hand to him. Taking her hand in his own, he sent Maud a concerned look. Suddenly chilled, she crossed to the sofa by the hearth and the blazing fire. Daisy took the empty space on the sofa next to her. They both sat contemplating the burning logs; the trip down to the kitchen hadn't yielded any clues.

The door opened again and Magnus strode in, looking furious, his sister a little way behind. Ailsa took a seat, while Magnus stomped over to the fire and stood in front of it, his hands behind him, his back to the flames. The very picture of a laird dispensing justice, Maud thought.

The door opened again and Finlay entered carrying a tray laden with tea things. After him came Isobel, her nervous eyes darting from Magnus to Maud and Daisy. Finlay set the silver tray down on the sideboard. Isobel placed the two cake stands beside it. Daisy eyed the cut scones topped with jam, slices of fruit cake and little sugar cakes.

'Thank you,' Ailsa said to the servants. 'You can leave everything there. I will serve today.'

Finlay and Isobel left the room and silence fell, broken only by Ailsa dispensing cups of tea and cake and the murmuring of thanks. As she sipped her tea, Maud saw through the window that the mass of dark cloud had moved away from the castle. Perhaps there would not be a storm, after all.

Magnus cleared his throat. 'We all know by now what happened to Sandy McNeish this afternoon, here in this very castle and under our noses.' He stared round the room, glaring at Daisy. 'Andrew and Mr Dalgleish have taken the sergeant to an outbuilding to keep the lad cool for the Fiscal. For those who might think this an opportunity to investigate, kindly refrain from any attempt to examine the sergeant's body. But just in case some of you cannot help yourselves' – his glare was directed at both Maud and Daisy – 'know that I have ordered the outbuilding door to be secured. In the morning, the groom will take the boat to inform the police office on the mainland of the sergeant's murder.'

Maud drew in a silent breath. There was little time now to solve the murders before the authorities arrived – and if they couldn't, what would it mean for Daisy? Could Lord Urquhart help? Could he wield his considerable influence on the situation? No, Magnus had made clear his opinion of Lord Urquhart less than an hour ago.

Maud glanced at Daisy and quietly let out her breath. 'Have you sent for the Procurator Fiscal?' she asked.

'Mr Greig is unfortunately away from the island at present, visiting his sister on the mainland. He'll return to Mull shortly, as long as the threatened storm doesn't hit.'

'In the circumstances,' Lord Urquhart said, 'it might be a

good idea if Miss McIntyre and Miss Cameron – of the M. McIntyre detective agency – investigate.'

'Oh-ho, you think so, do you?' Magnus glared at his house-guest. 'Well, I think that would most definitely not be a good idea – *in the circumstances*.'

'I'm not sure I take your meaning, Magnus,' Lord Urquhart said stiffly, letting go of Jane's hand and taking a step towards Magnus.

'I think you do, Hamish.' Magnus's tone was equally formal.

Lord Urquhart relaxed his posture. 'Magnus, you cannot possibly think either of the two ladies—'

'I don't appreciate your telling me what I think, Hamish. And truth be known...' Magnus straightened himself to his full height, put his hands on his kilted hips and thrust out his chin. 'If it wasn't threatening to be a beast of a night, I would throw the three of you out. Not only have you all deceived me,' Magnus went on, 'but one of you three could be the killer for all I know. Most likely it was Miss Cameron here. She was the one found with Sandy's dead body. As I see it, there was no time for anyone else to have stabbed the poor fellow. And I think we must all agree on one thing: whoever killed Sandy must also have murdered Neil.'

'That's ridiculous!' Maud started up from the sofa, before sinking back into it. It wasn't so ridiculous from their host's point of view, she could see that, but...

Jane began to wail. Ailsa rose quickly and went across the room to take her hand.

'Magnus,' Lord Urquhart said, his voice calm, 'Miss Cameron hadn't met Tremain until yesterday evening.'

'So she's led us to believe!'

'It's true,' protested Daisy. 'I'd never met the man before, or even heard of him.'

Lord Urquhart moved to sit on the arm of the sofa by Daisy. 'Since I have known the two ladies, I have formed a very favourable opinion of their honesty and dedication to their work. I would not have asked them here had I thought otherwise.'

Maud shot him a grateful look. Surely his social standing would help to protect Daisy.

Magnus appeared to be considering the matter. 'Very well, Urquhart. I won't throw her, or any of you, out – but I will have Miss Cameron locked in her room until the police arrive.'

'You can't do that!' Maud leaped to her feet.

'What about *habeas corpus*?' Daisy cried.

'Bring out the dead?' Jane looked bemused.

'The literal meaning of *habeas corpus* is *you shall have the body*,' Lord Urquhart explained. 'In effect—'

'It's a summons demanding that a prisoner be brought before the court to determine whether the detention is lawful,' Maud interrupted. 'But—'

'It does not apply in Scotland,' Lord Urquhart finished her sentence.

'What is this,' growled Magnus, glancing from Maud to Lord Urquhart and back, 'some sort of double act?'

Maud would have laughed if the matter were not so serious. 'I believe the Criminal Procedure Act 1701 has the same effect in Scotland as *habeas corpus*.'

'Then we'll apply for that.' Daisy's tone was hopeful as she looked to Maud for confirmation.

Magnus scowled. 'And who do you think will hear the matter?'

'The court, of course.' But Maud felt the legal ground shifting under her feet.

'And the local court is...?' The laird had a triumphant look on his face.

Maud realised the problem. 'It is you, Mr Carmichael.'

'It's me.' He gave a satisfied nod. 'Even if it were another magistrate, I doubt he would free Miss Cameron in the circumstances. There have been two murders already in this house. I'm simply detaining her to prevent a third.'

'Surely—' began Maud.

'And as I have no wish to speak to you again, Miss McIntyre, I will stay in my own chamber until the police get here. I suggest the rest of you do the same.'

Ailsa spoke up. 'Magnus, please—'

He put up his hand to indicate he wanted to hear no more on the topic, snatched up a slice of fruit cake and stomped out of the room.

'Oh dear,' Ailsa said, after a short silence. She glanced uncomfortably around the room. 'I'm sorry, Miss Cameron. My brother is usually of an even temper, but occasionally he can be nothing short of irrational.'

'I suppose it's not really irrational,' Daisy said. 'It does look as if I might have done it.'

'Did you?' Jane stared at her with wide, frightened eyes.

'Of course I didna!' Daisy recovered herself. 'Och, well...' She gazed at the cake stands on the sideboard. 'I'd better have one or two of those wee scones and another cup of tea, in case your brother decides to starve me while I'm locked up in my room.'

Maud admired her assistant's stoicism, but it was no joking matter. When the police replacements arrived, Daisy would be arrested for the sergeant's death, if not also for Mr Tremain's. Maud knew she must hurry to solve the case before they arrived.

The penalty for murder was hanging.

THIRTEEN

Later that evening, Maud tried the handle to Daisy's bedroom. As Magnus had instructed, the door was locked.

'Daisy,' Maud called softly through the door, 'are you all right?' She heard a thumping sound coming from the room.

'Happy as a haggis in the mating season,' came the cheerful reply.

'Were you given dinner?'

'Aye. Our host isna going to starve me, after all.'

'That's a relief.' Maud smiled, which she knew her friend would hear in her voice. 'Please try not to worry about this turn of events. I'm sure I can find the real murderer.'

'I dinna doubt it, Maud.'

'I know that.'

'I ken I canna come out, but I'll do what I can from here. I've got my notebook, after all.' Maud heard Daisy rustle the pages for her benefit. 'I'll work on what we've got so far.'

'I know you will, Daisy. Remember to put a line through the three questions we got answers to this afternoon.'

'Just a minute... Here they are. Numbers three and six: what are the rooms above and below those of the two victims, and where were the below-stairs folk at half past seven this morning. What do you think about crossing off number two?'

'Remind me which question that was.'

'Who knew of the priest hole.'

Maud thought for a moment. 'Yes, I think if you agree, that can also be deleted. If Magnus didn't know of it, then it's extremely unlikely anyone else did, other than whoever stole the statuette. And we won't know the answer to that question until we catch the culprit. I suppose the question about why the killer waited until morning to stab Tremain can also go.'

'That's number nine.'

Maud looked quickly about her. The corridor remained empty, but she kept her voice low. 'I'm not convinced Tremain's murderer did hide in the cupboard. The sergeant's killing has shown us a hiding place isn't necessary for the work of this man.'

'Or woman,' Daisy amended.

'Present company excepted.'

There was a pause. 'Done,' Daisy said through the door. 'That's five questions down now and seven to go: why would someone want Neil Tremain deid, whose head is a hair short, who or what was Neil frightened of to make him lock his door, why did Ailsa dislike Neil, who inherits Neil's estate...' She paused.

'Yes, Daisy? That's only five.'

'There's also the two questions that'll have the same answer really: how did the murderer get into the room and how did he get out of it?'

'Hmm, yes. Those two are the crux of the matter. Well, let us see what tomorrow brings.' Maud looked towards the window at the end of the corridor, where a lighted oil lamp stood on the sill. Natural light had faded some hours earlier, before they had eaten dinner in the great hall. She'd seen the black clouds swirling over the castle as if the fast-approaching storm knew of the goings-on inside and wished to send a warning to the unwary. Maud shivered.

'It looks as though the weather will prevent the groom crossing to the mainland police any time soon, which will give us a little longer to bring this case to its rightful conclusion.'

'Shouldna take us too long now,' said Daisy. 'We've got the answer to almost half the questions, which means we're nearly halfway to solving the case.'

'We are.' Maud's voice sounded more positive than she felt. 'I'll come back and talk to you again tomorrow morning. Is there anything you need at present?'

'Nae, I'm fine, thanks. Isobel brought up some of those scones and a novel for me from the library.'

'Any written by Miss Maisie Smart?'

Daisy laughed. 'Good night, Maud.'

'Sleep well, my friend.'

With a heavy heart, Maud went to her own room. She could understand why Magnus believed Daisy was responsible for Sergeant McNeish's death, but why couldn't he see that the same person had killed Neil Tremain, and that Daisy had no motive to murder either man? There seemed to be no way anyone, including Daisy, could have got in and out of Tremain's locked room. But that was exactly what someone had done.

Maud let out a deep sigh. Daisy was locked up and relying on her, and she must not falter. She'd had time to consider Daisy's comment about the murderer possibly making one of them his next victim, but she dismissed the idea. As long as her assistant was as good as under arrest and about to be charged with the crimes, the real killer would see Daisy, and probably Maud too, as no threat.

Maud, though, was very aware of the even greater need to solve the mystery now that her friend was at risk of being hanged for the murders.

While Daisy was working through the information they had

so far, Maud would do the same. As she hadn't written anything down herself, perhaps making her own new list would reveal something hitherto hidden.

Maud carried the lamp from the mantelpiece over to the little writing table. In the far distance came the sword-gleam of the first lightning, making her catch her breath. Then, taking her notebook from her leather satchel, she drew out the chair and sat down. She opened the book, picked up the fountain pen placed neatly on the table, uncapped it as she thought for a moment and wrote *Suspects List* at the top of the new page before underlining it. The black ink flowed smoothly in a satisfying manner.

She lifted her pen from the sheet. Who to begin with? She had no real main suspect. The assailant in *The Mystery of the Yellow Room* turned out to be the least likely person, which of course is exactly who it should be in fiction. But in real life? Wasn't it one's nearest and dearest, as Kirsty had pointed out? Maud would start with Tremain's daughter.

1. Jane Tremain. Motive:

Maud could think of only one motive for Jane. *Money*, she wrote. With her father dead, and assuming her mother was also deceased and Jane the only child, she probably stood to inherit a handsome sum.

Maud paused. There were two murders to investigate and this motive would apply only to the first one, not the second. She would need to take the two separately.

Maud looked again at what she had written. There was sufficient space under the heading, *Suspects List*. She added *Re the Murder of Neil Tremain.*

Maud returned to Jane and wrote the next subheading. *Alibi.*

Dr Munro had given the approximate time of death as

between seven and half past eight in the morning. Maud wrote the only thing she could: *Asleep in her room.* She added a question mark and looked at the shining blob of ink at the bottom of the shape. Weren't all those above-stairs going to have the same tenuous alibi – that they were alone in their bedroom and asleep? How could she prove otherwise?

She glanced at the window and beyond the glass saw the sky purple in the lurid storm-light. In the distance came the rumbling of approaching thunder.

She turned back to her notebook and added a new subheading.

Opportunities: Jane left the drawing room after dinner the night before Tremain's murder, for approximately fifteen minutes, allegedly to fetch a lost handkerchief from her room.

Maud didn't see how this could be relevant, given the time of death stated by the doctor, but she wrote it, anyway.

A further notion struck her and she quickly added: *If Tremain had stolen the bronze statuette* – and, she thought, it very much looked as though he had – *did that mean he had financial problems? Had Jane found out there was little to inherit and killed her father in a fit of rage?*

Maud sighed. Jane was a shallow creature, but she didn't seem the type to plan a murder. Whoever had killed Neil Tremain was cold and calculating.

2. Ailsa Carmichael. Motive: Hostility clear between suspect and deceased; reason unknown. Alibi: Asleep in her room? Opportunities: Ailsa left the drawing room after dinner the night before, to go down to the kitchens to speak to cook about the morning's breakfast arrangements.

Again Maud had included an irrelevant fact, but it could

turn out to be important. Was it possible, she suddenly wondered, that Dr Munro had made a mistake about the time of Tremain's death? That would make a big difference to the investigation. But no, she reminded herself – when he was found, Tremain's body was still warm, there was no doubt about that.

She was getting along more quickly now. But when she looked at what she had written, there was little, if anything, of substance. The wind howled down the chimney, sending a fall of soot on to the fire, threatening to extinguish it, as she ploughed on.

3. *Magnus Carmichael. Motive:*

Maud hesitated. What motive could he have? The two men were old friends she had been told, and she was aware of nothing to dispute that. Had Magnus – who, when roused, seemed to have a temper – decided for some reason that Tremain was the statuette thief? She wrote: *Possibly believed Tremain had stolen his bronze lion. Alibi: Asleep?* She could think of nothing for *Opportunities.* Maud yawned; it had been a long day.

Next, 4.

With a jolt, Maud realised the only other person above-stairs not yet mentioned was Lord Urquhart. He had been on the very first suspects list she and Daisy had ever drawn up – the one in the Duddingston case. Interesting that she should think of that now. Anyway, it was only fair that she consider all the evidence in this current investigation, including anything that might point to his possible involvement. Daisy's life was at stake.

Lord Urquhart, she wrote. *Motive:*

No possible motive came to her mind. Admittedly, she didn't *want* to think of any motive, but she had a professional duty to at least try. She tried. Very hard. No, nothing; not even the smallest of motives came to mind. Very well, then. *Alibi*: *Asleep in bed. Opportunities: Does he wear pyjamas in bed or simply slide those long limbs between the cool sheets...*

Maud stared aghast at what she had written. She hastily crossed through that last sentence, blotted the ink and turned over the page.

Anyone could have left their bedroom earlier that morning – but how did that help, when there was no way of entering or exiting Tremain's room? Maud was getting tired of all the questions coming back to this crucial point: how did the killer get in and out undetected? She and Daisy could make no progress until they had solved that conundrum.

There was also the sergeant's death to consider. The motive here at least was straightforward: undoubtedly to prevent the officer from naming the murderer. Even if McNeish hadn't solved the case – and Maud thought it unlikely that he had – the killer feared the police officer would soon work it out. The missing page, whatever it contained, would be reduced to ashes on the villain's fire by now.

A further, dreadful thought came to Maud. Had Daisy been set up for McNeish's murder? No, the real killer couldn't have known that she would return, and so soon, to the policeman's room. It was more likely that her sudden return was a lucky coincidence for the killer, Maud thought angrily.

She needed to focus on the murder of Neil Tremain. If she could solve that, the rest would follow. She decided to consider again the precise order of events leading up to the discovery of Tremain's body.

On the page in front of her, Maud drew up a timetable.

6 a.m. Kirsty the kitchen maid up and working.

6.30 a.m. The rest of the servants up and about their tasks.

8 a.m. Below-stairs eat their breakfast in the kitchen.

8.20 a.m. Finlay, the butler-cum-valet-cum piper, leaves the kitchen to clean and polish the laird's boots in the boot room next door.

8.30 a.m. Servants' meal finished and all busy with their jobs. Isobel takes breakfast tray to Ailsa. Finlay goes to assist Magnus. Andrew, the temporary valet, takes a can of hot water to Tremain's room but gets no reply.

Shortly before 9 a.m. Andrew comes back with fresh hot water. Still no reply. Alarmed, he runs downstairs to the first floor where he knows Finlay is assisting Magnus. Andrew returns with Finlay and Magnus. Alerted by Magnus's banging and shouting, Lord Urquhart then Maud and Daisy join the group, which now includes all the servants, milling around in the passage outside Tremain's door.

9 a.m. Dr Munro arrives. Ailsa and then Jane appear on the scene. Doctor breaks down the door. Tremain is found dead. Doctor says death occurred within the last hour, two at most – that is between 7 and 9 a.m. Andrew had first knocked on the door at 8.30 a.m. to no avail – ergo, Tremain must have been killed between 7 and 8.30 a.m.

9.30 a.m. William Greig, the Procurator Fiscal, and Sergeant Sandy McNeish arrive at the murder scene.

Maud read what she had written. It looked so simple, so straightforward. And it was. Sometime between the servants carrying out their duties and finishing their breakfast, Neil Tremain was stabbed.

She shook her head. Something wasn't right. There was a red herring somewhere – but where? What was she missing?

Maud gasped as a flash of lightning streaked across the room. She gave a wry laugh. If only the answer would come to her in a similar flash of light. She rubbed her forehead. It wasn't unknown for storms to cause headaches, although if she were about to have one, it wouldn't be caused by the pressure in the air. It must be rather gratifying, she thought idly, to be a doctor and deal with the ailments of a grateful patient rather than be a detective and deal with the complaints of a grumpy...

Another jagged flash of lightning lit up the dim room, burning bright for just a second. The doctor – they had forgotten the doctor. She settled back with a soft satisfied laugh as thunder rumbled in the distance.

They had not given him any consideration in the investigation as he had arrived *after* Tremain's murder. But he had been present shortly before the murder of the police officer. So, too, had Magnus and Lord Urquhart, of course, but she had these two down as possible suspects in Tremain's death, unlike Dr Munro. She and Daisy were convinced the same person had killed both men, and she had been in danger of losing sight of that.

But if it had been Dr Munro, how had he performed the feat of murder through a locked door when he wasn't even in the castle? And what was his motive? There was no suggestion he and Tremain had ever met before dinner last night. If she and Daisy could discover whether the doctor had a motive for doing away with Neil Tremain, that would be a step forward in the investigation.

A whip of light flashed in the sky and thunder rolled. Maud started counting quietly and reached only three before there came a clap of thunder so loud it was as if the roof had fallen in. 'It's so close,' she murmured. The storm must be almost above the castle.

If only it would pass, she could take the short crossing to the island of Ulva. There must be some clue in Tremain's house on the tiny island. But then, Maud reminded herself, when the storm was over, she would truly be investigating on her own. The police would come from the mainland and Daisy would be taken away.

A soft knock on the door brought Isobel. 'Grace thought an extra candle might help you get through this storm, Miss McIntyre.' The maid set on the dressing table one of the two saucer candlesticks she carried, and lit the wick using the box of matches she took from her apron pocket.

There was a tremendous crack as a bolt of forked lightning tore across the sky, the flash so bright that for a split second the room was lighter than day. Isobel's face as she stood, startled, was blanched by it. A clap of thunder followed almost at once.

Maud got up and crossed to the window, seeing only her reflection in the glass. She opened the window to watch. The trees were thrashing back and forth. Then came another bolt of lightning, zigzagging down on to the front lawn, bathing it and the tree-lined driveway in an eerie light. Another roll of thunder pealed through the sky. She closed the window and the shutters, and turned back to the room.

'It's the crack of doom, miss,' whispered Isobel, standing in the room and shivering.

For a moment, Maud was almost inclined to agree with her. But she gathered her wits and sought to reassure the frightened girl. 'It's nothing but a storm, Isobel, and it will pass soon.'

'Yes, miss.' The maid swallowed. 'Will you be going to bed shortly, miss? Only I can take the warming pan now if you wish.'

'Yes, thank you, Isobel. I won't be long.'

The maid slid out the metal pan by its long wooden handle. 'This other candle is for Miss Cameron.' She gave Maud a quick, shy smile. 'Don't be concerned about your friend, miss. I'll do what I can for her.'

As the girl left the room, the first drops of rain began to fall. A patter at first on the windowpane, but soon it grew louder and spots the size of tuppenny pieces hit the glass. An intermittent electric flicker and the low distant grumbling of thunder showed the storm was retreating. Before long, the heavy rain turned the room dark, the light of an oil lamp and the candle not equal to the fight. Daisy would be safe for a while longer.

Maud felt suddenly weary. She desperately needed some sleep if her brain tomorrow were to be as bright as the lightning this evening. Daisy deserved no less than Maud's absolute best and that wouldn't happen if she failed to rest.

She drew the door curtain on its portiere rod and climbed into bed, relishing the comfort of warm sheets. After the exhausting events of the day, she thought she would fall asleep as soon as her head touched the pillow. But precisely because of the day's troubling events, she failed to sleep. After lying awake for what seemed an interminable time, she sat up, drew the blanket around her, felt for the matches on the nightstand beside her bed and lit the candle. She would read for a while. Perhaps *The Mystery of the Yellow Room*, which she hadn't quite finished, would give her some clearer idea on solving the locked-room mystery. The sky rumbled overhead. Plucking the book from the stand, she turned to where she'd inserted the bookmark and began the final chapter.

Rain lashed against the window as Maud read on until she'd finished the book and set it down. When searching Tremain's bedroom, she thought she had considered all the same possibilities that Joseph Rouletabille, the amateur detective in the novel, had contemplated. But she hadn't. What Maud had overlooked, she now discovered, was the timing of the injuries. In *The Mystery of the Yellow Room* this was crucial. Could this also be the case with Neil Tremain? She and Daisy, along with everyone else, had assumed the mortal injury had been inflicted an hour or two before he was found. But what if the time between the assault on Tremain and his subsequent death had been much longer than they'd all assumed?

She started up in the bed; she really needed to speak to Daisy. But it was the middle of the night and her friend would be fast asleep.

For Maud, though, sleep was further off than ever. The clock over the stables struck one.

She looked around for something else to read, but there were no other books in the room. 'The library,' she murmured, then wondered if it was a good idea to leave the relative safety afforded by her locked door. Daisy's observation about their possibly being next had unsettled Maud a little.

Quickly, she got out of bed, pulled on her dressing gown and picked up the candle. She looked at the poker in the hearth, but she had no free hand to carry it. Desperately hoping no one would hear her, and that she needed no weapon, she stealthily opened the door.

FOURTEEN

The oil lamp in the corridor had been extinguished and the darkness was intense. There was no light visible under the door opposite her room; Lord Urquhart had retired for the night. Maud noticed Jane's door was likewise dark, as was the late Neil Tremain's, as she passed it on her way to the stairs.

She went cautiously down the spiral staircase, one hand on the rail and the other holding up her candle. Here there were no windows and rain beating against glass couldn't be heard. She strained her ears to catch any sound other than her own soft footsteps and thumping heart. The blades of the weapons displayed on the curved walls glinted in the flickering light of her candle. The first floor was as dark as the second floor.

She reached the ground floor and started across the great hall. Outside it was pitch black and the high narrow panes of stained glass glimmered only with the faint reflection from the dying fire. Heavy shadows fell around the stone walls and deep into the corners to the side of the huge fireplace. Two ornately carved, high-backed chairs faced the hearth where the embers burned low.

'Good evening.'

Maud jumped. Almost immediately, her legs felt like water. She turned towards the two huge fireside chairs. 'What are you doing here?'

His body still hidden by the high-backed chair, Lord Urquhart's dressing gown-clad arm appeared holding aloft a book. 'As you can see.'

She stared at the hand holding the book, his elbow supporting the now slowly waving forearm. Then his face came into view as he lowered the book and leaned out over the chair's padded arm.

'Yes, all right.' Her voice sounded faint even to her own ears. 'You've come down for a book and decided to sit by the fire to read. But there isn't enough light for you to do that, so I'll ask you again. What are you doing here?' With a horrid jolt, she was certain she had said those very words to him only the previous afternoon, in the corridor outside Tremain's room.

'May I beg a light?' He indicated the candle Maud held.

Silently she crossed over to the chair and held it out to him. He lifted his own candle from the table, tilted the wick towards hers and the flame caught.

'That's better,' he said softly, his eyes sparkling in the candlelight.

'Are you going to answer my question?' she demanded, feeling her strength come flooding back.

'I thought I just had, but I'm happy to explain it in more detail if you wish. But you first. What are you doing here?'

'I couldn't sleep, so I came to get a book from the library. Now you tell me.'

'I couldn't sleep either. I'd finished the book I brought with me, so I came downstairs to borrow one from the library. Which I did. And on a whim, I decided to read by the fire. When I heard someone coming down the stairs, I extinguished my candle. I thought it might have been the murderer. I sat here by the fire and waited to find out who it was. I was thinking to pass the evidence on to you, Miss McIntyre.' He gave a broad smile. 'But wait, *you're* not the murderer, are you?'

'Oh, for goodness' sake!' Maud turned on her heels. 'I'm going to the library.'

Lord Urquhart sprang from his chair and followed.

Without the glow from a hearth, the two candles were barely adequate to light the darkness of the passageway. She was cautiously making her way along, taking care not to stumble on the flagstones, when a hand slid around her waist. With a sharp gasp, she stiffened. *How dare he!* She had seen his affection for Jane and here he was dallying with her.

'I think you have mistaken me for someone else.' Maud's cold fingers curled about his and lifted his hand away.

'Who on earth can you mean? Surely not Jane—' He broke off with a shocked look on his face. 'Wait, what was that?' he whispered urgently, stepping to her side. 'Don't move. Listen.'

'What? What was what?' Oh dear, thought Maud, his proximity was affecting her ability to speak the King's English. As they stood together, she held her breath and strained her ears. 'I don't hear anything.' He was playing with her again, she thought.

'I thought I heard footsteps,' he murmured. 'I must have been mistaken. But, here, take my hand. It's better that we stay close together.'

She took his large hand and her pulse throbbed with pleasure. 'Your hand is warm,' she said accusingly. 'Does nothing alarm you?'

'Not much,' he said. 'I'd better go first.'

She sighed at the arrogance of the supremely confident male, but let him lead her along the passageway. When they reached the library, she let go of his comfortable hand and at once felt a little lost. Telling herself to stop being so childish, Maud gazed around the lofty-ceilinged, shelf-encircled shadowy room. Suddenly the task of choosing one from such a

vast collection and so late at night seemed unappealing. A gust
of wind and rain carrying a scatter of small debris struck the
large un-curtained window and she jumped.

She raised her chin, walked with purpose over to one of the
shelves and holding up her candle selected a volume at random.

Spinoza's *Ethics*. Perhaps not suitable bedtime reading.

Behind her she heard Lord Urquhart's soft voice. 'Some say
the philosopher is notoriously difficult to understand.'

'Nonsense. His opinion is that we always act in accordance
with what we think is most profitable to us. You must surely
agree with that, Lord Urquhart.'

Clasping the book under her arm, Maud turned and
mounted the stairs back to her room, leaving him standing in the
library. Whether the matter concerned Jane Tremain or his
mysterious behaviour, her early instincts had been right.

Lord Urquhart was no longer to be trusted.

Maud woke in the morning to the sound of wind rattling the
wooden shutters. Behind its moan, she heard the distant,
roaring boom of the sea. She climbed out of bed, pulled her
dressing gown around her, drew back the curtains and threw
open the shutters. Rain streamed down the windowpane. The
thunderstorm had passed, but there would be no boats going out
today. Neither the weather nor the Sabbath would permit that.

Isobel arrived with a brass can of hot water for Maud to
wash. As she knelt and coaxed the fire back to life, Isobel
confirmed to Maud that the laird had indeed taken to his room.

'He is constantly grumbling and ringing for something or
other, so I hope the wind and rain will stop soon and then he
can leave his room and... Sorry, miss,' Isobel whispered as she
got to her feet. 'I don't want Miss Cameron arrested. I don't
believe she committed those two murders – or even one of
them,' she added.

'Thank you, Isobel. That is kind of you to say so. I *will* find the real murderer.' Maud spoke with a confidence she didn't feel. 'How is Miss Cameron this morning?'

The maid brightened. 'She's in good spirits, Miss McIntyre. I've already taken up what she requested for breakfast.'

'Quite a large tray, was it?' Maud smiled.

Isobel laughed. 'Aye, it was.'

The day that Daisy's appetite disappears, Maud thought, doesn't bear thinking about.

As she performed her morning *pliés*, *elevés* and *relevés*, Maud thought about the events of last night. What had seemed a possible answer to the case now seemed unlikely in the cold light of day. In *The Mystery of the Yellow Room*, the victim had, crucially, been attacked some hours before she had sustained the mortal injury. But there had been no sign of any assault on Neil Tremain, only the fatal thrust of a sharp implement into his heart, causing immediate death. Nonetheless, she must tell Daisy and get her opinion.

As to Lord Urquhart's mystery appearance in the great hall, Maud had no idea what to make of it. He'd sidestepped giving her a satisfactory answer, but his being there was still niggling at her. What was it he wasn't telling her?

Maud finished with a *sauté*, leaping upwards with both feet pointed and landing neatly back in a *plié*.

She washed and dressed in a white long-sleeved blouse with a high lace collar, and her dark tailored suit with a straight skirt. She swept up her hair loosely into coils, before making her way downstairs to the dining room.

Lord Urquhart was the only person in the room. He rose politely as she entered. 'Good morning, Miss McIntyre.'

Maud noted his attire: dark suit with waistcoat and a high, round-collared white shirt and necktie. He also was dressed for church.

'Good morning to you, Lord Urquhart. After yesterday, I

wonder you can be so calm.' Maud herself seethed. How could
he behave as if the extraordinary events had not taken place?

'The storm did cause me to lie awake for a while,' he said,
deliberately misunderstanding her.

Andrew entered with a covered silver dish and placed it
next to the others arranged on the sideboard. The conversation
she wished to have with Lord Urquhart would have to wait
until they were alone.

She went to the sideboard and Andrew lifted the lid from
the new dish.

'Kedgeree.' Maud smiled at him. 'One of my breakfast
favourites.' She helped herself to a plate of the buttery smoked
haddock, hard-boiled egg and rice. Andrew stood by waiting to
lift the lids from the array on the sideboard.

Lord Urquhart had resumed his seat, and she took the one
opposite him. He had finished his plate of eggs, bacon and
sausages.

Andrew moved to the table, carrying the silver coffee pot.
'Miss McIntyre?' he murmured.

'Thank you, Andrew.'

The footman poured the steaming dark liquid into the cup
in front of her on the table, before doing the same for Lord
Urquhart, then returned to his position at the sideboard.

'Can I help you to some milk?' Lord Urquhart asked her,
lifting the small jug on the table.

'Thank you. Just a splash,' she said a little icily. Avoiding
eye contact, Maud pushed her cup and saucer towards him.

She inhaled the aroma of coffee and felt its reviving proper-
ties flood through her. Instantly, she felt better disposed towards
Lord Urquhart and ate a forkful of kedgeree.

'It must be hard for Miss Cameron, confined to her room as
she is.'

Maud heard genuine concern in his voice.

'That's exactly why I must solve these murders before the

police arrive.' She glanced at the window, still being battered by the rain. 'At least the officers won't be here just yet.'

'Miss McIntyre, forgive me for suggesting this...' His voice was strangely formal and he shifted a little in his chair.

'Yes?' She was aware of an edge of suspicion in her voice.

'Now you are minus a detective, I wondered if *I* can help you in any way?'

Maud narrowed her eyes. He had been trying to charm her into letting him work on an investigation with her since almost the first moment they met. She glanced at Andrew, busy with the dishes on the sideboard, his back to them. She leaned forward and lowered her voice.

'You can hardly think I am about to trust *you*.'

He mirrored Maud's actions and lowered his voice to match hers. 'I behaved foolishly last night.'

She looked at him hopefully. 'Does this mean you are going to tell me what you were *really* doing?'

'Miss McIntyre, I'm sorry, but I am not at liberty to do so.'

Maud gasped. The effrontery of the man.

'I realise now,' he went on, 'my proper course would have been to make up a plausible story.'

'You think I would have believed you?' she scoffed.

'I don't see why not. I believed your story about coming down for a book.'

'That's because I *did* go down for a book!'

Maud glanced again at Andrew and saw that his back had stiffened. If he hadn't been listening before, he was certainly doing so now.

Lord Urquhart sat back and regarded her admiringly. 'I do think you're wonderful, you know.'

Maud stared at him and likewise sat back. A warm feeling spread through her. But did he really admire her? Wasn't it Jane Tremain and her silly ways that he preferred? 'Why?' she asked.

'Because you are a detective.'

'What is wonderful about that?' Not a declaration of love, then. 'Is that why *you* want to investigate cases, because it would make you seem wonderful too?'

He raised an eyebrow. 'No, that wouldn't make *me* seem wonderful. I'm a man.'

'So, I'm wonderful for doing the job because it comes under the domain of men and I'm a woman?' She drew a breath. 'A woman can do nearly everything a man can do. And sometimes she can do it very much better!'

He frowned. 'I never said that women were inferior.'

'You did with your eyebrow.'

He began again. 'I've somehow said this all wrong. Let me start again. I have always admired a woman with brains.'

'You'd be surprised how many of us have them.'

A frown deepened on Lord Urquhart's brow. 'What I mean is, it can't have been easy to set yourself up in a man's world.'

'It wasn't. It isn't.'

'You're an exceptional woman.'

'You can't get out of telling me what you're up to with a compliment. I make it a rule not to be that self-indulgent.' She sat up straight. 'I'm an ordinary woman who has been fortunate enough to be able to use her brains. No, I don't think it would be a good idea for you to *help* me, Lord Urquhart. I need someone who will take the work seriously and, more importantly, someone I can trust with my life.'

He learned forward in the chair, his look earnest. 'You can trust me, Miss McIntyre. I do take it seriously. It was I who got you both into this mess, after all.'

'We came here to do a simple theft investigation. It's not your fault that Daisy is now locked up under suspicion of murder. I will say, however, that I'll be charging you for the murder investigation if Daisy needs money for a defence advocate.'

'I'll certainly pay the bill, but let's hope it doesn't come to that; and I assure you that I have a personal interest in the outcome of the investigation. I consider you and Miss Cameron personal friends, so please let me help.'

An interest? What did he mean? Surely he wasn't intending to propose to Jane Tremain?

Lord Urquhart was gazing at her; he was waiting for her reply.

It might be useful to have another person with her as a witness when she visited Ulva, Maud thought. The journey would also give her the opportunity to discover the real reason he was staying at the castle. She had the strongest sense that it was more than a stolen bronze cast in the shape of a lion.

Andrew began clattering the lids on the silver dishes, but Maud was sure his ears were twitching. She lowered her voice and leaned a little closer to Lord Urquhart on the other side of the table once more. He leaned his head towards her.

'You can come with me to Neil Tremain's house on Ulva tomorrow. The partnership is just a temporary arrangement, you understand. You know Daisy and I found the missing statuette in his bedchamber. I'm not saying there is a link between the theft and his murder, but it is possible.'

'What is possible?'

Maud and Lord Urquhart jumped at the sound of the sharp, feminine voice.

FIFTEEN

Maud and Lord Urquhart hastily drew back from each other and looked up as Jane entered the breakfast room.

'Oh dear, am I interrupting a charming little tête-à-tête?' She gave a silky smile.

'Of course not,' Maud said crossly. She took a sip of coffee and burned her mouth.

'It's just that you both looked so... intimate.'

Smarting at the pain in her mouth, Maud flushed. Really, the young woman was quite unpleasant. Wasn't she supposed to be grieving for her dead father? Instead, she was insinuating there was some romantic intrigue going on. Weren't two murders in the same day intrigue enough?

With a swish of purple silk, Jane slipped into the seat next to Lord Urquhart and looked at him. Clearly, she was expecting him to say or do something.

He rose. 'Can I get something for you from the sideboard, Miss Tremain?'

'We know each other well enough by now for you to call me Jane,' she purred.

He gave a slight dip of his head. 'Jane.'

'Just a slice of toast for me, please. And a little butter and marmalade. Just a little. I must think of my figure.'

She gave a pointed glance at Maud's plate heaped with kedgeree. Maud ignored her, but resolved when she had finished what was on her plate, she would to go to the sideboard and get her own toast and load it with butter and marmalade.

Jane clicked her fingers at Andrew, who came forward and poured her a cup of coffee.

'So, what is possible?' she asked when Lord Urquhart was again seated, her gaze going between the two of them. 'The subject of your conversation just now. I sense a mystery.'

'The only mystery, Miss Tremain, is who is the murderer amongst us.' It took effort, but Maud kept her voice soothing; after all, this woman's father was one of the victims. 'Do you have any notion who would want to kill your father?'

Jane, sobered, shook her head. 'We weren't very close, as you might have gathered, so I don't know much about his personal life. But I can't imagine anyone hating him enough to kill him.'

'Your mother, Miss Tremain,' Maud went on, 'if you don't mind my asking, is she still with us?'

'If you mean is she still living, the answer is no. I have no real memory of her, as she died when I was a young child.'

'And yet you say you are not close to your father?'

'He sent me to live with his sister, my aunt.' Jane's tone was brusque. It was obvious she had not forgiven her father for this. 'My aunt was kind, but...' She shrugged.

'You don't know why he sent you away?'

'To get rid of me, I assumed. What other reason could there be?'

Extreme distress at the death of his wife? A feeling of being unable to cope with a young child, especially one of the oppo-site sex, on his own? Neither was a good reason for sending away your child, but Maud had heard that it happened.

'You have no brothers or sisters?' she asked.

'No.' Jane shook her head. 'My aunt died about a year ago, so I am now quite alone in the world.' She sent a quick, sideways glance at Lord Urquhart.

'I'm sorry to have to ask you this, Miss Tremain,' Maud went on, determined not to be distracted, 'but do you know why your father left his position at the shipyard?'

Jane sent Maud a sharp look. 'You are well informed.'

'Always desirable for a detective.'

Jane sighed. 'In answer to your question, no, I don't know why he left when he did. Some sort of upset, my aunt said at the time.'

'An upset?'

'I'd already been fostered out to my aunt, so I can't be certain, but I think it was something to do with where he lived. He had a bad temper, as you've probably gathered for yourself, so perhaps he assaulted a neighbour.'

'One last question, if I may,' Maud said. 'Was there a reason why you were visiting him at present?'

Jane flushed. 'No.'

Ah, so there was, Maud thought. Jane sent Lord Urquhart a quick glance, and the reason was clear. The young woman knew her father was to visit Clachan Castle where Lord Urquhart was also a guest. Goodness, what some young women will do to get their man...

'What are you plans for today, Jane?' Lord Urquhart asked.

'I haven't yet decided.' Jane looked towards the window, where the rain still lashed the glass. 'Although I don't think there is much that *can* be done today.'

At least you are free to walk about the castle, Maud thought, unlike poor Daisy. 'I wonder if it's possible to get to the kirk this morning,' she said.

'Perhaps not the eleven o'clock service,' Lord Urquhart replied, 'but the evening one might yet be possible.'

Jane pouted. 'If we were in Edinburgh, there would be no end of activities to amuse us.'

'And so we must make our own entertainment,' Maud said briskly. 'Do you play whist, Miss Tremain?'

'Yes.'

'If we can persuade Ailsa to play too, that will give us two partners of two.'

'That is a good idea.' Jane smiled. 'You ask Ailsa to partner you and Lord Urquhart will partner me.'

'I'd be delighted,' he said.

Was he being civil, Maud wondered, or did he really mean it?

'Or, better still,' Jane went on eagerly, 'we could play a game of sardines.'

'Do you not think we are a little old for hide and seek?' Lord Urquhart looked uncomfortable.

'It's the reverse of that game, Lord Urquhart,' Jane smiled, 'as well you know. It's not for children.'

Indeed, thought Maud. One person hides and everyone else searches for the hidden person. When a seeker finds the hider – was there such a word? – they quietly join them in their hiding place. It can get very... cosy in the space.

Maud decided to forego toast and marmalade and leave them to it. Excusing herself, she rose from the table. Lord Urquhart politely got to his feet and his eyes met hers with a look of hurt in them. Did he want her to stay? She couldn't tell. But even if he did, she would not sacrifice her self-esteem, and anyway, there was no time to play games of any type. She needed to keep her mind on Daisy's predicament, and the only way to resolve that injustice was to hand to the police whoever it was who *had* committed the two murders.

She turned away and walked out of the room. Did she hear a peal of female laughter as she closed the door behind her? No matter. Lord Urquhart was old enough to know what he was doing.

In fact – Maud's steps slowed as she climbed the stairs – why had he not already married? Dashing and eligible, he was also of an age a gentleman ought to be married. And Jane was a beautiful young woman – with a head as empty as it was beautiful.

Maud reached her room. She drew her notebook and pencil from her bag, climbed onto the bed and plumped up the pillow, turned to a clean page and wrote.

1. Either Lord Urquhart is attached to Jane Tremain or he is not.

2. If he is not so attached, then her pursuit of him will cause him no distress.

3. If he is so attached, then either the attachment is reciprocal or it is not, and JT is an outrageous flirt.

4. If it is reciprocal, then JT's pursuit of him will cause Lord U no distress.

5. If it is not reciprocal, Lord U will suffer distress whether I intrude or not.

6. If Lord U will suffer distress whether I intrude or not, my intrusion cannot be the cause of Lord U's distress.

7. It is therefore logically impossible for my intrusion to cause Lord U distress.

Maud stared at what she had written. What had she been thinking? She needed to save her energies for investigating the murders. She loved Daisy dearly and would do whatever she needed to save her friend's life. Maud told herself that what she'd felt last night with Lord Urquhart – emotions for him she had successfully quashed in the past – was irrational. She was a rational being and she would concentrate on facts.

With an exclamation, she tore the page from her book and threw it onto the fire. The flames consumed it within seconds. Solving the two murders was of paramount importance and she was wasting time on schoolgirl drivel. Chastened, she hurried along the corridor to Daisy's room and knocked on the door.

'Daisy? It's me!' Maud called. 'How are you?'

After a short time, Maud heard Daisy's voice on the other side of the door. 'Bearing up, Maud. It's just a wee bit frustrating, nae being able to do any real work on the case.'

'I know what you mean. Jane Tremain and Lord Urquhart are talking about playing a game of sardines, for goodness' sake!'

'*Tsk*, and on the Sabbath too.'

'If you had seen her with him this morning, you'd think him in danger of becoming as frivolous as she.'

Daisy laughed. 'Are you sure his lordship is as keen as Miss Jane? There's something about that lassie—'

'There certainly is, Daisy. She's angling to be his wife.'

'You dinna sound very pleased about that.'

'Well, it's just that...' *Just that what?*

'If you dinna want him, Maud, why shouldna he choose someone else?'

Maud could give no answer to this. 'This is a ridiculous conversation, Daisy,' she said. 'We need to concentrate on getting you out of there.'

'Have you worked out a way of entering a locked room?'

'Sadly, I can't. If only I knew the person in this castle who can.'

'You canna do any good standing there, Maud, so go and do whatever you need to.'

'I will be of no more use today than if I were also locked up,' Maud told her ruefully. 'Whist, sardines...'

'What is it, Maud? What's got your brain ticking?'

'I have two things to report, Daisy,' she said, lowering her voice. 'No, three.'

'I canna hear you through the door. You'll have to speak up a wee bit.'

Maud cleared her throat and raised her voice a little. 'It's difficult to have such a conversation in this way. Anyone could hear.' She looked around. The corridor was empty, but it felt too public. 'I will tell you the third item, though. Jane has no mother or siblings.'

'Right, Maud, I'll cross that off our *Questions* list. That's only six left needing answers.'

Maud prepared to leave. 'I'm sorry that you aren't able to come to kirk today, Daisy.'

'Nae doubt Magnus thinks I'm beyond redemption.'

Maud smiled. 'If there's nothing you need, I'll go now and come back later.'

'Just do your best.'

Maud retraced her steps down to the ground floor and wandered into the library. Last night's Spinoza lay unread on her nightstand. She browsed along the bookshelves. A few volumes on Scots law by Home, two books by Hutcheson on moral philosophy... and a number of mystery novels. Fergus Hume, Conan Doyle – Magnus can't be all bad, Maud thought with a wry smile – Arthur Morrison; all the classics. She continued to examine the spines of the books. E.W. Hornung with his Raffles stories, Edgar Allan Poe and *The Murders in the Rue Morgue*, a locked-room mystery.

A sudden thought came to Maud. Magnus's instruction had been that Daisy should be locked in her room – not that anyone else should be locked out. How foolish of her not to have thought of that earlier!

Maud sped down the stairs to the servants' hall.

'Isobel!' she cried, bursting in to the kitchen.

The room was steamy and a hive of activity. Kirsty was washing up posts and pans, trying to keep up with Mrs Baillie as she cooked lunch.

'Isobel,' called the cook, looking up from beating eggs. 'Whatever are you doing? Pay attention to Miss McIntyre.'

The girl had turned, holding a tray with a small china teapot and strainer, cup and saucer, milk jug and sugar bowl, and a plate of small almond macaroons.

'Please allow me to take Miss Cameron's mid-morning tea tray up to her,' Maud said quickly.

'This is it, miss, but are you sure?' The maid glanced uneasily at Mrs Baillie.

The cook had transferred her attention to Kirsty. 'Have you put the kidneys to soak, girl?'

'Not yet, Mrs B.'

'Then do it now, for goodness' sake. I'll be needing them for the kidney omelette for those upstairs. Begging your pardon, Miss McIntyre.' The cook was already looking around for something else she had thought of.

Isobel took advantage of her preoccupation. 'Thank you, miss,' she murmured, passing the laden tray to Maud and indicating the door key which lay next to the plate of biscuits.

The tray was much heavier than Maud had expected. Goodness, how did such a slip of a girl as Isobel manage to carry such weights countless times a day? Maud felt chastened, thinking of the servants in her father's house.

As Maud hefted the laden tray out of the kitchen, she heard Mrs Baillie say, 'Isobel, don't just stand there when there are bedrooms to be cleaned.'

Maud made her way back up the stairs. On the ground floor, the sound of Finlay's and Andrew's voices came to her through the open door of the great hall, chatting as they laid the table for luncheon. She continued up the staircase. On the first floor, she knew that Grace and her mistress would be talking in Ailsa's room. Maud paused on the stairs for a moment, wondering if she should try to listen through the door, but the tray was growing heavier by the minute. Maud moved on, up the stairs to the second floor and along the corridor, past the closed doors first of Jane's room and then of her own. Daisy's bedroom was the last one on this side of the corridor. With relief, Maud reached the door.

A series of irregular thuds came from inside Daisy's room. What *was* she doing?

Maud set the tray down on the long rug and took up the key. 'Daisy,' she called softly through the door. 'It's me.' She unlocked the door just as it was wrenched open by Daisy on the other side.

'Maud!' Daisy gave her a huge smile. 'How did you manage that?'

Maud laughed. 'It wasn't magic. I simply realised that Magnus had ordered you to be detained in your room. He didn't say anything about keeping the rest of us out, so I offered to bring up your mid-morning refreshment.' She bent and picked up the tray.

Daisy stood back from the door. 'I never thought that one day you'd be waiting on me!'

'It's my pleasure.' Maud stepped into the room.

Daisy closed the door. 'Here, give me that.' She made to take the tray.

'And spoil your experience of me waiting on you? I think not, Daisy Cameron. I'll put it on the writing table.' Maud did so and turned to her friend. 'What was that noise, Daisy? I've heard it from your room before.'

Daisy tucked her brown and cream blouse more neatly into her skirt. 'Just me walking up and down. There's only so much reading and gazing out of the window that a body can do.'

Maud wasn't convinced, but her friend would tell her in her own time.

'You off to kirk?' Daisy asked, looking at Maud's dark tailored suit.

'It seems it's not possible this morning because of the weather.' She gestured towards the window, where rain streaked down the pane. 'Perhaps later this afternoon. But Daisy, how are you?'

'It's nae even one day since I've been locked in here, you ken.' Daisy dropped into an armchair and Maud took the one opposite. 'But it feels like a lifetime.'

'Even one day in isolation can be hard when there's so much to be done.'

'Anyway, I was asleep for eight of those hours.' Daisy sounded her usual chirpy self.

'So, if you slept well, are you ready to discuss the case?'

'More than ready.' Daisy rose, threw another log on the fire and took her notebook and pencil from the drawer of the writing table. 'No more putting these down the side of an armchair for me.' She pulled a wry face as she returned to her seat.

'Tea first, before it goes cold.' Maud got to her feet, poured Daisy a cup of tea and handed it to her, before offering the biscuits.

'Thanks, Maud.' Her face lit up. 'Almond macaroons – my favourite.' Daisy took the plate and balanced it in her lap on top of her notebook.

'Are there any biscuits you don't like?' Maud asked with a smile. Daisy never seemed to put on weight, regardless of the amount of food she consumed.

'Nae really,' Daisy admitted.

'Have you had any new thoughts?' Maud asked, sitting back down.

'Just a minute. Where's your tea and biscuits, Maud?'

'I'll have mine shortly.'

'Have a macaroon, then?' Daisy held out the plate to Maud.

Maud shook her head. 'Have you any new thoughts on the case?'

'The only person I've seen since being locked in here is Isobel, but I did manage to find out a few things.' Daisy took a gulp of tea and ate a tiny macaroon, before setting the cup and saucer and the plate by the side of her chair.

She flipped open her notebook. 'I asked Isobel, ever so discreetly, if she kent why the laird and his sister hadna married. Nae to be nosy, but in case it was relevant to our investigation.'

'It could well be. Any information is worth having.'

'Isobel told me that a long time ago Magnus had a fiancée, but she died of consumption and he never wanted another woman after her.'

'That's a romantic story, but...'

'Aye, it doesna take us any further forward. As to Ailsa, she has never wanted to marry; the castle and the family name mean everything to her. At least, that's according to Grace, who Isobel got this from.'

'So there's no suggestion of a past attachment between Ailsa and Tremain? A woman scorned and all that?'

Daisy shook her head.

'And yet there's some sort of history between the two of them. Ailsa's dislike of Neil Tremain was clear on our first day here.' Maud could hardly ask her hostess outright why this was the case. 'Perhaps we can find out more about that through one of the other servants later on.'

Daisy sent Maud a quick glance, as if asking would she, Daisy, get the opportunity *later on*?

Maud gave her an encouraging smile. 'If the weather eases a little tomorrow, Lord Urquhart and I are going to visit

Tremain's house on the isle of Ulva, to see if we can find any clues in his background to help solve his murder.'

'Lord Urquhart? Maybe Jane Tremain isna as secure in his affections as she thinks she is.'

'Lord Urquhart has offered to help me on this case only during your temporary absence, Daisy.'

'Oh aye?' Daisy said with a smile.

'But only if you don't mind. Although I confess I could do with his help.'

'Maud, two heads are better than one, as we've always said.'

'I'm sorry it can't be the two of us working together.'

'Until then, do you have anything new?' Daisy leaned over to pick up her cup of tea.

'Oh yes.' Maud smiled. 'I've had *two* breakthroughs.'

SIXTEEN

'First,' said Maud, 'a very strange thing happened last night.'

'What?' Daisy sat up quickly, almost spilling her tea into the saucer.

'I couldn't sleep, so about one o'clock I went down to the library to look for something to read.'

'A library's the best place to find a book.' Daisy grinned.

'And I came across Lord Urquhart—'

She raised an eyebrow. 'Also in the library in the middle of the night looking for something to read?'

'It was as I was passing through the great hall. He was sitting in one of those large chairs by the fire, but in the shadows as if he were hiding.'

'Hiding? Who from?'

'That's the question. He's being evasive about it. He said he'd come downstairs for a book, but I don't believe him.'

'Why?'

'It was far too dark to read where he was sitting.'

'So you think the book was to cover his being out of bed after hours?'

'When you say it like that it sounds as if he's a schoolboy at boarding school.'

They were quiet for a moment.

'What's the second thing?' Daisy asked. 'You said there were two.'

'Before I went downstairs, I finished reading *The Mystery of the Yellow Room*. And it turned out that the time of the attack on the victim wasn't exactly when everyone had thought.'

'You mean you think the doctor got it wrong in Neil's case? That doesna sound right.'

Daisy popped another macaroon into her mouth as rain hammered against the window.

'I agree that we know his body was still warm. I'm not really sure what I mean.' Maud pulled her notebook from her pocket. 'I've drawn up a list of suspects of those above-stairs.' She opened to the page *Suspects List* and read out what she had written on Jane, Ailsa, Magnus and Lord Urquhart. 'I was convinced our strongest candidates were the first two, that is Jane and Ailsa; Jane's motive being money and Ailsa's her hostility towards Tremain for whatever reason. Have another talk with Isobel, Daisy. Find out why Ailsa holds a grudge against him.'

'All right.'

'Then last night I realised Dr Munro is also a likely suspect.'

'Why?' Daisy wrinkled her brow. 'He wasna in the castle when Neil was murdered.'

'But he was in the castle when Sergeant McNeish was murdered.' Maud noticed she had not added him to her list. 'Lend me your pencil, Daisy. I've left the pen in my room.'

Daisy passed it to her.

'Suspect number five,' Maud went on, reading aloud as she wrote. 'Dr Munro. Motive...' She paused and looked at Daisy. 'Here, I am at a loss,' she admitted and added a question mark. 'Alibi: Suspect not present when Tremain murdered.' Maud looked at her assistant. 'We agreed that whoever murdered Tremain must also have killed the sergeant?'

Daisy nodded.

'And we know that those present in McNeish's room just a minute before he was stabbed were you and me, Magnus, Lord Urquhart and the doctor?' Maud scribbled a note to this effect in her book and looked at Daisy.

Again, Daisy nodded in agreement.

'And that Ailsa and Jane were visiting the stables to check on the new horse at this time?'

'Apparently.'

'Assuming this is true – and we know from the search made by Magnus and Lord Urquhart immediately after we discovered the policeman's body that Jane's room was empty – then neither of them could have killed McNeish.'

'Which means our main suspects are now the three gentlemen?'

Maud sighed. 'It would seem to be the case. And yet I can think of no motive for the doctor – or for any of them – to kill Tremain. The murder of the sergeant was done to stop him uncovering the truth. If we concentrate on Neil Tremain's background, perhaps we'll discover *why* he was killed. There must be something there that will help us find the answer.'

'We must hope so, Maud.' The colour drained from Daisy's face. 'All I ken is Lord Urquhart is a good man and I dinna want you to rule out any help. My life depends on you solving this case.'

The remainder of Sunday morning passed slowly for Maud. Without Daisy actively involved in the investigation, she felt lost. Daisy was as good a detective as she was, but what Daisy could do much better than Maud was to put her troubles to one side and get on with the job.

Magnus emerged briefly from his room to take morning prayers in the hall for the servants, and Maud made sure she kept out of the way of Lord Urquhart and Jane Tremain. Let the two of them play sardines if that's what they wish, she thought.

But their company couldn't be avoided at luncheon, eaten in the dining room which faced the front of the castle. Through the window, Maud saw between the trees a shining wet expanse of sky and water as if merged into one. The clouds appeared to be moving more slowly, but still the tops of trees swayed in the strong wind.

'I think what these suffragettes are doing is ridiculous,' Jane was saying, cutting her kidney omelette into very small pieces.

'In what way?' Maud asked, returning her attention to the room and forking up a portion of her own omelette.

'Oh, everything really,' Jane said vaguely.

'Wanting votes for women?' suggested Ailsa in a cool tone.

'Well, not precisely *that* – although I do think we can safely leave important decisions to the men.' She cast a flirtatious glance at Lord Urquhart. 'Don't you agree, my lord?'

He took a sip from his glass of wine. 'What I do think is ridiculous, is that women have no vote. This is the twentieth century.'

Jane flushed. 'I suppose it depends...'

'On what?' Maud took another bite of her omelette.

Jane drew a breath and started again. 'What I mean is, I think that window-smashing, setting fire to letter boxes and so on is too much.' She picked up her glass of red wine.

'I have to agree with you there, Miss Tremain,' Maud said. 'This new militant phase of the Women's Social and Political Union is dangerous, and I'm not sure it will have the desired effect.' Maud admired the series of disguises adopted by the eldest of Mrs Pankhurst's daughters, Christabel, as she fled to Paris to avoid arrest, but not the WSPU tactics.

A gust of wind and rain rattled the window. Jane jumped, causing wine from her glass to splash over her apricot blouse. She let out an oath. Not such a calm and elegant Gibson Girl, after all, thought Maud with a degree of relish. During the shocked silence Jane mopped at the crêpe de Chine fabric with her napkin.

As they ate, Maud took discreet glances at the others around the table. Ailsa, Jane, Lord Urquhart. All possible suspects. She really could not believe *he* had murdered anyone. But could Ailsa or Jane have stabbed Tremain? For that matter, was it likely that Magnus had stabbed the sergeant? Perhaps brother and sister had acted together for some unknown reason. It would certainly throw the police off their scent. Ailsa could have told Magnus exactly how she had killed Tremain, and Magnus could have replicated the method with the murder of McNeish.

She was clutching at straws, Maud told herself, and was grateful when the luncheon came to an end. For lack of anything better to do, she made her way to the library, crossed the room and leaned against the wall of the recessed window, gazing dismally out at the dripping trees, sodden lawn and steady rain. She wondered which outbuilding the police sergeant was in and if she should don her coat and saunter round to it.

'What a foul day,' she heard Lord Urquhart say as he came to stand beside her.

'Perfect for fishing.' Maud pictured her three older brothers going out with their fishing rods when they were all children, but they would never let her join them. It's a funny thing, but now that she could go out and fish if she wanted to, she had no desire to do so. She smiled at the thought.

'Something amuses you?' he asked.

She told him about her brothers and Lord Urquhart

laughed. 'I cannot imagine you as a funny little girl in pigtails and a pinafore.'

'I was never a *funny little girl in pigtails,*' she said in a severe voice, trying not to laugh.

He looked down at her. 'I don't believe you were. I suspect you were a serious child always with her nose in a book.'

'Not always...'

'A book by Conan Doyle, as soon as you were able to read his works.'

'Well, that is true.'

They stood together for a moment longer.

'I'm going out,' Maud announced suddenly. 'Being in the rain outside is better than standing indoors watching it fall.'

'I agree. We need to find McNeish and examine his body. We only have Munro's word that the killings are of the same type, and he's a loyal friend to this household. And Magnus stormed out of the room in outrage over blotting Finlay's good name; there's a strong loyalty there too.'

A sudden gust of wind moaned down the chimney, startling Maud. 'You mean that Daisy, being both an outsider and of a lower social class, would be an acceptable villain?' She couldn't keep the horror from her voice.

'I mean only that it's possible.'

'I did consider that the killer might have chosen to frame Daisy as the policeman's murderer,' Maud faltered, 'but I dismissed the idea. The real killer couldn't have known she would be the first to enter Sergeant McNeish's room.'

Nonetheless, a shiver went down Maud's spine at the remote possibility of her friend being singled out as a scapegoat.

A short while later, shod in her sturdy button boots, Maud took a mackintosh and a black sou'wester from a selection in the lobby and slipped them on. She found Lord Urquhart waiting for her at the open front door, also suitably attired and holding a large furled umbrella.

He smiled. 'You haven't changed your mind, I see?'

'Of course not. I'm not about to let a drop of rain or two stop me getting some fresh air.'

His eyes travelled from her boots to her hat as he considered her rainproof costume. 'How charming you look, even when dressed in such an outfit.'

She frowned. He was making fun of her. Of course Jane Tremain would not wear such *practical* clothing.

'What have I said to deserve that look?' he asked, an eyebrow raised.

She would not give him the pleasure of hearing her explain her feelings. 'Nothing, my lord.'

'My lord? Now I know it's serious.'

She gave a light laugh and immediately chastised herself for sounding – unintentionally – like the coquettish Jane.

'I meant it, you know,' he said in his deep, warm voice, and a wave of pleasure swept over her.

He stepped out onto the porch and unfurled the black umbrella. A gust of wind took hold of it and almost blew it inside out. He wrestled with it and got it under control, while Maud, clamping the sou'wester to her head, struggled to close the front door behind her.

He crooked his arm towards her. 'Ready?'

The rain had lessened considerably, but she pulled up the collar of her mackintosh to keep drops from trickling down her neck, took his arm and they stepped outside.

'I thought we should avoid the garden and walk down the driveway,' he said, raising his voice above the wind moaning through the branches of the trees. 'This will have the merit of keeping our feet dry while we discuss the plan.'

'Daisy would say that the best way of keeping feet dry would be to stay indoors.' Maud smiled as they set off at a brisk pace down the avenue leading away from the castle. The driveway was strewn with twigs and leaves torn from their branches.

'Miss Cameron is right, as always.'

She glanced up at him. He had a calm, kind set to his face when he didn't think anyone was looking. 'You know that Daisy is innocent?'

'I've never doubted it for a moment. She is not a killer, but one of Edinburgh's finest detectives.'

They walked on in silence for a while, the wind whipping at their raincoats and hats.

'How well do you know our host?' Maud asked.

'Not very. Magnus is an OF, of course, as am I.'

'An OF?'

'An Old Fettesian. Magnus and Tremain boarded together and so they were close. At least, I understand they were as boys. I wasn't at the College at the same time.'

'Magnus told us that Tremain visited occasionally, but did Magnus ever visit him?'

'Not as far as I am aware. That is something you would have to ask him.'

'I'm not sure he'll talk to me at present, so you should ask him. How did you come into contact with Magnus if he doesn't move in society?'

'Fettes has a journal which enables its *alumni* to keep in touch with the school and with each other, should they so wish.' Lord Urquhart guided Maud around a large puddle in the drive.

'Why did you contact him?'

He glanced down at her. 'What do you mean?'

'Only what I said. The age difference must mean you have little in common, and I can't believe the pull of the old school is sufficient.'

He gazed ahead as they walked. 'As I told you, I learned of

the bronze statuette he was thinking of selling and quite fancied it for myself.'

'Hmm. And now that the lion has been found, are you still interested in it?'

'I have examined it, and it is just as I imagined.'

'That's an evasive answer.'

He smiled. 'If you say so.'

What was he hiding? she wondered.

While they had talked, the rain had stopped and a weak sun had emerged, but twigs continued to crack as they broke off tree branches in the wind.

They reached the end of the drive.

'Shall we turn back?' he asked.

Maud nodded and they did so. 'I hope we can cross to Ulva tomorrow,' she said. 'This waiting around is unbearable. The only good thing about this weather is that it has prevented boats crossing to and from the mainland. Are you sure the ferry to Ulva will be in use?'

'The wind is still too strong for the longer passage,' he told her, 'but we should be fine for the narrow stretch of water between Mull and Ulva.'

Now they were on the return walk, she could see the castle's outbuildings through the trees, their grey slate roofs washed to a darker shade with the rain. Mr Dalgleish, wearing an old sack over his shoulders to keep off the wet, came out of the shed and moved slowly around the corner.

'Poor Sergeant McNeish's body is in one of those barns,' Maud murmured.

As soon as the words were out of her mouth, she ducked under the creaking tree branches and set off at a pace across the wet lawn towards the buildings. The neatly cut grass became undergrowth as she drew closer. Behind her she heard Lord Urquhart struggling with the umbrella as he followed.

'Leave it behind!' she called over her shoulder and hurried

on. Skirting around the stables, Maud came to two stone outbuildings. The larger one was double height and had no windows, only a long stretch of skylights to provide natural light. Together, she and Lord Urquhart heaved open the heavy sliding door. The cavernous building was gloomy inside but empty, the concrete floor cleared of straw, presumably ready to house beasts when the weather grew cold. A room to the side proved to be an Aladdin's cave of sorts, full of items the family must have gathered over the years. Certainly there was no policeman's body here.

She moved along a rough path to the smaller structure. This had a window and Maud peered in, but the glass was so dirty and cobwebby she could see nothing. Lord Urquhart walked round to the door and tried the handle.

'The sergeant's body must be in here,' he said. 'The door is locked.'

Maud felt the desperation show on her face.

Lord Urquhart took Maud's hand and pressed it to his chest. She could feel his heart beating beneath her fingers.

He smiled at her, his grip strong and dependable. 'Together, Miss McIntyre, I promise we will prove that Daisy is innocent.'

SEVENTEEN

By five o'clock, Maud had pinned on her picture hat with its black feather and had drawn on her gloves. She was on her way out of the front door, throwing a warm fur wrap around her shoulders, when a deep, familiar voice called her back.

'Miss McIntyre!'

She turned to see Lord Urquhart. 'I will accompany you to kirk, if I may?' He looked very smart in his well-cut dark overcoat, necktie and homburg. He's too handsome, she repeated to herself. Too charming. Too *deceitful?*

'Of course.' She strove for nonchalance in her voice. 'Does Jane not wish to join us?'

'I did not see her to ask,' he said indifferently.

Good, thought Maud.

She had asked Finlay to bring her car round, and it was standing in the courtyard, its wet paintwork shining in the light from the oil lamp in the lobby.

'You didn't drive here from Edinburgh?' she asked, as Lord Urquhart slid into the passenger seat beside her.

'No, I took the train to Oban and from there the ferry to Tobermory. Magnus picked me up in his pony and trap.'

'So, without my assistance you'd be in for a long walk.'

'I have long legs, so I think I'd manage. But yes, I'd have to walk.'

They drove in silence along the winding roads, the trees making a tunnel over them. It was as if the tangled, swaying branches were weaving an enchantment around them, she thought whimsically. But there was Neil Tremain murdered in a locked room, Sergeant McNeish killed in a room no one had time to enter and Daisy imprisoned in her room at the castle. This was no fairy tale.

The few miles to the village were soon covered. They drove along Main Street by the side of the darkening bay. Small, moored boats bobbed in the shelter of the harbour, while turbulent waves were a blizzard of white far out to sea. Past the Carmichael Arms, the grocer's shop and the post office, all closed for the Sabbath, and up the hill to the parish kirk.

Maud parked, climbed out and, buffeted by the wind, they hastened towards the wide doors standing open in welcome. A little terrier, waiting patiently outside for its master, eyed them as they passed into the church.

The air inside the kirk was chilly and Maud was relieved to see coal stoves had been lit for the service. The pews were full and there was the familiar smell of a mix of ancient wood and old hymn books. Candles glowed on the altar and in every window, the stained glasswork and brass candlesticks gleaming in their light. The church had few flowers, but Maud was sure they were saving the blooms for the following Sabbath. It would be the autumn equinox and therefore the harvest festival, when the congregation would bring an abundance of gifts of food and flowers to the kirk as a sign of thanks to God for a good harvest. She hoped the crops had already been brought in, given the damage the storm must otherwise have done.

Maud and Lord Urquhart dropped their offerings in the plate beside the door, walked up the aisle and sat in the Carmichael family's pew as Ailsa had requested. She had declined to come, too upset by the events that had taken place at the castle.

There were prayers and hymns. Maud's mind drifted before the sermon was delivered. She looked around, wondering if anyone in the congregation would approach them with some snippet of information to help free Daisy. She prayed for help, for some sort of enlightenment from on high. After the service Maud and Lord Urquhart came out of the church, he dutifully cranked the engine for Maud and she drove back to the castle. A wasted journey for Maud the detective; Maud the woman hoped her prayers would be answered. The storm clouds had brought the darkness on early and they passed cottages where warm lamps glowed behind un-curtained windows, then shadowy fields and hedges.

'Tell me,' he said, as her motor car wound through the country lanes, 'what made you want to be a detective?'

'That's easy to answer. I possess an insatiable curiosity and I'm not well-suited to the round of amusements which make up the futile existence of some parts of society.' She glanced pointedly at him, which was wasted as he was gazing at the road ahead. 'The belief that women should be gracious and charming at all times,' she went on, 'seen rather than heard. That's not for me.'

'So I have observed.'

'Not gracious or charming?' she teased him.

'Seen rather than heard.' A smile appeared on his lips and was gone again. He was quiet for a moment and then seemed to come to a decision. 'In light of what you have said, about a futile existence, I expect you are wondering what I generally do with myself all day.'

'Certainly not.' Maud coloured at her outright lie, glad that he couldn't see her blush in the darkness.

He paused and then said, 'I will tell you, anyway. I'm a newspaper correspondent.'

He suddenly rose in her estimation. 'I've not come across your name. What do you write about?' Perhaps he covered the stories around the suffragette movement or the inadequacies of government.

'I write under a pseudonym for *The Sketch*. Their *Scottish Man About Town* column.'

'*The Sketch*,' she said. 'For *cultivated people who in their leisure moments look for light reading.*'

'*Imbued with a high artistic value.*' He finished the quote with a grin.

'How could I have forgotten that aspect? You once told me, shortly after we first met, that you had no gainful employment.'

'Some might say that's true, writing such a column.'

'But you wanted to put your time to some use, at least?' She glanced again at his profile and in the darkness could just make out that his expression was an endearing mix of serious and shy. She turned her attention back to the road and softened her voice. 'I'm afraid I know almost nothing of your life.'

'I can tell you in half a dozen sentences. My father gambled away the bulk of his inheritance at card tables. He cheated on his wife, my mother. Their marriage lasted only a few years and she went back to America. As I grew up, he either rebuked or ignored me. His debts meant he was forced to sell his property in England, but he managed to keep the country estate in Inverness-shire which is now mine. That, and the journalism, is more or less my sole source of income.'

In those few words, it was as if a space had been crossed between them. 'Which explains why you're not married.'

He laughed. 'Miss McIntyre, I admire your style.'

'You mean my bluntness.'

'Indeed, I do not.' He shrugged. 'The story is all too common amongst my father's peers. I am more fortunate than others, in that he had retained some property which I inherited.' Maud sensed him glance at her. 'I'm enjoying our working together on the investigation.' She heard the smile in his voice. 'My mind rebels at stagnation.'

'Sherlock Holmes!'

Lord Urquhart laughed. 'You are not the only one who reads Conan Doyle.'

They reached the massive iron gates standing open and drove along the tree-lined gravel drive, the lights from the castle illuminating its smooth lawns.

She could work with this man, Maud thought – but only until Daisy's name was cleared and the real killer unmasked.

'It's only a little over twenty miles,' Lord Urquhart told Maud, as they prepared to set out for Ulva early the following morning to catch the ferry, 'but the road is very narrow.'

'Is there another route?' she asked, tying a silk motoring scarf around her hat and head. Yesterday's gale had blown itself out, but it had left a blustery day, so she added an extra knot under her chin.

'There is and it's shorter, but it would take us considerably longer as the road is even more narrow and winding.'

'The first route it is,' she agreed, settling herself comfortably into the driver's seat of the Napier.

Because her appearance was not of importance, unlike her arrival on Mull, and, unlike yesterday evening's drive to the village, they would be travelling some distance, Maud had dressed as recommended by Dorothy Levitt in her chatty little handbook *The Woman and the Car*. Maud wore a two-piece blue tweed skirt and jacket set, with a simple blouse and a jumper for warmth. Soft leather gauntlet gloves covered her slim hands and a pair of unflattering driving goggles protected her eyes. She had decided against Miss Levitt's recommendation that the woman driver should carry a little hand-mirror in a convenient place, so that she may hold the mirror aloft from time to time in order to see behind while driving in traffic. There was no traffic on Mull.

They drove in companionable silence, south from Tobermory along the east coast and then west towards the tiny hamlet of Ulva Ferry. Most of the oak and ash trees had lost their leaves in the storm, but the lochs lining the roads were delightful, yet Maud's mind was on other things.

They drew into Ulva Ferry, parked and climbed out. Maud removed her driving goggles and dropped them into the motor car. Across the narrow strip of water, a small boat was moored outside a low building nestling in trees.

'How do we summon the ferryman?' Maud said, wondering if they would be required to jump up and down and wave their arms to attract attention.

'Here's how.' Lord Urquhart gestured to a small building behind them. A white wooden panel attached to the wall had a painted notice instructing passengers to slide the panel to red. Lord Urquhart slid the panel along, revealing a block of red colour underneath.

'Simple, but effective.' Maud smiled.

They walked a short way down the slipway and almost immediately the ferryman emerged from the boathouse on the opposite side of the Sound of Ulva. They watched as he climbed into the small boat and began to row. Lord Urquhart slid the board back to white, again as instructed, and before long the ferryman reached where they stood waiting.

'Thank you,' Maud said, as the man held out a hand and assisted her into the boat.

She untied the silk motoring scarf wrapped around her head and knotted it loosely around her neck. Lord Urquhart

paid the ferryman, they took seats on the short wooden bench
and the boat set off across the narrow strait. The water was clear
but grey, reflecting the overcast sky.

'Are you here on holiday,' the man asked pleasantly, pulling
on the oars, 'or visiting someone on the island?' Mull gradually
receded.

'We're looking for the house of Mr Neil Tremain,' Maud
told him. She glanced at Lord Urquhart. They had earlier
discussed that Tremain's housekeeper, with no telephone
service on either island and no post possible because of the
storm, was unlikely to have heard of his death. The boatman's
next words seemed to confirm this.

'Och, you'll easily find Tremain's house. It's the biggest one
on the island. An Taigh Mòr means The Big House.' He indicated the mountain looming ahead of them. 'That's the highest
point of Ulva – it's called *Beinn Chreagach*, the rocky
mountain.'

Seeing Maud's look of alarm, he added, 'But you won't be
needing to cross that to reach Mr Tremain's house.'

'Do many people live here?' Lord Urquhart asked.

'Not as many as used to. At the beginning of the last
century there were some six hundred souls spread across
twenty-two townships, villages you might call them. Now there
are barely fifty folk.'

'The clearances?'

'The potato famine didn't help, but aye, the clearances.' The
ferryman negotiated a sudden shift in the wind.

'I've heard of the infamous Sutherland clearances,' Maud
said.

'We had them here too. A lawyer from Stirling bought the
island' – the ferryman spat over the side of the boat – 'and when
he wasn't making enough money from the kelp industry, he
ordered the evictions. The people – his tenants – were given

little or no warning; the thatches of their houses were burned and they were forced to live on almost nothing. Many were taken to what's now known as Starvation Point, to exist as best they could on shellfish and seaweed, which meant they starved to death.'

'That's dreadful.' Maud felt desperately sorry for the island people of old.

'Aye, it surely is.' The oars dipped rhythmically in and out of the water until the boat drew level with the slipway. 'Here we are,' he announced. 'Just come back to the boathouse when you're ready to return.'

Lord Urquhart climbed out and helped Maud from the boat.

'Where does the name Ulva come from?' she asked the ferryman, as he turned to go back inside the building.

'It's Old Norse for wolf island.'

'I hope there are none left,' Maud said, only half joking.

'Officially, the last wolf in Scotland was killed in the seventeenth century, miss, but there's those who reckon they still see them today. I'll be thinking what they are seeing is the ghost of that lawyer.'

Maud laughed. 'That's a relief.'

They set off, her leather satchel bumping against her hip and the wind gusting about her skirts as they walked along the track leading inland from the water's edge.

'I don't think we have to worry, Miss McIntyre,' said Lord Urquhart, slowing his stride to match hers. 'I know there have been reports of wolves surviving in remote parts of the Highlands as late as some thirty years ago, but I'm sure there won't be any here.'

'I believe wolves can swim.' Maud couldn't stop herself from glancing around.

'They can, but I'm sure if there were any here, the ferryman would have warned us.'

'He did in a way, although his warning was about a different kind of wolf.'

Lord Urquhart laughed. 'From Stirling.'

Ahead of them was a low cottage, built with drystone walls packed with earth and roofed with thatch of turf. There was no chimney for the smoke to escape through and the smoke was making its way through the roof. Outside a few hens scratched idly in the earth. As Maud and Lord Urquhart drew close, the hens flapped away, squawking.

The door was open and they could see a young woman inside sweeping the packed-earth floor. The blackhouse consisted of only one room: one end for livestock and, with a partition between them, the other end the living space for humans. How hard her life must be, Maud realised.

'Are you thirsty or in need of a rest?' Lord Urquhart broke into her thoughts. 'We might be able to trespass on her hospitality.'

She smiled and shook her head.

They continued walking, a goat observing them, wary but unmoved. A flock of small, black Hebridean sheep with two pairs of horns grazed on the hillside. As Maud and Lord Urquhart drew closer, the sheep ran, startling a red deer. He barked his annoyance, his antlers impressive as he stared down at the two-legged intruders.

Maud once more turned her thoughts to what they might find at Tremain's house. She and Daisy had been told by Finlay that the man was a recluse, so did this mean he lived entirely alone? Maud wondered. Presumably Tremain kept a servant or two – perhaps a husband and wife – to run the place.

Maud and Lord Urquhart continued to pick their way along the track, negotiating tree roots, moss and rocks. She grew warm from the walk, despite the wind which blew off the water, flattening the grasses and whipping at their clothing. They passed the occasional derelict cottage, roofless and with neglected

patches of green that must once have been used to grow potatoes and cereals. What a hard life it must have been here, Maud
thought, and perhaps still is. Yet this was where Neil Tremain
had chosen to live.

After a while, they came across a man repairing a drystone
wall and stopped to ask for directions.

'An Taigh Mòr? I doubt Tremain will let you in.' The man
shrugged. 'Aye, it's only a wee bit further on. You can't miss it.'

And he was right.

EIGHTEEN

Neil Tremain's house was solid and substantial against the scudding grey clouds. An imposing building, but one that lacked the sense of activity that was usual with such houses. Maud looked up at the windows but had no sense of anyone in the rooms. 'It looks very secretive,' she observed as they walked up to the closed oak door. Lord Urquhart lifted the large iron ring and rapped three times.

They waited. He was about to knock again, when they heard the sound of a bolt being drawn back and the door was opened.

'*Fáilte.*' The traditional Gaelic welcome wasn't reflected in the suspicious look the middle-aged woman gave them.

Maud smiled at her. 'Is this the house of Mr Neil Tremain?'

'Aye.' The housekeeper frowned at them.

'We have a slight acquaintance with Mr Tremain,' went on Maud, determined to stick to the truth as much as possible, 'and have come across from Mull—'

'I'm sorry, but you've had a wasted journey. The master's away from home at present.' The woman began to close the door.

'Perhaps we might be permitted to come in for a short while,' Maud put in quickly, 'before we return to Mull? I am Miss McIntyre and this is Lord Urquhart.'

The woman's eyes grew wide at Lord Urquhart's name, and she opened the door again. It was astonishing, Maud thought with a degree of annoyance, how a title gave access.

'I'm Eppy.' The housekeeper bobbed a curtsy at him. 'Your lordship.'

He smiled at Eppy. 'Mr Tremain said we should visit. It was foolish of me not to write and let him know, but we were in the area and thought why not? It seems a shame to have come all this way and be denied a tour of this historic house.'

Was it historic? Maud wondered. It was large, but it didn't look old and it looked to be rather plain.

'Well, I suppose...'

'Thank you so much. We have no wish to disrupt your work and won't stay long.'

'There's only me here,' Eppy said, 'but as Mr Tremain rarely leaves the house and never entertains, there's precious little for me to do.' She held the door wide for them to enter. 'He's away visiting an old school friend at the moment.'

That much was true, then, thought Maud.

'Can I offer you a cup of tea?' Eppy closed the door behind them.

'That would be delightful,' Lord Urquhart said.

'The drawing room is clean and tidy.'

'The kitchen will be perfect, thank you, Eppy,' Maud said, guessing the housekeeper would be more relaxed there. 'We have no wish to make extra work for you and I expect the fires aren't lit when Mr Tremain is away.'

Eppy glanced at Lord Urquhart, clearly thinking his lordship should not be made to take tea in the kitchen.

'I would be very comfortable there,' he reassured her. 'I'm

not unused to the kitchens of a great house. I spent many happy hours in them at home when I was a boy.'

'Well, if you're sure, my lord.' She led them along the corridor.

The sense of an empty, unloved house was marked. There were no sounds of activity behind any of the closed doors they passed, no scent of flowers, no warmth from hearths making its way into the passage. Any paintings that might have once graced the walls were gone, no books left casually on the hall table. Their footsteps echoed on the flagstones.

They descended a flight of stone steps at the end of the corridor where Eppy threw open a door. This was clearly her domain. Warmth from the stove greeted them and the rich smell of meat cooking.

'Judging by that aroma,' Lord Urquhart inhaled deeply, 'you must be a good cook.'

Eppy's cheek coloured a little. 'My mother did teach me well.' She seemed to recollect her manners. 'Can I offer you some dinner? There should be enough,' she added doubtfully.

'That's very kind of you, but we must return to Mull very soon,' Maud said firmly.

Must we? Lord Urquhart's look said to her. *Isn't there time to eat first?*

Perhaps this wasn't so different from working with Daisy, after all, she thought.

'The cup of tea would be welcome, though.' Maud smiled brightly as she removed her leather gauntlet gloves and placed them on the table.

As Eppy turned to put the kettle on the stove, Lord Urquhart pulled out a chair at the table and sat down, prepared to enjoy his tea. Maud discreetly indicated the kitchen door. He drew his brows together in a frown. Goodness, she thought, this is not an encouraging start for a detective duo. She gestured with a jerk of her head and mouthed *the study*. His face cleared and he gave a slight nod as Eppy turned round and picked up the brown teapot.

'Eppy, may I tidy myself up?' Maud spoke apologetically, touching a hand to her hat.

'Yes, miss. I will show you the way.' She went to set the teapot down again.

'I wouldn't mind a taste of your wonderful stew, Eppy,' Lord Urquhart said. 'It reminds me so much of my childhood. And I can tell you stories of my helping Cook when I was a boy.' He smiled.

'I'm sure his lordship would enjoy a chat with you. If you could just give me directions to the necessary facility?' Maud hoped very much the house *had* the necessary facility.

'Up the stairs and back along the corridor, then up the next flight of stairs and it's the first door on your right-hand side.'

'Thank you.'

Maud shut the kitchen door firmly behind her and set off hastily up the stone stairs from the kitchen. On which floor might Tremain's study be? Her own father's was on the ground floor as he liked to be able to step out of the french windows whenever he wished for a breath of fresh air. Very likely Tremain was the same. Did this house have french windows? She hadn't noticed any at the front of the building, but they would be at the back overlooking the garden.

She turned the handle of the first door she came to and tentatively pushed it open. Peeping in, she saw it was the dining room. There was a long table in the centre of the room with a large number of chairs set around it. The mahogany gleamed, but the room had an air of desolation. She softly closed the door and turned to the room on the other side of the corridor.

The door was locked. This must be Neil Tremain's study. Pulling the pin from her hat, she bent and inserted it into the lock and moved it around carefully until she heard the click she had been waiting for. If Magnus had asked her to pick the lock

of Tremain's bedroom, it would have saved damage to the door.
But Magnus hadn't known that Miss Maisie Smart possessed
such a skill. Maud straightened and pushed the hat pin back
into her hat. Turning the handle again, she opened the door and
entered the room.

A desk with papers and ink stood overlooking the unkempt
lawn. It seemed that Tremain had no interest in gardening or in
employing a man to do the work. On the floor was a once beautiful, now threadbare, rug and most of the surfaces were thick
with dust. Clearly Eppy wasn't allowed in here to clean. What
had happened to Neil Tremain to make him hide away like this?

Maud left the door ajar to listen for any sound of Eppy and
crept over to the desk. She set down her satchel and got to work.
The carved oak of the desk and chair needed a polish, but they
were not dusty, showing these at least were often used. She sat
in the chair and examined the papers on the desk: a letter from
his daughter Jane announcing her coming to stay and a number
of invoices apparently not yet paid. It seemed that Tremain
might have financial problems. Maud slid open the top drawer.
Inside lay an unopened box of cigars, a box of matches and
packets of indigestion lozenges. She closed the drawer and
pulled open the second one.

This contained sheets of unused writing paper with a letter-
head. The afternoon light was poor, so she removed the top
sheet the better to read it. Embossed along the top were the
words *Tremain Antiques, An Taigh Mòr, Ulva, Scotland.*

Maud gazed at it. Neil Tremain was trading in antiques.
And the addition of *Scotland* to his address suggested he was
doing business internationally.

At the sound of footsteps crunching up the gravel outside,
Maud's heart leaped in her chest. Rising from the chair, she
crossed quickly to the sash window and peered out from behind
the heavy curtain. It was only the postman. He must have

dropped the post through the letter box, for almost immediately he crunched away.

She let out a sigh of relief and turned her attention back to the desk. The third and last drawer held a leather-bound notebook. Maud lifted it out and opened it.

In beautiful copperplate, each entry listed the date, the item sold and the name of the purchaser, and the price.

Neil Tremain was not trading in *any* antiques, but in valuable bronze statuettes.

NINETEEN

Maud stood for a moment, staring at the entries. As she had guessed, without exception the buyers lived overseas. That would be the safest way of disposing of stolen property.

As she straightened, her eye lighted on a cupboard set into the wall. Not another priest hole, she thought wryly. She crossed the floor in a few strides and lifted the latch.

There on the middle of the shelf sat the bust of a Grecian lady modelled in bronze.

Maud frowned. She closed the cupboard door and strode back over to the desk. She looked at the notebook. It was documented evidence of criminal activity, so should she be handling it? She hesitated for a moment, deciding what to do, then in one swift movement she snatched it up, opened the flap on her satchel and dropped the book inside.

She looked up at the sound of footsteps. Her heart beat faster in her chest. Hastily she stepped into the passage, shutting the study door quietly behind her. She barely had time to move along the corridor, before the housekeeper and Lord Urquhart appeared.

'Ah, Miss McIntyre.' The housekeeper looked relieved. 'There you are. You found what you were looking for?'

'Yes, thank you.' Maud smiled, walking along the corridor towards them as if she had just descended from the room where she had gone to use the facilities.

Lord Urquhart sent her an apologetic glance. 'Eppy was beginning to think you'd got lost.'

'Your tea's gone cold,' the woman added pointedly.

'Oh, have I been that long? If you don't mind my saying, I was wondering why the house seemed so unloved.'

Eppy stiffened. 'I do my best, miss.'

'I didn't mean that you don't take great care of the house. What I meant was there's nothing quite as forlorn as a lighter square on a wall where once a painting hung, don't you think?'

'Mr Tremain has no interest in paintings.'

'Well,' said Maud, 'we'd best be going. We've taken up enough of your time.'

'But I haven't given you the tour yet.'

'Thank you all the same. You've been most kind.'

'Indeed you have, Eppy. Thank you for your hospitality.' Lord Urquhart, polite to the last, gave Eppy a small bow of the head and was rewarded with a smile.

He turned to Maud. 'Are you ready, Miss McIntyre?'

Maud nodded and set off for the door. Within minutes, she and Lord Urquhart were standing on the front step with the door closed and bolted behind them.

Lord Urquhart pulled Maud's driving gloves from under his arm and handed them to her. 'I thought you might need these.'

Maud drew on her gloves before she took a further step – one must maintain standards, wherever one was.

'Was the trip worth it?' He buttoned up his coat against the stiff breeze.

'It was very profitable.' She walked briskly down the path, Lord Urquhart by her side.

'Really? That's a relief.'

'I was almost caught in Tremain's study, though. I would have thought you could have entertained the woman for a little longer. Surely that is something a gentleman such as yourself *can* do.'

'One thing a gentleman does *not* do is flirt with servants.'

'Oh, well yes, of course. I'm sorry.'

'So, tell me, what did you find in his study?'

Maud shook her head. 'Wait until we are out of sight of the house.'

A few minutes later, they turned onto the track leading back to the ferry. Now she could talk about it, Maud could hardly contain her excitement. If only Daisy were here!

'I found sheets of writing paper headed with the name *Tremain Antiques...*'

'He's been running an antiques business? He never mentioned that.'

'That's not all. There was an accounts book with details of the sales he's made of – guess what? No, never mind, I will tell you. Bronze artefacts. He's been trading in bronze artefacts over the last few years.'

'Good Lord! That certainly explains why he had the lion hidden in the priest hole.'

'Yes, it does. But there's more...'

'What more could there be?'

'Another bronze! I found a bust in a cupboard in his room.' She sent him a glance. 'If that turns out to be on the police list for stolen items in the area, we'd have proof that he stole Magnus's lion.'

He frowned. 'But do we have proof? The housekeeper could destroy the sheets of paper and the account book if she suspects what we were up to.'

'Eppy couldn't destroy the bronze, although she could hide it. But I don't see how she could suspect us of anything. She didn't see me coming out of the study, and she doesn't know yet that her employer is dead. More importantly, I have the accounts book here.' Maud patted her satchel and smiled.

'You have the accounts?' Lord Urquhart sent Maud a broad smile. 'Well done, Miss McIntyre. Very well done indeed.'

'Thank you.' Brisk and businesslike as ever, Maud carried on. 'Although, I might have committed theft. I've taken the property of another without his consent – but then, can one steal from a dead man? I suppose it would be from the beneficiaries. No matter, I will tell the police that I had a good reason for taking the book, and once they've seen it, I'm sure they will agree. They will realise I was protecting the evidence from possibly being destroyed.'

'The housekeeper was certainly suspicious of something.'

'What makes you say that?'

'The locked door when we arrived; that is unusual in rural houses. And her attitude; Highlanders tend to be welcoming and friendly.'

'But you managed to win her over, all the same.'

'It comes with the title.'

Maud laughed and shook her head. 'Years of working for a man as grumpy as Tremain would make a person unpleasant. What did you learn from her? Did she work for him when he lived in Glasgow?'

'No, she's barely been off this tiny island. She told me she started as his housekeeper when Tremain moved here ten years ago.'

Maud sighed with frustration. 'We need to find out what happened in Glasgow. His daughter doesn't know—'

'Or *says* she doesn't.'

Maud nodded. 'True.'

'But what about Magnus?' Lord Urquhart asked thoughtfully. 'When Ailsa started to say something about that period in

Tremain's life, he interrupted her with a comment about it being old history.'

'You should speak to Magnus and see if you can learn why Tremain left his well-paid employment and moved here,' said Maud. 'He had sufficient money to buy that substantial house, but since then he seems to have been short of funds and turned to stealing *objets d'art*. There must be a link somewhere in this to his murder, don't you think?'

They walked on, the wind gusting.

'We should hurry,' said Lord Urquhart, looking up at the grey clouds being blown across the sky, 'in case the weather worsens again, or the ferryman decides he's had enough for the day and retires to his warm hearth and a nip of whisky.'

'Mmm, that does sound good.' Maud smiled, before a sudden thought hit her. Her stride faltered.

'What is it?'

'Oh dear, the housekeeper will know I went into Tremain's study, as the door is no longer locked.'

'It was locked?'

'Of course it was locked. I had to pick it.'

'You *picked* the lock? Well, well, Miss McIntyre.'

'How else could I have got into the room?'

'If she doesn't suspect you were up to no good, she won't think to check the door.'

'Perhaps not.' Tears suddenly welled in her eyes.

Lord Urquhart looked down at her. 'Why are you so sad?'

'I've just remembered the police will arrive at the castle shortly, once they can cross over from the mainland...' The confidence in Maud's voice faded away. She saw Daisy in her mind's eye, struggling with two burly uniformed officers who held her between them. Maud glanced up at Lord Urquhart. What she was thinking must have been written on her face.

He gave her a reassuring smile. 'We've cracked one case today – we found out who stole the bronze. Next on the list is to find Tremain and McNeish's murderer. And we will. Never fear, Miss McIntyre, we will, because Daisy is depending on us.'

Back at Clachan Castle mid-afternoon, Maud found Isobel hastening up the stairs with a linseed poultice.

'For the laird's sister,' the maid said, pausing for a moment to explain. 'All this damp has brought her down with a chill.'

'Please tell her I hope she feels better soon.'

'Yes, miss. You've missed your luncheon. Shall I ask Mrs Baillie to make something for you and his lordship?'

'Perhaps some extra sandwiches for his lordship at tea time,' Maud suggested. 'But you must be rushed off your feet, Isobel. Let me take Miss Cameron's tea tray up to her.'

'Thank you, but she's already had her tea, miss.' Isobel excused herself, continued up the staircase and turned onto the first-floor corridor.

Maud climbed to the second floor and tapped on Daisy's door. 'Daisy, it's me, Maud.'

'And who else would it be, sounding exactly like you?'

To her astonishment, Maud heard the sound of a key being turned in the lock and the door opened. Daisy laughed at the look on Maud's face.

'Come in.' She stood back, gesturing grandly.

Maud stepped into the room. 'I thought you were locked in.'

'I was – I am.' Daisy closed the door behind them and locked it. 'See! Isobel and the others have taken pity on me and given me the spare key on condition that I keep the door locked when Magnus and his sister are about. But with the two of them taken to their rooms, they dinna know that Isobel smuggled me down to the kitchen for their midday dinner. I'm going to be taking my meals with them now for as long as we can get away with it.'

Maud smiled. 'How kind of them. I think you would pine

away with no one to speak to for hours on end. But are you sure Finlay doesn't object? As the laird's man, he might well.'

'He was there when I was and didna say anything, so I reckon I'm safe.'

'We will have lots to tell each other about our respective mornings, but first I need to change and join the others for tea. I'll return afterwards.'

'Where did you two get to this morning?' Jane asked in a peevish tone at they took tea in the small sitting room.

'We merely went for a drive,' Lord Urquhart said, piling his plate with tongue and mustard butter sandwiches from the sideboard. He had dismissed Finlay and Isobel, saying he and the two ladies would be informal this afternoon and help themselves.

'You might have asked me,' went on Jane. 'It was very boring here with no one to talk to.'

'I did look for you, Miss Tremain, but you were not to be found.' Maud hated to lie, but needs must.

She shot Maud a sharp glance. 'Then you couldn't have looked very hard.'

'What a beautiful costume.' Maud was keen to change the subject, but she was also speaking the truth.

Jane was wearing a white dress with a deep neckline, not suited to afternoon tea with only two others – but one of those others was Lord Urquhart.

Jane immediately smiled. 'I wore this when I was presented to the King and Queen at the Palace of Holyroodhouse last July.'

Should she mention, Maud wondered, that she and Daisy had more recently enjoyed dinner with their majesties at the palace, after they had solved the Fort William choir murders? Maud sighed. No, that would be churlish.

'If you could have been there, Miss McIntyre,' Jane went on. 'It was during the King and Queen's coronation tour. Lord Urquhart was present, of course.' Her lips curved into a coquettish smile.

Maud glanced at Lord Urquhart. His dark eyebrows were drawn together.

'The presentation was for debutantes, and naturally members of the peerage were also invited. That was where I first met Lord Urquhart.' Jane looked at him from under her eyelashes.

'Do tell me about it, Miss Tremain.' Maud had not wished to be a debutante and her father had respected this, but it would be interesting to hear about the event given it was where Jane had met Maud's newly appointed and very temporary detective.

'Oh, it was a splendid occasion.' Jane's face assumed a faraway look. 'We entered the palace under the archway and the Holyrood High Constables with their tall hats and batons standing in a row. Then there was a long stretch of corridor, with flights of stairs and the Royal Company of Archers – they're the King's Body Guard in Scotland, you know. They were dressed in their green and crimson. Finally, we were in the throne room where the King and Queen sat on the dais on two gilt thrones. He was dressed in red, blue and gold. And she was so lovely and shimmering.' Jane sighed.

There was a moment's silence, until a log fell in the grate, sending a shower of sparks up the chimney. Maud and Lord Urquhart exchanged an impatient glance, aware they had a case to solve.

'We were all in a daze by the time we were presented,' Jane went blithely on. 'And then we were ushered into the long gallery, with long buffet tables and powdered footmen in the royal livery.' She laughed softly. 'The whole room seemed filled with the plumes of the three curling white ostrich feathers we debutantes had to wear in our hair. I decided not to have more than one glass of champagne, just in case, you know. I didn't want my headdress to get caught on anything. That would have been shameful.'

Lord Urquhart offered the cake stand to Jane and she absent-mindedly took a thick wedge of Victoria sponge – which Maud suspected the cook had meant for Lord Urquhart – and bit into it. He moved on to Maud. She helped herself to a buttered scone.

'Of course, Lord Urquhart was there,' breathed Jane. 'So tall and dashing in black knee breeches and coat...'

Maud saw him flush at her words.

Jane was still speaking, delighted to be the centre of attention. 'We were shown how to allow our fan – furled, of course – to droop across the body towards the floor while performing a deep and elegant curtsy: down on the left knee, up on the left foot, three short steps to the right and curtsy to Her Majesty, head lowered as you make your obeisance, raised to look at Their Majesties as you rise. Smile with your eyes only. Gather your train with grace over your left arm. Never turn your back on the throne.' She took another large bite of the sponge cake.

'Goodness,' Maud said. 'That is quite a procedure.' And an expensive one to take part in. Little wonder that the finances of Jane's father were depleted.

Maud did a quick calculation. Debutantes were launched into society at the age of seventeen or eighteen with a formal introduction to the monarch and a debut at a ball, followed by a whirlwind six months of cocktail parties, dances and special events. Jane must therefore be eighteen or nineteen years of age and clearly, given her presence here at the castle, hadn't 'taken' during her six months. Don't despair, Maud wanted to tell the young woman, you are still young and life can offer many opportunities.

'Oh.' Jane stared aghast at the remains of cake on her plate.

Finlay returned to the sitting room, approached Lord Urquhart and cleared his throat. 'Beg pardon, your lordship, but in the absence of the laird and Miss Ailsa, I felt I should let you know that Dr Munro came earlier to ask after matters. When I informed him the lady had taken a chill, he apologised that he couldn't stay as he was on his way to see a patient who needed urgent medical attention, but that he would call at the castle later.'

'Thank you, Finlay. I'm sure both Miss Ailsa and her brother will be pleased to see the doctor.'

'So would I,' added Jane. 'We need another man at table if there's to be just the three of us. I hope Ailsa invites him to dinner. If she doesn't, I will.'

As soon as she could excuse herself, Maud darted upstairs to Daisy's room. From within there came the sound of a hard object hitting the floor and a smothered oath from Daisy. A short delay and then the door opened and an eager Daisy let her in.

'What was that noise?' Maud asked.

'Och, I knocked into yon lamp. I caught it in time and nae harm done.' Daisy gestured to the oil lamp on her writing table. 'Take a pew.'

Maud sent her a look to indicate she knew there was something Daisy was not telling her, but it failed to embarrass her assistant. They settled back in the comfortable armchairs.

'You first,' Daisy said.

Maud recounted their visit to Ulva, informing her of the headed letter paper and accounts book, bronze bust and lack of any of the usual adornments found in houses of a certain size. 'And so, Daisy,' she concluded, 'the theft of the lion, and other statuettes, was because Tremain was in desperate need of money.'

'Nae wonder he doesna have a valet,' Daisy said. 'I wonder, though, how he kent about the secret cupboard?'

'I don't think we'll ever know the answer to that. I can only assume he was looking for somewhere to hide the bronze for the duration of his stay and, as you suggested, had spotted the knob in the back of the wall cupboard – and the priest hole was revealed.'

'So we've solved the theft.'

'But not the murders.' Maud's heart went out to her friend. Could Daisy maintain this brave face for much longer? 'I'm not sure why, but I have a feeling that the answer lies in Neil Tremain mysterious flight from Glasgow.'

Daisy looked up from examining the accounts book, now in her lap. 'I might ken the answer to that.'

TWENTY

'You think you know why Tremain left Glasgow?' Maud said to Daisy, her voice incredulous. 'Then tell me!'

'When Isobel smuggled me down to the servants' hall to eat with them...'

'Yes?' Maud urged her on.

'They told me how the finger is always pointed first at the servants—'

'That's not entirely true in this case. We had to consider Andrew because he was the last person to see Neil Tremain alive – and no one is actually pointing the finger at him.'

'Not yet,' Daisy amended.

'True. But we discounted Andrew when the sergeant was murdered. All the servants were in the kitchen at the time.'

'Aye, and they said the fact that I used to be a lady's maid will go against me in court when I'm up for the policeman's murder.' Daisy stared at the book in her lap, despondent.

'When did they find out you'd been a maid? You didn't tell them, did you?'

'I didna have to.' Daisy looked up with a smile. 'Servants *always* know.'

That was probably true, Maud thought with dismay. 'Listen, Daisy. Lord Urquhart and I will give you excellent character references, and so will my father – but it won't come to that,' she added quickly.

'Anyway,' Daisy went on, 'they see me as one of their own, which is nae a bad thing right now. And while I was downstairs, I learned that the good doctor once had a wife and daughter.'

'Did he? What happened to them?'

'Sadly, they're both now deid.'

'Do we know why? I mean, how it happened?'

'No one below-stairs kent that.'

Maud sighed. Not only was it proving difficult to find out about Tremain's background, it seemed it was also the case with Dr Munro.

'Oh, and they reckon below-stairs that Jane Tremain is going to make a strong play for his lordship.'

Maud spluttered. 'Going to make? I think she's doing so already.'

'Does it matter? After all, you've told me in the past that you're just good friends.' Daisy cast her a look. 'You'd better snap him up before she does.'

'I'm not interested in *snapping him up*, Daisy. Now tell me, did you discover why Tremain and Ailsa disliked each other?'

'It seems there wasn't a problem until...'

'Let me guess: Tremain moved from Glasgow to Ulva?'

Daisy nodded.

'Let us consider the remainder of the questions we need answered.'

Daisy placed the accounts book on the floor and took her notebook from down the side of her armchair. 'It's a handy place to keep it,' she said in response to Maud's questioning look.

'The questions we have left,' Daisy went on, 'are to do with Ailsa disliking Neil, what was Neil feart of, the hair we found, why someone would want him deid and how the killer managed to carry out both murders.'

'If we look first at number one—'

'That's question number eleven on the list,' Daisy added.

'Thank you. Could the reason, whatever it was, that Neil moved to Ulva, be sufficient for Ailsa to have killed him?'

'You mean, something that happened in Glasgow *before* he flitted to the wee island? Aye, that's possible. Or it could be that Neil's done something bad to her *since* he flitted to Ulva. We canna say. She might think she has a sufficient reason, even if we don't.'

'Hmm. Very well, the next question: what had frightened Tremain so much that he locked his bedroom door that night?'

'Number ten on the list.'

'There's no need for us to consider the question numbers, Daisy, only the questions themselves,' Maud said gently.

'I'd say Neil was feart he was going to be discovered with the statuette.'

'That's very possible. But we had better keep it on the list, for the time being at least, in case it's something other than that.'

'Remember you and his lordship had put the wind up him that afternoon?'

'Yes, but was the sound of someone talking or footsteps in the corridor enough to make him afraid?'

'Perhaps if he wasna expecting any noise, with everyone downstairs watching the play, including the servants.'

'But not all of them were. We know that Kirsty wasn't, as she reported seeing Lord Urquhart coming down the stairs.'

'Are you adding Kirsty to our list of suspects?'

Maud referred to her notes again. 'I don't know... We do know that between 7 and 8.30 a.m., when death took place, the servants were first engaged in their respective tasks and then in eating their breakfast. Surely it would have been noticed if anyone were absent from breakfast.'

'Not necessarily. When you do the same thing at the same time every day, it's easy to assume that what should happen did happen. It depends on the distractions going on at the time. Like Finlay popping out to clean the laird's boots ten minutes before the others left the table.'

'Hmm. But now we're back to the question of how anyone could get into the locked room.'

'What about the hair?' Daisy flicked back through her notebook and produced the long white strand. 'I still think that finding it under the bed is suspicious.'

'And yet I don't think either Magnus or Ailsa hid under the four-poster and then crawled out to murder Tremain.'

'I canna see it either,' Daisy admitted, a little despondent. 'And they were both at the dinner table when he went upstairs. Shall we put it down to Isobel having to do the cleaning of this place all on her own and nae having the time to do a thorough clean?'

'Yes. After all, it could have lain there for some time, long before Tremain arrived. The hair could have wafted under the bed months ago. It could belong to another guest who'd never met Tremain.'

'Right you are.' Daisy put a line through the question, got up and dropped the hair on the fire. 'That's question number five.' She caught Maud's eye, smiled and returned to her seat.

'That leaves us the crucial questions of *why* would someone want the man dead and *how* on earth did the murderer get in and out of the two rooms. If we could work out that last question, I'm sure we would have the answer as to *who* he is.'

'Do you think the doctor has anything to do with Tremain's murder?'

'A man he'd never met before? I find it highly unlikely.' Maud retrieved her own notebook from her satchel.

'But what if his mind was turned by the loss of his family and he'd snapped and killed Neil Tremain?' asked Daisy.

'But why Tremain? No, I think not, but let me look at my suspects list again.' She did so. 'Jane, Ailsa, Magnus, Lord Urquhart, Dr Munro. No one from below-stairs. I should add Isobel and Andrew.'

Daisy frowned. 'Why Isobel?'

'We know that Tremain had suffered from heartburn the previous night. That seemed genuine enough. And that Tremain was given bicarbonate of soda, which Isobel took up to his bedroom. Couldn't she have put something – perhaps poison – into the preparation?'

'Dinna forget that Neil was stabbed, nae poisoned.'

'Andrew, then, because we know he was the last to leave Tremain's bedroom the night before he was murdered and he was the first to enter the room in the morning.'

'You're wrong there, Maud. The doctor and Andrew went into the room together that morning and we were both witnesses to that.'

'Did they go in at exactly the same time?' Maud turned back the pages in her notebook. 'Here it is. I'll paraphrase. *Shortly before 9 a.m. Andrew comes back with fresh hot water. Still no reply. Alarmed, he runs down to Finlay and Magnus. The three men return and are joined by the rest of the servants alerted by the banging and shouting. Lord Urquhart, then Maud and Daisy, join the group outside Tremain's door. Dr Munro arrives and breaks down the door. Tremain is found dead.'* She looked up at Daisy. 'I've not noted the exact order the two of them entered the room.'

Daisy thought for a moment. 'I mind Andrew standing back to allow Dr Munro to break down the door... I think the doctor went in first, but Andrew must have been immediately behind him.'

'What about Dr Munro and Andrew acting together for some reason? The two who found the body?'

'Didna some folk believe that Jack the Ripper was the various policemen who found the bodies of the women?'

'That was far too fanciful a theory and it came to nothing.' Maud frowned. 'My head is spinning, Daisy. At this rate when the doctor comes to see Ailsa, I'll need to ask him for something for a headache.' She sighed. 'Was there anything else, anything at all, that the servants told you?'

'Mrs Baillie said the strong wind's been causing havoc with the kitchen range.'

'Daisy...'

'I wrote down what they told me about that night,' Daisy went on more seriously, 'in case it was of any use. Let me find the right page.' She leafed through her notebook. 'Here we are. Dinner was served upstairs at eight o'clock. About nine o'clock, Isobel had just finished tidying up in the bedrooms, drawing the curtains and laying out the nightwear, and was back downstairs when Dr Munro rang to ask for bicarbonate of soda and water for Mr Tremain.'

'The doctor asked for the powder and the water as two separate things? Isobel didn't mix the preparation in the kitchen?'

'She said he asked her not to do that, to be sure Mr Tremain was given the right proportions.'

'No matter,' Maud said. 'Dr Munro gave the time of Tremain's death as the following morning.'

'But we should keep the doctor as a suspect?'

'Yes, we should.'

Daisy frowned. 'Even though he wasna in the castle when Neil was murdered and nae weapon was found on him or in his bag?'

Maud nodded.

'And even though he'd had nae opportunity to kill Sandy McNeish?'

'Even though.'

'So, is there anyone *nae* on our suspect list?'

'Let me think. Grace, Mrs Baillie, Kirsty, Mr Dalgleish, Peddie the garden boy...' Maud paused as another thought came to her. 'Did Isobel stay while Tremain took the medicine?'

'Nae, she needed to get back to her next job, helping Kirsty with washing the dishes. Andrew said he would bring down the empty glass.'

'And what happened next?'

'The doctor gave Neil the powder mixed with water, saw that he drank it and then he left to go downstairs, where he played whist with you. Andrew stayed for a short while after, to check he had all he needed for the night. Neil was crabbit as usual, but – not as usual – he told Andrew he would lock his bedroom door because of the earlier stushie. That was you and his lordship, Maud.'

'I think so.' Maud coloured slightly. 'Go on.'

'Then Andrew went downstairs to start cleaning the glass, silverware and cutlery.'

'Did anyone see him do that?'

'Everyone was in the kitchen, so aye.'

'And then?'

Daisy checked her notes again. 'Mrs Baillie the cook went off to bed, Kirsty followed as soon as she was able, as did Isobel. Finlay and Andrew had to stay upstairs to wait on us in the drawing room...'

Maud nodded. 'We can vouch for them.'

'And Grace stayed downstairs waiting for Ailsa to ring to help prepare her for bed. Finlay had to do the same for Magnus. When the doctor left the house—'

'What time was that – can you remember?'

'Nae long before we all went to bed, which was about half past ten.'

'I remember that Dr Munro said he would let himself out and not to trouble Finlay.'

'Aye. Finlay said he'd just been securing the downstairs

shutters in the rooms that wouldna be used any more that evening. He saw the doctor go out through the front door and as the doctor left, he had called good night to him.'

'And then Finlay made safe both the outside doors?'

Daisy nodded.

'We know that Neil Tremain wasn't murdered that evening, but it's useful to have a note of where everyone was.' Maud sighed. 'As we know, the great detective himself – Sherlock Holmes – says: When you have eliminated the impossible—'

'Whatever remains, however improbable, must be the truth,' Daisy finished. 'Aye, Maud, you've fair drilled that famous quote into me!'

We know that the murderer didn't enter through the door, window or chimney and that he wasn't concealed in the room, Maud thought, remembering the rest of Holmes's discussion with Watson.

But how did the killer commit this seemingly perfect crime?

TWENTY-ONE

'How is the patient, doctor?' Maud asked over dinner.

Maud had suggested that the four of them – Lord Urquhart, Dr Munro, Jane and herself – might eat in the dining room this evening, as it would be more pleasant with their reduced number. The log fire burned with a soft crackling, sending green and blue flames up the wide chimney, and it would have felt quite cosy if the servants hadn't felt it necessary to uphold the grandness of the castle and set the table for the small party to be spread out.

'Miss Carmichael is suffering with a cold, nothing more,' Dr Munro replied. 'It was most kind of her to ask me to stay for dinner, although unfortunately she didn't feel quite well enough to join us herself. I'm sure she will be up and about again in a day or two.'

'I'm sure that you will take great care of her, Dr Munro.'

'Rest assured I will, Miss Tremain.'

Jane gave him the warmest of smiles. 'Dear Ailsa. She is always thinking of others and now it's only right that others take care of her.'

Maud took a sip of red wine as she politely listened to the

conversation and wondered if the woman had transferred her affections from Lord Urquhart to the doctor. Or was she casting her net in both directions? Maud chastised herself for such a vulgar expression.

Jane was a sight to behold in a burgundy satin evening gown, its bell-shaped skirt swishing as she walked. The plunging neckline and matching ribbon tied in a bow around her long neck were as if Jane had wrapped herself up as a gift to a special someone.

The young woman chatted animatedly to the doctor, her ruby earrings flashing in the firelight. Maud absently fingered one of her own earrings, the pearl a delicate shade of pink. The matching bracelet looped around her wrist slid slowly towards her elbow as she watched Jane flatter the doctor. Maud felt comfortable in her less-elaborate costume of silver-grey, which complemented her fair hair. The slim dress with its wide dark grey belt shimmered in the candlelight.

Maud studied Jane. Two men dead, Maud thought, one of them this girl's father, yet she was carrying on as if nothing had happened. She understood Jane hadn't been close to her father, but he was her father and for that alone Jane should be showing some sort of mourning. Maud sighed and glanced across the length of the table at Lord Urquhart. He seemed bored.

Lord Urquhart, being of the highest social status, had been seated at one end of the table and Maud, the more senior of the two females, at the other end. It gave Maud a momentary pang to realise her years were the reason for her position. And another pang to note that the bow around Jane's neck faced Lord Urquhart.

'Your pearls are quite beautiful, Miss McIntyre.' Jane indicated to Maud's softly gleaming pink pearls, each the size of a pea. 'And the grey gown is very becoming. Ladies with pale hair can be so easily outshone by brighter colours, and of course the older you are, the larger the pearls can be.'

Maud heard Lord Urquhart's sharp intake of breath, but Dr Munro's face held only polite interest.

'Worth is the only dressmaker who understands me,' Jane continued. 'And Paquin can cut a bodice as nobody else.'

'I know nothing of such matters,' the doctor murmured.

But Jane hadn't yet finished on the topic. 'Have you heard of either of them, Miss McIntyre? I mention them only because I believe it's due to their expertise,' she purred, looking down demurely in such a manner as to display the full luxury of her lovely eyelashes, 'that I am the object of so much admiration.'

Oh, for goodness' sake, Maud thought.

The silence that followed was broken by Dr Munro. 'You are a most attractive young lady, Miss Tremain.'

Jane looked gratified.

'It is difficult to comprehend,' Lord Urquhart said, 'that we are all seated here as if it were a normal evening, when Mr Tremain and Sergeant McNeish are dead.'

Jane let out a cry, a hand shooting up to cover her mouth. The doctor stared at Lord Urquhart, a look of disbelief clouding his face. Maud carried on eating, grateful to Lord Urquhart for bringing the subject back to what was important.

'Did you know him well, Dr Munro?' he went on.

'Who?' the doctor asked.

Had there been a beat too long before Dr Munro replied, or was that Maud's imagination?

'Sergeant McNeish,' said Lord Urquhart.

'Oh, not really.' Dr Munro dabbed his mouth with his napkin. 'I mean, he is – was – the local bobby and I'd pass the time of day with him when we met, but that wasn't often.'

'Not much crime on Mull, I imagine?'

'Very little. Where I used to live the police had their own doctor to call upon, but it's not been deemed necessary here. This is the first murder case I've been involved in.'

'You've mentioned that you used to stay in Glasgow?'

'I did.' The doctor took a sip of wine.

'Quite a different way of living,' Lord Urquhart mused.

'Very.' Dr Munro was not to be drawn on his move to Mull. 'There have been a few thefts on the island over the years, but nothing more,' he went on.

'Were the thefts solved?' Lord Urquhart asked, keeping his tone neutral.

'Unfortunately not. I believe it was what you might call thefts of specialist items, but you'd need to ask the sergeant about that.'

After an uncomfortable pause, during which they all realised afresh that such a conversation could not happen, Dr Munro spoke again. 'I wonder what you have made of the two deaths, Miss McIntyre, in your professional role? If it isn't too distressing for us to talk about, Miss Tremain?'

Jane shook her head. 'I want to know who is responsible. But perhaps it would have been better if Miss McIntyre had really been Miss Smart. It would seem fictional detectives always solve the crimes they investigate, when real-life detectives are apparently not so clever.'

Maud blinked. 'I'm sure all detectives do their best, fictional and real.'

'I'm sure they do, Miss McIntyre.' The doctor's tone was soothing. 'Have you any suspects at all?'

'Rather too many, I'm afraid.'

'But some in the castle must be ruled out, surely?'

He's fishing to see if he's on our suspect list, Maud thought. 'Those on the list are those who need to be there.' She gave a pleasant smile.

'Dr Munro,' Lord Urquhart put in, 'I would be interested to know your opinion on the use of the instrument that killed the two men. Was a degree of strength required or would the murderer have needed a knowledge of anatomy?'

'Because some pointed object had been driven at a single

thrust into the heart?' The doctor thought for a moment. 'If the implement had hit one of the man's ribs, then some strength would indeed have been needed to penetrate to the heart, but this didn't happen. Of course, it could be that the fatal blow was simply a fortuitous one.'

'Could a killer be fortunate enough to get the right spot on two such occasions?' Maud asked.

'In the case of the police officer, the thrust was not so accurate, but nonetheless it did the job, if I may use that expression.' He sent a concerned glance towards Jane. 'I'm sorry, my dear.'

Jane sniffed elegantly behind her lace handkerchief.

The doctor gave her a sympathetic smile, then continued. 'This leads me to believe the killer had needed very little knowledge of human physiology.'

'The second murder was committed in a hurry, which affected the killer's aim,' Maud put in.

Dr Munro inclined his head in agreement. Even so, Maud thought, the murders must surely involve some basic knowledge of human anatomy.

'I'd like to learn first aid.' Jane looked expectantly at the doctor.

Dr Munro frowned. 'Why do you say that?'

Maud groaned inwardly; for a doctor he was a dolt. To get you back onto her favourite subject, Maud thought: Jane herself.

'I might have been able to help my papa.'

'Oh no, my dear. He was already beyond anyone's help. But if you're interested in medicine, you could train as a nurse,' he told her. 'With the political situation in Europe darkening, it seems that war is inevitable. In which case, there will be a great need for nurses.'

Jane wrinkled her pretty little nose. 'Must conversation turn to war? Can't we talk of something else?'

'Of course,' Dr Munro said. 'What would you like to discuss?'

'Oh, I don't know.'

'Home Rule for Ireland, perhaps?' Lord Urquhart sent her a look of innocent enquiry.

Maud picked up her napkin more to hide a smile than to dab at her lips. She kept up with world politics and the newspapers had been full of the Third Home Rule Bill. It had been introduced by Prime Minister Mr Asquith in Parliament in April.

'*Home Rule is Rome Rule.*' Maud murmured the slogan of the mainly Protestant north, which feared the largely Catholic south. The northern part of Ireland claimed one hundred thousand marching Ulster Volunteers, all vehemently opposed to a home-rule island governed from the south.

Jane shrugged. 'Let them do whatever they want. It's nothing to us, after all.'

'It's not as simple as that,' Maud said, replacing the napkin in her lap. 'If there is civil war in Ireland, it will affect us here too.'

'Back to talking about war again.' Jane toyed with the food on her plate.

'We can talk about something less contentious, such as Captain Scott's expedition to the Antarctic,' suggested the doctor. 'They will have reached the South Pole and be on their way home by now.'

'Really?' Jane didn't sound impressed.

'Mrs Scott is to meet her husband in New Zealand at the end of the year.'

The little group at the dinner table discussed the British expedition and the success of Scott's rival, the Norwegian, Captain Amundsen. But Maud could see that Jane was just going through the motions of polite conversation and had no interest in the matter.

How the young woman could think she and Lord Urquhart would make a suitable match, Maud could not imagine. Maud pondered on the curious lack of perception shown by some women in their choice of husband. Mary, Queen of Scots, for example. Admittedly she'd had no say in the matter of her first husband. The five-year-old Queen of Scotland, Mary, was betrothed to Francis, the four-year-old heir to the French throne, in 1548. They were married in Notre-Dame Cathedral ten years later.

But her second husband was the arrogant fop Henry, Lord Darnley, murdered in a garden less than a mile from Holyrood-house. And Mary's third husband was the swaggering James, Earl of Bothwell, who was reputed to have murdered Darnley, before fleeing Scotland and living the rest of his life imprisoned in Denmark.

Maud was idly trying to imagine what kind of man would make a suitable husband for Jane as the table moved on to the pudding course. She'd come to no satisfactory conclusion when she noticed Jane was counting the plum stones she had arranged round the edge of her plate.

'*Tinker, tailor, soldier, sailor, rich man,*' murmured Jane.

Maud was certain the young woman had taken care to help herself to the desired number of plums to see whom she would marry. Jane would not have risked going on to poor man, beggar man, thief.

Dr Munro turned to Maud. 'How is Miss Cameron?'

'She is keeping her spirits up, thank you, doctor.'

'It is most unfortunate that Magnus's ire has fallen on Miss Cameron,' Lord Urquhart added. 'Miss McIntyre and I are certain she is not the guilty person.'

'It is hard to imagine that she is,' the doctor agreed.

'Perhaps someone has framed her for the murders,' Jane remarked casually.

Maud looked at her sharply. She and Lord Urquhart had

talked of this earlier and now Jane was suggesting it. Had he discussed the case with Jane? Surely not.

'Why would anyone do that to Daisy?' she asked.

Jane shrugged. 'I have no idea.'

Maud turned to gaze out of the window. The mountains of the Ardnamurchan peninsular were obscured by mist. Her investigation seemed equally shrouded in haze. She needed longer to solve this case. 'We must hope that the police boat from the mainland will not be able to cross tomorrow.'

'Must we?' Jane frowned. 'I'd have thought the sooner the officers arrive, the better.'

Maud turned sharply back into the room. 'And have Daisy, who's been falsely accused of murder, arrested and taken away?'

Jane looked shocked at Maud's outburst. 'You mean Miss Cameron?'

'Of course I do. I have not yet solved the crime, Miss Tremain, but I intend to do so before the police arrive.'

TWENTY-TWO

Maud woke to find the bedroom grey. Padding across the floor, she opened the shutters and looked out. The whole of the island, as far as she could judge from the window of her bedroom, was wrapped in fog. The mountains were invisible, the Sound of Mull was recognisable as water, and that was all.

This was now the third day since the two men had been murdered and, as yet, she and Daisy had no real information on the identity of the killer. Maud had passed a sleepless night plotting and planning. She meant what she'd said to Jane Tremain about solving the case before the police arrive, but would she be able to do it?

Daisy had spent long enough locked in her bedroom, Maud decided. If Magnus and Ailsa were going to spend the day in their respective rooms, then she and Daisy would venture forth. More needed to be learned about Dr Munro.

She washed and dressed quickly in her high-necked white blouse, a camel-coloured waistcoat and matching skirt with a double row of buttons down the front, and hurried downstairs to the dining room, pleased to see that none of the other house guests were yet present. She ate a hasty breakfast of porridge, staying only long enough to ascertain from Andrew that their host and his sister would not be leaving their bedrooms for this morning at least, and then she mounted the stairs to Daisy's room. A couple of soft knocks brought her friend to the door, already dressed warmly for the day in her dark green skirt and long cardigan belted at the waist.

'Have you had your breakfast?' Maud asked, as she entered her friend's room.

'Aye, thanks. You're early.'

'Good. We need to go immediately. The Carmichaels are supposed to be keeping to their rooms for the morning.'

'Go? I'm getting out?'

'Yes.'

'Right you are.' Daisy stepped out of the room, waited for Maud to do the same, and quietly closed the door behind them.

'I'm not convinced Dr Munro is as innocent as he would have us believe,' Maud said, as they descended the stairs. 'Some years ago, something happened to him in Glasgow—'

'As it did to Neil Tremain.'

'And the doctor came here yesterday supposedly to check on Ailsa—'

'Which may or may not be true. He said all she has is a cold.'

'Perhaps her age makes him cautious about it possibly developing into bronchitis. But I think the real reason for his return last night was that he wanted to find out how the investigation was progressing. And, more importantly, if he's a suspect.' Maud put her finger to her lips as they drew level with the first floor. The Carmichaels' respective rooms were along the corridor, but it was better to be safe than sorry.

'So, what are we going to do this morning?' asked Daisy, as they went down the next set of stairs that would bring them to the great hall.

'We're going to visit the doctor—'

Daisy stopped. 'You're going to spring me from my prison?'

'I don't know where you get these expressions from. Let us say that I am releasing you into my custody. Keep moving.'

'Sounds good to me, however you want to phrase it.'

Maud smiled as they reached the great hall and saw no one there. 'Dr Munro lives just outside the village, so we can walk there,' she whispered.

Daisy's face fell. 'Have you seen the weather?' She gestured towards the windows. 'Can we nae drive?'

'That's precisely why we can't drive, my friend. Visibility is poor and I don't want us to have an accident. Besides, the footpath takes a shorter route than the road.'

Daisy huffed. 'What if I get caught?'

'The servants are on your side. They won't say a thing, if they even see us leave.' Maud ushered Daisy across the stone-flagged floor.

'What if the doctor's nae in?'

'So much the better. He's bound to have a housekeeper and we are likely to learn more from her than from him.'

'Nae if she's anything like that Eppy on Ulva.'

'Let's hope she's not.'

Maud and Daisy had almost reached the door to the lobby when Isobel came out of the dining room, feather duster in her hand. Ignoring her astonished face, Maud informed her they were going for a walk. In the lobby they pulled on coats, hats and gloves and went out.

Daisy shivered as the foghorn sounded from the Tobermory lighthouse, its deep intermittent hum sounding eerie in the fog-enclosed world. She pulled her coat around her more tightly. 'Are you sure about walking, Maud?'

Maud was reminded of the beginning of Dickens's *Bleak House*. Fog up the river, on the marshes, lying in the yards, drooping on the barges... But this wasn't London, and here the fog clung wetly to trees and shrubs.

'It will provide good cover for us, Daisy, and especially for you if it's widely known that you have been imprisoned in the castle on suspicion of murder.'

'Since you put it like that, I suppose it's best I foot forward.' Daisy went down the stone steps and onto the driveway. 'This fog really is thick.'

Maud came up behind her and linked her arm into Daisy's. 'If we walk together, we will at least know where the other is.'

They set off down the avenue, Maud moderating her stride and Daisy's shorter legs hastening to keep pace. They walked in silence, broken only by the low pitch of the foghorn, both concentrating on keeping the gravel beneath their boots. Once or twice one of them strayed onto the lawn, but the feel of springy turf beneath their feet brought them quickly back onto the gravel avenue. At last they reached the stone pillars marking the end of the drive.

'Phew.' Daisy let out a breath. 'I can't keep up that concentration all the way to the village.'

'You won't need to, Daisy. Look.' Maud gestured around them. 'It's surprising what difference even half a mile can make.' Now they were a little closer to the coast, visibility was slightly better. 'Come on. We'll still need to exercise care, but we won't need to be afraid of missing our steps and falling into the Atlantic Ocean.'

They set off along the footpath towards the village. The few cottages they passed had their lamps lit and drifts of grey smoke from the chimneys rose straight up into the windless air to mix with the fog. *A similar veil hangs over our case,* Maud thought.

Before too long, they reached the brae going down to Breadalbane Street, set a few roads back from the sea. The fog was patchy here and less dense than in the countryside where the castle stood, so they had no difficulty finding the row of attractive two-storey houses.

'Wait, Daisy.' Maud paused at the end of the street. 'I don't want to speak to the doctor.'

Daisy groaned. 'You mean we've come all this way for naething?'

'I mean I would rather speak to his housekeeper.'

'So what are we going to do if the mannie himself opens the door?'

'I've thought of that. First, we'll see what we can discover through the window...'

Daisy's eyes lit up. 'You mean we're going to case the joint?'

'Where do you get such language from? Not *The Queen* magazine.'

Daisy grinned. 'From *Tit-Bits*.'

They resumed walking.

'It's a pity we havena got a disguise, a tinker woman or something,' Daisy muttered.

'We thought nothing more would be required than posing as a lady crime novelist and her secretary,' Maud pointed out.

They continued along the road, passing no one in such weather, until they reached a house with a blue door on a corner of the street.

'This is it,' Maud said in a low voice. She lifted the latch on the side gate, positioned in the middle of a blackthorn hedge, and led Daisy through the garden. They quickly reached the side of the house where their feet sank into soil.

'Bother,' Daisy hissed. 'We're standing in a flower bed.'

The mist lay in wreaths around the garden and they felt their way around the stone wall of the house. Through the lit window of the kitchen at the back, they could see a female servant preparing a hot meal.

'It looks like the doctor will be home for luncheon,' Maud murmured.

A black cat jumped from the top of the garden wall and onto the roof of a shed, making them both jump and turn in its direction.

'A black cat means good luck,' Daisy commented.

It raised its face to the sky and uttered a long caterwaul. From inside the house came the howl of a large dog.

'Or maybe not,' she added.

The cat called again and the dog was responding in its own mournful way when the kitchen window was thrown open.

'*Thalla leat!*' shouted a disembodied female voice.

Maud felt no translation was necessary to know the woman was instructing the cat in no uncertain terms to go away. The feline, undeterred, put back its head once more and opened its mouth.

Out from the window flew a bucket of water. The cat screeched and fled, as the window shut with a bang and peace reigned once more.

'I hope human visitors get a warmer welcome,' muttered Daisy.

Maud glanced at the other windows. 'I think that black cat might have been a bit of luck, after all, as there's no sign of movement or a light anywhere else in the house. The doctor must be out.'

'We should check the front too.'

They crept around the house, keeping below the level of the window sills. When they reached the front door, Maud stopped and beckoned Daisy close.

'Our story, Daisy, is that we are staying at the castle, stepped out for a walk and the mist came down rather quickly. We were hoping for a cup of tea with the good doctor, before making our way home again.'

Daisy smoothed down her coat and adjusted her hat. 'Right you are.'

Maud took a deep breath and lifted the door knocker. She rapped twice.

After a minute, the door opened and a handsome woman of middle years stood there, her hair a cloud of blonde-white and wearing a housekeeper's black dress.

'Can I help you?' she asked, an enquiring smile on her face.

'We are Miss McIntyre and Miss Cameron,' Maud began, 'and wondered if Dr Munro was at home.'

'I'm afraid he's out on his visits.' She looked down at Daisy and her brow furrowed. 'Would it be a medical emergency?'

'Och, no.' Daisy spoke up. 'We're staying up at the castle, came out for a wee walk and then the mist came down.'

'And you were hoping the doctor would invite you in for a cup of tea?' said the woman, saving Daisy from having to finish the rest of their explanation.

'I can see now that's not possible.' Maud's tone was regretful.

'Why, of course it is. I'm sure he would want me to give you tea.' The housekeeper smiled. 'And a piece of my shortbread.' She stepped back to allow them to enter.

As soon as they were in the hall and the front door closed behind them, a huge, shaggy, grey-haired dog emerged from the back of the hall. It scampered along the polished floor, skidded on the hall rug and came to a halt at Maud's feet. Panting, it gazed up at her, its small ears semi-erect in excitement, its tongue lolling.

The housekeeper laughed. 'I think he likes you, Miss McIntyre.'

Maud looked at the dog. Saliva hung in a long drool from its mouth, its long head was flat and its hairy tail reached almost to the ground. An interesting-looking animal. 'A Scottish Deer-hound,' she said. She'd seen the breed depicted in a painting owned by her father, a snowy landscape by Joseph Farquharson, and knew the dogs had been bred to cope with the cool and damp Highland hills and glens. As she gazed back into its dark eyes, she remembered that they were famed for being gentle and friendly, docile and eager to please.

'I prefer wee dogs myself,' Daisy said, but she gamely held out a hand to the animal's nose for it to sniff. It did so.

'As you are friends of the master, he won't mind my taking you into the sitting room,' the woman said. 'I am Mrs Lamont, by the way. Dr Munro's housekeeper.'

Maud extracted her foot from under the deerhound's paw and followed Mrs Lamont and Daisy. The hall was furnished with a narrow oak table along one wall, and as they passed, she noted it was strewn with an interesting variety of odds and ends. Dog collars, a shoehorn, a number of ancient tweed caps, a couple of pipes, a tin of tobacco and – rather sweetly – a small mug crammed tightly with brightly coloured, daisy-like asters. It was very much a bachelor's house – no, a widower's, Maud reminded herself.

The door to the sitting room stood open and Mrs Lamont ushered them in. The dog padded in behind them and jumped up onto the sofa. It lay down, making itself comfortable.

'Please, take a seat. I've just made a fresh pot, so it won't take long.' Mrs Lamont left the room, walking with quick, light steps.

Maud and Daisy looked about them. A large bureau, its writing flap open, was littered with papers, and there were more papers behind the clock on the mantelpiece. Two book-cases full of books stood against a wall, with yet more papers on top of them. A fairly good landscape in oils hung on one wall, but the leather of the armchairs was scratched by the dog's claws, and the cushions and the loose covers of the sofas and chairs hung limp. Maud's fingers itched to set this room to rights.

Daisy nodded towards the writing desk. 'There could be something amongst the doctor's papers,' she said softly.

'I'll have a look,' Maud whispered. 'Keep an eye on the door.'

'Dinna you mean keep an eye on the dog?'

Maud glanced at the animal sprawled on the sofa. Its doleful look went between her and Daisy, its brows twitching as it tried to assess the situation.

'Both door and dog,' Maud said.

She hurried over to the bureau and began to search through Dr Munro's correspondence lying there. Invoices, receipts, various letters; nothing that seemed pertinent to the case.

The dog let out a sudden bark. Maud started. The sheets of paper slid from the desk to the floor. Daisy stifled an exclamation and crossed to her side. The pair knelt down and began to gather up the pages.

'I can't possibly put them back in the right order,' Maud breathed in dismay.

'I shouldna worry. There looks to be nae order.'

As they hesitated with the papers in their hands, Maud's eye fell on a single sheet of printed paper which had slipped from the others when they fell to the floor. She hastily put her rough pile back on the desk and swooped down to pick up the stray sheet. It was a piece cut from a newspaper.

FEARFUL DEATH OF A CHILD IN GLASGOW

'What's this?' Maud said softly.

'What does it say?' Daisy dropped her collection of papers on top of Maud's and looked at the clipping in Maud's hand.

'*About half past three o'clock on Tuesday,*' Maud read aloud, '*Mr Neil Tremain was proceeding from his home in Bath Street in his motor car, and when turning a sharp corner of a street in the city into Holland Street, Clementina Munro, the four-year old daughter of Dr Roderick Munro and his wife...*'

They both froze at the sound of approaching footsteps.

They stared at one another, then towards the dog. To their combined relief, the dog was snoring.

Maud recovered first and hastily slipped the newspaper cutting back under the papers on the desk before perching on the sofa.

Look natural, she mouthed to Daisy.

Daisy looked with distaste at the armchairs and cast around for inspiration. She hurried to the empty hearth, turned to face the door and attempted to lean her elbow on the mantel.

Maud frowned in alarm at her petite friend, before composing her own features into an expression of innocence. Mrs Lamont entered, carrying a tray with the tea things. Maud's eyes followed her across the room as she set the laden tray on top of the papers strewn over the writing desk.

'Here we are.' Mrs Lamont beamed.

Maud let out a silent sigh. Clearly the disorder on the desk looked no different from before.

'Miss Cameron,' the housekeeper went on, 'you do look uncomfortable over there. Please have a seat.'

Daisy gingerly sat in one of the armchairs.

'It's so nice to meet some of Roddy's friends,' the house-keeper went on, busying herself with pouring out the tea.

Roddy? Daisy mouthed behind the woman's back.

Mrs Lamont sounded more like his wife or sister than his housekeeper, Maud thought. Jane Tremain could be wasting her time with the doctor. Maud wondered if there was a Mr Lamont.

'Have you worked for him long?' Maud asked.

'Aye. Since before the terrible tragedy.' Mrs Lamont turned and handed Maud a cup of tea. The name they had just read in the newspaper article, Neil Tremain of Glasgow, had to be the same Neil Tremain now lying dead at the undertaker's.

'A tragedy, indeed.' Maud had no wish to disabuse the

housekeeper of their slight acquaintance. She affected a thoughtful air. 'How long ago was that now?'

'Ten years it will be – this coming week, in fact. Charlotte was a lovely lady and their wee lassie was such a delight. To think only four years old when she was killed.' Mrs Lamont shook her head. 'They loved that little girl, their only child and all the more precious for that.'

She turned back to the tray, took up the second cup and saucer and passed it to Daisy.

'So you were with him when he stayed in Glasgow?' Daisy said.

'I couldn't leave him after what happened. As if the bairn's accident wasn't bad enough, then his poor wife drowning herself in the Clyde.' She sighed deeply.

Maud's heart gave a lurch. The news was even worse than she had feared.

'That was the final blow for the doctor,' went on the house-keeper, 'so when he decided to move here, to try to get away from the memories, I came with him. My husband had died some years earlier, you see, and there was nothing to keep me in Glasgow.'

The dog gave a loud snore, waking itself up. It opened one eye, gave a thump of its tail and closed its eye again.

Mrs Lamont regarded it fondly. 'Maida's been with him for seven years. You're getting old now, aren't you, boy?'

The dog's tail gave another thump.

'Maida? That was the name of Sir Walter Scott's dog.' Maud had visited the Scott Monument in Edinburgh. It shows Scott seated, resting from writing with a quill, the deerhound by his side and gazing up at his master.

'That's where the name came from. Now, just you both help yourselves to a piece of that shortbread.' She gestured to the biscuits. 'The master will be back in about half an hour for a cup of tea himself, so if you have the time you'll be able to see him.'

As soon as she had left the room, pulling the door to close behind her, Maud and Daisy sprang from their seats. Maud slid the newspaper cutting out from under the papers and read the news item in a low voice.

'*Clementina Munro, the four-year old daughter of Dr Roderick Munro and his wife, ran from her garden into the street in front of the motor car, was hit by the motor car and fell to the ground, one wheel passing over the unfortunate child's body, crushing the bones. Death almost instantly followed.*'

TWENTY-THREE

'The puir wee toot,' Daisy murmured.

Maud looked at the handwriting on the top of the piece. 'The Glasgow Herald. Wednesday 17th September 1902.'

'Look! There's another piece stuck underneath.'

Daisy was right. Glued by the top left-hand corner, and dated a few days later, was a second news item. Daisy read it aloud.

FINDING ON THE DEATH OF CLEMENTINA MUNRO
There being no witnesses to the fatal accident on 16th September other than Mr Tremain and Mrs Roderick Munro, and both agreeing that the young child had run out in front of the motor car while chasing after a cat and that the motor car was not going more than about ten miles per hour, the Procurator Fiscal recorded a finding of accidental death, having come to the conclusion that no individual was to blame for Clementina Munro's death.

'So Tremain was not prosecuted,' Maud said. 'That must have been difficult for the Munros.'

'And poor Mrs Munro, who doesna even seem to have a Christian name of her own, seeing her own wee girl killed in front of her eyes. She must have felt she was partly to blame. Nae wonder she killed herself.'

They were both quiet for a moment.

'Drink your tea quickly, Daisy,' Maud told her. 'We don't want to risk being here when the doctor returns. He won't believe our story.'

Daisy eyed the shortbread on the tray. 'Have we got time for a wee piece?' Her gaze turned to the seats in the room. 'But I'm nae sitting again. All the chairs are covered in dog hairs.'

'Three minutes, no more.'

Daisy took a biscuit, nibbled it as quickly as possible and gulped down the contents of her cup. Maud finished her tea and set the cup back in the saucer.

'Next,' she said, 'we must visit the stationery shop and buy a map of Glasgow.'

The dog began to stir on the sofa. It lifted his shaggy head and looked at them.

Daisy plucked another shortbread finger from the plate.

'Daisy, there isn't time for a second piece,' Maud told her.

'Och, it's nae for me,' she said. 'It's for Maida. Here, boy.' She threw him a shortbread finger. 'Put that behind your ear for later.'

The dog opened his mouth and caught it in mid-air.

'Very amusing,' said Maud, 'but we have a serious task in front of us. It looks like we have an answer to question number one on our list. Dr Munro had a good reason to want Tremain dead. If the recently deceased Neil Tremain lived in Bath Street, and it must surely be the same man, then Dr Munro is now at the top of our suspect list.'

. . .

The stationer had no street maps for sale, but he directed Maud and Daisy to the small bookshop close by. It had narrow aisles and a shuffling proprietor who looked like he'd not left the premises for fifty years. He returned Maud's greeting – '*Latha math*' – and left the pair to browse.

Maud could not resist a bookshop, so she picked an aisle at random and wandered down it. Historical non-fiction, second-hand books with ragged covers, biographies... There at eye level on the next shelf was a volume by R. Austin Freeman. Maud knew the author's name but not the title: *The Singing Bone*. It must be his new publication. She pulled it out.

The book was the latest in the Dr Thorndyke Mysteries, a collection of stories in which the reader knows the killer's identity long before the medical detective enters the scene. The question was not who committed the crime, but how would he be caught? A very good question, she thought. If Munro is the murderer, how will she and Daisy be able to prove it?

'I've found what we want,' Daisy said, coming up to her, a folded map in her hand. 'It looks like you've found something too.'

'I'll pay for them both and then I had better get you back in time for your midday meal below-stairs. We don't want your absence noticed and Isobel reprimanded.'

Maud opened her purse and counted out the money as the proprietor wrapped her purchase in brown paper. She paid him and they went out with their parcel into the fog.

The village remained quiet. A line of washing not retrieved in time hung limply in a side garden. Further along the road a horse stood alone and forlorn with its cart as the dampness settled on its blinkers. The fog thickened and swirled around them.

They had almost reached the stone pillars marking the

beginning of the avenue leading to the castle, when a short, elderly woman appeared out of the shifting fog. She wore a dark grey dress, a yellow neckerchief and round her shoulders a light grey shawl. For a brief moment, Maud was reminded of Walter Hartright's encounter with the mysterious woman in white in Wilkie Collins's novel, before she gathered her senses again.

'Are you lost, madam?' she asked.

'Not at all, my dear. I am looking for my cat. I don't like her to be out in this weather.'

'I'm sure she will come home presently,' Maud said.

Through the fog Maud could now see behind the woman an open garden gate with a path beyond. She could just make out the shape of a cottage visible at the end of it.

'Are you going up to the big house?' The elderly woman's eyes were bright, birdlike.

'We are,' Maud said.

'I heard there was some trouble up there.'

'There was, but I'm sure it will be sorted out soon.'

'Let's hope so. Lady Ailsa doesn't do well when things go wrong. Well, I'll be getting back indoors now.'

'We'll wait until you're safely in,' Daisy told her.

The woman walked sprightly down the garden path and with a wave of her hand disappeared into her cottage. Maud closed the low gate and as she did so she saw the name painted on the wood. Shieling Beag. 'That must be Ailsa's old lady's maid, Lizzie.'

'I think you're right, Maud.'

They walked on and before long turned between the pillars and into the castle driveway.

'I think the fog is lifting a wee bit.' Daisy sounded nervous. 'Do you think—'

'We have our number one suspect now, Daisy.' Maud knew her friend was thinking of the police boat.

'Aye. All we need now is to show opportunity and method.'

'That's it.' Maud kept her tone positive and linked her arm through Daisy's.

The castle loomed into view; through the mist the oil lamps glowed in some of the windows. Maud glanced at her wristwatch. 'Ten minutes to midday. There is just time for you to return to your room.'

Daisy nodded. 'Isobel will come for me in another five minutes. Finlay is particular about starting the meal on time. Canna say I blame him, with upstairs luncheon to be served at one o'clock sharp.'

The front door of the castle stood open as usual, but the door to the lobby was closed because of the weather.

'I'll come to your room this afternoon as soon as I can and bring the map.' Maud touched the brown paper parcel she held under her arm and together they mounted the steps.

'Here goes.' Stealthily, Maud lifted the latch and eased open the inner door. She entered the great hall, thankfully standing empty. She beckoned Daisy in and closed the door quietly behind them, and they stole across the floor and up the spiral staircase, listening all the while for the sound of any activity. They felt a rush of relief when they reached the second floor without meeting anyone.

Daisy pulled the door key from her coat pocket and let herself in.

'I'll see you later,' she said, slipping into her room. 'Thanks for getting me out, even if it was just for the morning.' She closed the door.

Maud heard the key turn in the lock from the other side. She stared at the door. Was Daisy giving up? Maud frowned and felt the sting of unwanted tears.

With a small sigh, she went along the corridor and into her own room.

. . .

Over the oyster soup, Lord Urquhart addressed Maud. 'How was your morning, Miss McIntyre? I looked, but I couldn't find you.'

'I went for a walk.' She didn't meet his gaze. What she had just told him was true, but he might ask for further particulars.

'A walk?' It was Jane. 'What on earth is the point of a walk in such weather?'

'What is the point of a walk in any weather?' Maud replied with a shrug. 'To stretch my legs and exercise my limbs, to get a fresh perspective on matters.'

'On matters?' Jane's brows drew together. 'Does that mean you think you know who killed my father?'

'It means that I'm trying to work out who murdered both men.'

'And have you?'

'Not yet.'

Jane gave a loud sigh. She lifted her spoon and tasted the soup.

'And you, Lord Urquhart?' asked Maud. 'How did you pass your morning?'

'I came across a deck of cards and played a game of patience.' He sent her a glance that meant he was patiently waiting for when he could assist in the next part of her investigation.

Jane glanced swiftly at him. 'You could have asked me to play a game with you – a card game, I mean,' she added, sending him a look to suggest that she meant more than that.

Maud took a spoonful of the oyster soup. 'This is really very good.'

Jane gave a small, tinkling laugh as she smeared a tiny amount of butter on a thin slice of bread.

Lord Urquhart smiled at both women.

Maud narrowed her eyes at him, then spread butter thickly on a bread roll and bit into it. He is enjoying this, she decided as she chewed furiously. Well, if he thought he had two women fighting over him, he had another thought coming. And there would certainly be no detective partnership, not least because he'd still failed to tell her what he had been doing in the corridor outside Tremain's room that first afternoon. *And* in the great hall on Saturday night, sitting beside the dying fire in a vast draughty room when he could have been warmer in his bedroom.

'It seems Ailsa will be coming down for dinner tonight,' said Jane, nibbling daintily on her thin slice of bread.

'That's good news.' Lord Urquhart dipped his spoon.

'Yes, very good news.' Maud meant it. The little group of three was proving tiresome. As if to prove the point, Jane engaged Lord Urquhart in society news which was designed to exclude Maud quite thoroughly. So as she spooned up her soup, she concentrated her thoughts on what she and Daisy had learned this morning.

She had briefly examined the street map before luncheon and seen that Bath Street and Holland Street were close to one another. The piece in the newspaper had given them Dr Munro's motive for murder. If only they could find opportunity and method.

Suddenly, she remembered how Dr Munro had said he would let himself out when he left to visit the other patient on Friday evening. If the killer is indeed the doctor, she thought, then he must have returned to Tremain's room before he left the castle that night. After all, there had been no other opportunity before the man's dead body was found the following morning. If their suspicions were right, it must have been then that he murdered Neil Tremain!

'Is something amusing you, Miss McInytrre?'

Maud was startled out of her thoughts. She must have been smiling. 'Not at all, Lord Urquhart. Quite the opposite, I assure you.'

But her theory couldn't be correct, Maud realised with a sinking heart. Finlay had seen the doctor let himself out that evening. Could Dr Munro have returned to Tremain's room before leaving the castle? No, that would not work either. Tremain's death had taken place earlier that morning and not the night before. But then, she reminded herself, it was the doctor who had given the time of death. If he was the killer, then he would lie about that, wouldn't he? Then again...

'Is the ham not to your liking, Miss McIntyre?'

She looked at Lord Urquhart, confused.

'You were frowning,' he told her.

'I've never known a person make such extraordinary faces while eating.' Jane smiled prettily.

Maud stared down at the second course. When had that arrived? 'The ham and mashed turnip are excellent, thank you.'

As soon as luncheon was over, she excused herself, made her way upstairs and entered her bedroom. She waited until she heard footsteps and the door opposite her close – Lord Urquhart's, and then the door next to her room – Jane's. Maud sighed, then went over to the table and picked up the street map of Glasgow and the collection of short stories. Softly opening her door again, she tiptoed along the corridor to Daisy's room. She tapped lightly on the door and heard the key turn in the lock. Her assistant gestured for her to come in.

'You've brought the map,' Daisy exclaimed, closing the door. 'Spread it out over the writing table.'

Maud did so, and shoulder to shoulder they pored over it.

'There's the River Clyde.' Daisy pointed to the winding ribbon. 'That's easy to spot. And Glasgow Central Railway Station, just north of the river. Where's Bath Street and Holland Street?'

'I found it earlier using the index. They're here.' Maud pointed to them.

'Crivvens – they're nae far from each other!'

'I've checked the scale. They are less than a mile from each other.'

Daisy looked at Maud. 'So that's it, then. Our murderer is the good doctor.'

'I think so. But...'

'What?'

'Well, we know that he had a reason for hating Tremain—'

'An awfa good reason.'

'Yes, but more than motive is required to prove a case.'

'Opportunity and method. I ken.'

'If we consider the first of those, then when did he have the opportunity?'

Daisy thought for a moment. 'The night before, when he said he'd show himself out—'

'I've already thought of that. Finlay said he saw the doctor letting himself out. And Neil Tremain was murdered the following morning.'

'So the doctor says, but can we believe him?'

'I wondered that too, but I think we have to. Tremain *must* have been killed not long before the door was forced because his body was still warm.'

'What about Sandy McNeish. I ken *I* didna stab him—'

'I know that too. As do most of us here.'

'Aye, well, nae Magnus. But anyway,' Daisy went on, 'if we're agreed that whoever killed Sergeant McNeish also killed Neil...'

'We are.'

'There was no locked room on the second occasion, so when did Dr Munro get the opportunity to stab the sergeant?'

Maud and Daisy looked at each other.

'He must have been killed by one of the five of us – that's you and me, Lord Urquhart, Dr Munro and Magnus,' Maud said. 'Can you remember the order we all left the policeman's room?'

Daisy was shaking her head. 'I canna be sure. I mind the men standing back to let us go out first, but after that... It might have been the doctor who was last to leave, but I canna be sure.'

Maud tried to picture the scene again, but she couldn't. It was as if the horror of seeing Daisy standing over Sergeant McNeish's dead body had wiped the image from her mind.

'Do you agree, Daisy, that there are only three people who possibly had a motive for killing Tremain: Jane, Ailsa or Dr Munro? Jane because she may have discovered her father had no money and was furious. Ailsa because – oh, I honestly don't know why she would do such a thing. Dr Munro we now know had a strong motive. Do you think Tremain turning up here and staying at the castle pushed Munro over the edge? Could dining with the man who killed his beloved child have turned a normally peaceable man into a cold-blooded killer?'

'I do, Maud. I think it's more than possible. Neil Tremain ruined the doctor's whole life.'

Maud sighed heavily. 'You're right. But how to prove it?'

They studied the map silently for the next few minutes.

'We ken only one of three people could have killed the sergeant,' Daisy said. 'Magnus, Lord Urquhart or Dr Munro – because we ken we didna.'

Maud nodded. 'We are agreed that the two murders are the work of the same person. Ergo, it must be Dr Munro as he had a strong motive. But how could he have entered a locked room to stab Tremain?'

'This case just goes round and round, Maud.'

'And how could he have slipped into McNeish's room, stabbed him and slipped out again, all without being seen and within barely a minute? It's simply not possible. And yet, I'm *certain* he did it.'

TWENTY-FOUR

'The fog appears to be lifting. Miss McIntyre. Will you allow me to take you out to dinner this evening?' Lord Urquhart had been the first to arrive in the small drawing room for tea. He leaned back on the sofa, his legs crossed at the ankles. To the casual observer, he was a gentleman without a care in the world.

'I'm not sure that's appropriate, given poor Daisy is still incarcerated in her room.' Maud's teacup clinked slightly in its saucer as she smoothed the back of her skirts to sit in the chair opposite.

'There's nothing you can do to help her at present,' he said, 'and the tension in the castle is proving most uncomfortable.'

'We can't leave Miss Tremain to eat her dinner alone.'

'Are you suggesting she comes with us?' He smiled.

Certainly not, Maud thought. Before she could formulate a suitable response, Lord Urquhart spoke again.

'She won't be alone, because Ailsa will be down to dinner this evening.'

'Won't that appear terribly impolite, to leave our hostess like that?'

'I will speak to Ailsa. I'm sure she won't mind.'

'Well,' Maud said, still uncertain on her friend's account, 'you must first let me know that Ailsa isn't offended. I shouldn't like to make things worse.'

Jane stepped into the room and nothing further could be said on the topic.

As soon as she could excuse herself, Maud went to the library to look for a copy of *Who's Who*. She was certain Magnus would have the volume and he did. She turned the pages until she found the entry she was looking for.

Urquhart, Lord Hamish Alexander Jonathan Edward Maurice (Baron). Born 22nd May 1882. She did a quick calculation. That made him thirty, just four years older than her – not that his age was of any interest to her, but the need for detail in all things was important. She read on. Educated at Fettes College, then read Classics at the University of Edinburgh and spent a few years in the Royal Navy.

Maud frowned. Why only a few years? As she pondered this, a vision sprang to mind of Lord Urquhart's tall and muscular figure in his naval uniform. This vision smiled at her and her legs turned to water. What is the matter with you, Maud McIntyre, she chastised herself. He's just a man...

But was he? He was something of an enigma. Sometimes, he acted as if he wished to court her, but didn't he do that with every available female? She couldn't take him seriously. But if she was to solve this case and free Daisy, she should accept any help he offered. Her mind was made up. If Ailsa – and Daisy – had no objection, she would have dinner with him this evening.

'Of course you must go out for dinner with his handsome lordship!' Daisy laughed. 'There's naething to be done here at the moment.' Maud and Daisy were seated comfortably in Daisy's bedchamber.

'That's what he said,' Maud admitted. 'He's also spoken to

Ailsa, who is feeling better, and she assures him she won't be offended by our not having dinner here.'

'There you are, then. Go and enjoy yourself.'

'I don't know that it will be enjoyment, but I fully intend to find out why he was in the corridor that afternoon and more importantly the great hall the other night.'

Maud glanced at the book on Daisy's nightstand. It was the collection of Freeman's latest stories. 'What do you think of the book?' she asked.

'I've only just started it, but I will let you know if any of the stories answer our problem.'

Lord Urquhart was right that the fog was lifting, but the evening remained chilly. Maud wore her blue tweed costume and a warm jersey. She secured her hat with the scarf tied under her chin. He wore a cap, a dark suit of tweed, a warm scarf – and Maud's driving goggles. It was astonishing that he could look so *manly* in them. Secretly she studied his broad hands on the wheel, remembered how his strong arm had felt around her waist in the library that night. Of course, she had resisted him – how could she have done otherwise? – but it didn't stop her wondering what might have happened if she had not. Her gaze slipped down to his thighs as he pressed the clutch. Drawing in a silent breath, she clenched her hands tight as if they might of their own volition reach out to slide along the warm muscle. This would not do! She couldn't have feelings for a man she couldn't trust. He had still told her nothing of why he had been in the great hall. Clearly he hadn't been there to read a book.

Maud turned her attention to the scenery. She had forgotten how dark it got in the country. Hedges flashed past, illuminated only by the Napier's headlights, and fell back into the gloom behind them.

'It's kind of you to take me out to dinner, Lord Urquhart.'

'It's kind of you to allow me to drive your car. I was interested to see how she handles these roads.'

She smoothed the rug over her lap. 'Why do men refer to motor cars, as to ships, by the pronoun *she*? They are inanimate objects.'

He sent her a quick glance before turning his eyes back to the road. 'The tradition relates to the idea of a female figure such as a goddess guiding a ship and crew. By referring to vehicles as she, men confer on them qualities such as beauty, grace and strength – just as they would describe a beloved woman.'

She smiled into the darkness. 'Nicely put.'

They crossed a burn where willow branches dipped in the dark water. As they began to climb, Maud looked down and saw the glen was still wreathed in mist. At the top of the hill, she glanced back at Clachan Castle and found it looking sinister against the dark sky. An owl on the hunt swept on broad wings across the road. She didn't believe in portents of evil, but Maud had to force herself not to think of what might be happening in the castle this evening and to concentrate on the questions she needed to ask her dinner companion.

Lord Urquhart concentrated on the road as they travelled along the twisting narrow track in silence. Presently, they drew into a small village and came to a halt before The Drover's Arms, its lights sending out a welcome.

He placed his hand at the small of her back as they entered the modest-sized dining room. The room was bustling with diners and waiters, full of conversation and blessedly warm. They were shown to a corner table with a crisp white cloth adorned with a vase containing a sunny yellow dahlia.

Maud placed her small evening bag and gloves beside her on the table. 'This is very pleasant.'

He smiled. 'I'm glad you approve.'

The waiter returned and handed each of them a menu on a single piece of white card, before departing again.

Maud looked at the menu. 'Mmm, difficult to choose. *Veal ragout. Dressed venison...*' She looked up and caught him watching her. 'Is there a special reason for our being here?'

'Is one needed?' He smiled. 'Now, have you chosen?'

She needed answers from Lord Urquhart and the sooner they could get onto that the better. 'I'll have only a main course. The venison, please.'

'I will join you,' he said.

The waiter appeared, took their drink and dinner orders and went away. Before long, he returned with the bottle of champagne and poured two glasses.

'Perhaps there is an occasion to celebrate this evening,' Lord Urquhart said, raising his saucer of the bubbly wine.

'Oh?'

'That we are still alive.'

'You mean given that we are staying in a castle where two people have already been murdered?'

He nodded.

'I will drink to our being – and *staying* – alive, and to finding the murderer before the police boat arrives and Daisy is arrested.' Maud raised her glass. 'To being alive and to saving Daisy.'

With the sound of cutlery and china clinking in the background, Maud allowed Lord Urquhart to keep the talk between them light. It was pleasant, she realised, relaxing back in her chair, to be dinning with him alone. She bathed in his attention until the waiter brought their meal, then determinedly focused on the real reason she had agreed to dine with him and turned the conversation to important matters.

'What is your real occupation, Lord Urquhart?'

'I believe I have told you.'

'You have told me that you write the *Scottish Man About Town* column for *The Sketch*.'

'And that is true. I do.'

'What else do you do?'

'I don't understand.'

'Come, Lord Urquhart, I think you do.' She held his gaze.

He paused and rested his cutlery on the plate. He looked across the table at her. 'What I am going to tell you must go no further.'

Her heart lurched. Please don't let him say he was actually a thief, a gentleman thief like Raffles. Or, worse, a murderer... the murderer of Tremain and McNeish. She held her breath and inclined her head in agreement, giving every appearance of calm while inside her heart beat out a steady thud.

Lord Urquhart leaned forward and motioned Maud to do the same. He lowered his voice. 'I am an intelligence officer, working for the Secret Intelligence Service.' He watched her face for a reaction.

She let out her breath. 'Thank goodness.'

He blinked in surprise. 'Thank goodness?'

'All those occasions when I thought you were up to no good, you must have been there for your work,' she said. 'Duddingston House, hobnobbing with the wives of MPs—'

'I would not describe it as hobnobbing.'

Maud raised an eyebrow at him as she sipped her wine.

'Just the one MP's wife,' he protested, 'and before she was married.'

'You've been appearing in all sorts of places and behaving suspiciously ever since I have known you,' Maud went on, getting into her stride and continuing to exaggerate a little. 'Visiting coffee shops at all hours; staying with the King at Balmoral; in Fort William when the choir...' What was she saying? Surely the choir was nothing to do with secret intelligence?

'Fort William is close to army barracks,' he reminded her, his voice low, 'and therefore of some interest to my employers.'

'And now at Clachan Castle,' she concluded. 'I knew there was something about you, turning up at all these country houses.'

'It's easy to be invited when you are part of the set, and my society column helps. A surprising number of people want to be mentioned in it.'

'Tell me, Lord Urquhart, what are you doing on Mull for this service, of which I have never heard?'

'SIS is a new organisation. It began work only three years ago because of genuine concerns over the existence of a network of German undercover agents.'

'A possible European war?'

He nodded. 'We work to protect the United Kingdom from overseas threats. There are officers operating all around the world, gathering intelligence from people and organisations.'

'You mean,' she whispered, 'that you are a *spy*?'

'Yes, although we prefer the term *agent*. Our work must be done in secret to protect those involved.'

'So how did you become involved in the organisation?'

'I was recruited when in the Royal Navy.'

'Ah, so that explains...'

He smiled at her. 'Explains what, Miss McIntyre?'

She'd heard him use that tone of voice before. He was playing with her. 'Only that I happened to read your entry in *Who's Who*,' she remarked nonchalantly.

His smile widened and he placed his right hand on his heart. 'You looked me up? I'm touched.'

'Tell me,' she went on quickly, because he was about to distract them both, 'to whom is SIS accountable?'

'The government of the day, which means the Prime Minister has overall responsibility.'

Maud realised they had both stopped eating and were in

danger of drawing the waiter's attention. Lord Urquhart topped up her champagne glass; she picked up her knife and fork and he followed suit.

'So you are at the castle for reasons of the country's security?' she murmured.

'I am.'

'And does the bronze statuette play a part in this?'

He inclined his head. 'You are correct, Miss McIntyre. We knew information was being passed from somewhere in Scotland, but that was all. Magnus and his sister have always been content to remain at their remote castle and entertain rarely, so I needed to secure an invitation. Given my association with Fettes and my degree in Classics, it wasn't too difficult to obtain one.'

'I see. Let us start, then, with why you were hanging about on the second-floor corridor on the afternoon everyone else was watching the play.' Maud ate a forkful of the venison.

'*Almost* everyone else,' he corrected her, one eyebrow raised in challenge. 'I was shadowing Andrew. What were you doing?'

'You know very well what I was doing. Why were you shadowing Andrew?' Clearly she was going to have to drag the answers out of Lord Urquhart.

'Because... I believe he is working for the Germans.'

'Good heavens!' Maud's voice had risen an octave and with a start she realised other diners were looking her way. Suddenly she saw Andrew in a new light. Could he be the killer and not Dr Munro? Hastily she lowered her voice. 'And is he – working for the Germans?'

'I'm sorry, but I'm not at liberty to tell you any more than that.'

'Like everyone else in the country,' Maud said, 'I followed the trial in the High Court two months ago in the case of Dr Graves.' The German had arrived in Edinburgh in January under the cover of attending medical lectures. The newspaper had reported how he'd been kept under surveillance during his stay and was arrested the following month. 'He was the first person to be tried in Scotland under the Official Secrets Act passed last year.'

'It was unfortunate that the Crown was unable to do more than demonstrate that Graves possessed certain information about naval matters and had been using secret codes for communicating it.'

'I read that he was found to have a code book, but that most of the other items – maps, photographs and information about the new Rosyth naval base – could be read in specialist publications.'

'As a result,' Lord Urquhart added, cutting into his venison, 'he received only eighteen months' imprisonment, compared to the seven-year sentence he might otherwise have been given under the new legislation.'

'So, although Graves is now in Barlinnie Prison, there are other German agents working in this country?'

Lord Urquhart gave a barely perceptible nod. 'Yes, and they now suspect we're on to them, so I must ask that you do nothing to disturb my surveillance of the footman.'

'I don't know that I can promise that. Andrew must naturally be one of our suspects for murder and this conversation has made him look more likely to be the guilty person.' That was a little bit true, she told herself. She and Daisy *had* put him on their list for the killing of Tremain, but he had never been a serious suspect. Finding the newspaper cutting at Munro's house had propelled the doctor to the top of the list for both murders.

'Can you at least answer another question that has been bothering me?' she went on. 'Why were you lurking in the great hall in the early hours of Sunday morning?'

'It was related to the matter of Andrew and the statuette.'

'Hmm...' Maud drummed her fingers on the tablecloth and

thought for a moment. She was getting close. Why would a statuette be of so much interest to a spy? Maud tried to picture the
bronze again. Not a large object; a lion about six inches high
and on a base of roughly the same size.

Was that it? She glanced at Lord Urquhart, who was
watching her as he ate his meal. The base was perhaps of a
larger size than might reasonably be expected. Could there
be... Maud felt her pulse quicken... a secret compartment in the
base? Yes, it was entirely possible. She remembered reading
about something called a dead letter. A dead letter office was
established in London over one hundred years ago for
processing post that couldn't be delivered for some reason. And
wasn't there something called a dead letter box, which was used
to pass items or information between two individuals using a
secret location, meaning the individuals could avoid direct
meetings and maintain operational security?

'I think I know what it is,' Maud said with a smile.

TWENTY-FIVE

'Someone – you suspect it is Andrew,' Maud went on, 'had placed a message in a secret compartment in the base of the lion, for someone else to retrieve it. Or vice versa. And you had reason to believe the message was to be removed in the early hours of Sunday morning.'

The corner of Lord Urquhart's lips lifted in a smile. 'You are full of surprises, Miss McIntyre.'

It was her turn to smile. 'I do hope so.' She became serious again. 'Do you suspect Tremain of being Andrew's contact? No, that doesn't make sense. They could easily have passed information in the privacy of Tremain's room.' Lord Urquhart was not moved to reply. This was frustrating! She was close to the answer, Maud was sure of it.

'How do you find the venison, Miss McIntyre?'

Maud sighed. She would get no more out of him this evening. 'Delicious, thank you.'

'Did I ever tell you,' he began, setting his cutlery neatly on his plate and leaning back in the chair, 'about the time I was attacked by a red stag?'

'No, you did not. Was it an agent in disguise?'

He ignored her frivolous question. 'I was walking along a clifftop in the Cairngorms and, as I came over a rise in the heather, I was confronted with a very large stag. The great beast turned to face me, lowered his antler and charged.'

'Goodness!'

'I had a very similar thought. The stag tried to push me over the edge of the cliff, so I grabbed the antler, being very keen to stop the tines on his forehead from penetrating my stomach. Tines are only small, but they face forward with a sharp, curving point. He turned his head rapidly and a tine penetrated my thigh.'

Maud flinched. But Lord Urquhart hadn't finished yet.

'I struggled with the animal for what seemed like an age until eventually, the good Lord knows how, I managed to wrestle it to the ground. As I lay across its neck, my only thought was that I should go for its eyes. I forced a thumb into each eye. And then we both got up.'

'Good grief.' Maud's voice was faint.

'The stag butted me a couple of times, but I suppose the pain in his eyes made him reconsider and he ran off.'

Maud stared at him. 'Is this really true?' She began to imagine the whole spying story was also a fabrication.

'Of course it's true. I managed to get down the valley and to the house of the friend where I was staying. It transpired that I had sustained a wound close to my jugular vein.'

'Good heavens.' Could she think of nothing original to say?

'It was the rutting season and I later discovered that this particular stag – an Imperial with fourteen tines to his antler – was known as a bad-tempered brute.'

'So the work you're doing now seems a lot easier?' She gave a shaky laugh. If the animal had had sixteen tines or more, it would have been a Monarch, a giant of a beast, the largest of the United Kingdom's land mammals, but an Imperial is big enough. Lord Urquhart could have died in his encounter with the stag.

He laughed. 'Most definitely. And now I think it's time we returned to the castle.'

He lifted a hand to call over the waiter and in minutes the bill was settled. He ushered Maud towards the main door, and they emerged into a clear, dark night. Putting on his cap, Lord Urquhart offered his arm to Maud, and they descended the hotel steps.

She settled down under her rug. It was chilly and, since the fog had all but gone, the stars sparkled above the hills. The moon hung, orange and red, like a lantern.

'Almost a harvest moon,' he murmured.

The nearest full moon to the autumn equinox, Maud knew. Its light enabled farmers to work late into the night, helping them to bring in the crops from the fields. They drove along untarred roads with puddles gleaming in the moonlight; hedges and trees and cottages were black silhouettes as they passed. The lights of the motor car picked out everything in their glow, including a fat brown hedgehog on the grass verge waddling homeward.

Maud turned to Lord Urquhart to make a comment on the delightful little creature. His lips were pressed together in concentration. She gazed at his profile, looking a little forbidding now, but she remembered the occasions when she had secretly admired that noble profile. In the Ballater case when she had come across him waiting for her by his car; during the Fort William choir murders, with his head bent over the newspaper as he sought clues; on their way back to the castle after church only two days ago. Dark eyebrows over dark eyes, straight strong nose, sensuous mouth... Her heart gave a little skip. Yes, it *was* a physical attraction. Yet it was *much* more than that, she knew. He was intelligent and amusing and kind.

She felt a wave of unexpected pleasure. They were both

alive, the night was beautiful and... Her heart began to thud. Oh dear Lord. She realised with a pang that she loved him.

'I hope you aren't too cold?' he was asking her. 'It's a long way on a dark night.'

With an enormous effort, she forced herself to say in an ordinary voice, 'No, I'm not cold, thank you.'

'That's good,' he said.

But being in love was of no use at all. Yet for now, in this car and with him, she was happy. She felt such pure happiness welling in her heart that she was afraid he must notice. She thought of all the occasions when they had vexed each other, but it no longer mattered.

A side post at a crossroads loomed over the moonlit junction like a ghostly figure pleading for help, its arms outstretched. Maud caught her breath, a sliver of cold travelling down her back despite the warm rug. How could she have forgotten Daisy? Daisy, her oldest friend, who had been her lady's maid when Maud lived at her father's house in the country. The friend who then became her assistant when Maud started the detective agency in Edinburgh. Daisy, who had saved her from more than a life of boredom; she'd saved her actual life on more than one occasion. There was only one thing she should be focusing on until this was all over. Daisy must be saved from the clutches of the gallows at all costs.

'Glory be!' Daisy's mouth dropped open. 'His lordship is a *spy*?'

'Keep your voice down, Daisy,' Maud hissed. She was back in Daisy's room to discuss the events of the evening. 'I was as shocked as you at the revelation.'

'Who'd have thought it? I ken he has behaved suspiciously at times, but still...'

'It's not what we expected.' Maud flung herself into one of

the armchairs by the fire. 'I have to admit, though, it's a bit of a relief to know he's more Holmes than Raffles.'

'And working for Mr Asquith.' Daisy sat down in the opposite chair.

'That too.' Maud let out a deep sigh. 'I hope our Prime Minister appreciates Lord Urquhart's endeavours.'

She'd had time to ponder what Lord Urquhart had told her and what she already knew from reading the newspapers. For the last few years, rivalry had intensified between Britain – a long-established global power – and Germany with its growing imperial ambitions. Germany's policies had fostered a fear of hostile intentions, particularly of invasion and of German espionage. These fears were reflected in newspaper articles and in popular fiction. The Kaiser's efforts to create a more powerful navy had prompted the British government to build more warships for the Royal Navy. This naval arms race had brought about mutual suspicion between Germany and Britain, so perhaps the idea of a British secret agent was not so very far-fetched, after all.

'Lord Urquhart being a government agent explains a number of things about him as a man of mystery,' Maud went on. 'The trouble is that it's raised some new questions too.'

'Aye. Such as who is putting messages in the lion and who is taking them out?'

'And what, if any, connection it has to our murder cases. Did you find any useful ideas in the pages of the Freeman book?' Maud added, without much hope.

'I've only read the first story: 'The Case of Oscar Brodski'. That Dr Thorndyke fellow worked out the killer thanks to biscuit crumbs on the dead man's waistcoat showing he'd recently eaten. And that led to finding a wee tuft of fabric wedged between the dead man's teeth suggesting he'd been killed in a house with a carpeted floor. And the cinders in the grate contained shellac and so they were the remains of a hard felt hat... That's just a few of the clues. Naething we can use.'

Oh well, Maud thought, obviously not all detective stories could be of use to them.

Daisy was looking at her. 'I *do* have some news for you, though.'

Maud perked up. 'Yes?'

'Two things. I'll give you the least important first.'

'What is it, Daisy?'

'The gardener's boy, Peddie, was hanging about the kitchen back door – it seems he's sweet on Isobel...'

Maud smiled.

'He and I had a wee blether and he told me the castle has a bogle.'

Maud's smile widened.

'It's nae funny, Maud. You ken I'm feart of bogles!'

'Have you ever seen a ghost, Daisy?'

'Nae, but that doesna mean they dinna exist.'

'Very well.' They'd had this conversation before. 'And what did Peddie say about this bogle?'

'That it's an old woman – the Grey Lady, he called her – and he's seen her at night floating through the castle garden.'

'Has he seen her often?'

'Twice in the last year, since he started to work here.'

'She's not a frequent visitor, then. I wonder what he was doing in the garden in the dark.'

'It was to meet Isobel.'

'So the girl has also seen the spectre?'

Daisy shook her head. 'Isobel had gone back indoors by that time.'

'Did Peddie say when he last saw this ghost, this Grey Lady of his?'

'I didna ask him! I didna want to know anything more about

her. He might have told me she had her head under her arm.'
Daisy shuddered.

'Daisy, you're an investigator! You can't just decide not to investigate something of possible interest because of super-stition.'

'Well, aye.'

'What is your other, more important, item of news?'

'I learned over supper below-stairs this evening that Andrew had a German mither.'

Maud sat up. 'Good heavens! And no one thought to mention that before?'

'Nae doubt they thought it had naething to do with the two murders.'

'You say *had* a German mother?'

'She died a few years ago.'

'And his father?'

'He's still alive and stays in Edinburgh.'

'I suppose there's not an obvious link...'

Daisy sighed. 'I still canna believe that Andrew is a suspected German spy. He's too nice a chap.'

'I take it Andrew wasn't there when the others talked to you about him being of German descent?'

'Finlay said he had a stomach upset and didna want any supper.'

'Hmm. I wonder if Andrew's stomach upset has anything to do with a feeling that the net is closing in on him? Did the servants say anything else about him?'

'Only that he thought the Germans were doing a good job of running their country and we could learn a thing or two from them. They said he was always going on about how Germany might be a new country, but it's prosperous, more advanced than Britain and it has strong leaders.'

'It might be more industrially advanced,' Maud retorted,

'but the country is strongly shaped by militarism, nationalism and government authoritarianism.'

Daisy digested Maud's comments. 'That's a lot of isms, Maud, but nae any of them something to admire.'

'It seems as though Lord Urquhart is correct and Andrew is the spy in the castle. But to whom is he passing information? Assuming the bronze statuette has been used as a dead letter box before, it must be someone who stays in the castle, so that rules out Tremain and his daughter.'

'And Magnus wouldna have been thinking of selling it, and Neil Tremain wouldna have stolen it to sell.'

'True, Daisy. Who else, besides those who live here, has access to the castle?'

'The butcher?' Daisy suggested. 'He comes most days. But he only goes to the kitchens. If he tried to go up into the great hall, he'd be spotted.'

'Then the question is who else has access to the great hall?'

'The postie!'

'Of course. He brings the letters into the lobby and it's only a short flight of steps to the great hall.'

'Och, that doesna work. Lord Urquhart would have worked that out before we arrived. You said he was skulking in the great hall in the middle of the night, so he must be getting desperate.'

Maud and Daisy were quiet for a moment.

'Lord Urquhart asked that we do nothing to disturb his surveillance of Andrew,' Maud said. 'I'm convinced the doctor is our prime suspect and so we should leave Andrew to Lord Urquhart.'

'And yet Andrew could be Neil's killer.'

'Yes,' Maud admitted. 'He could very well be.'

The following morning, Maud climbed out of bed, pushed open the casement and drew in a deep breath. The air had been washed clean, the morning light frail and blue, and for the first time in days, she heard birdsong. Her thoughts turned to Daisy and the predicament she was in. The police boat would be on its way – if it wasn't already. Time was of the essence. She needed to tell Lord Urquhart what she had learned last night about Andrew from Daisy and in return he must tell her all he knew. There could be no other way.

She washed and dressed in a black skirt and pink blouse with a black and white striped tie. This was an important day – the day she would clear Daisy's name – and a smart blouse was required. Her hair secured in a bun at the nape of her neck, Maud hastened down the stairs. She must catch Lord Urquhart before he left the breakfast table. If she did not, it might be hours until she saw him again and that could prove to be too late.

'Good morning, Miss McIntyre.'

To Maud's relief, he was seated at the table and tucking into a plate of bacon and kidneys. Unfortunately, Ailsa was also there.

'Good morning to you, Lord Urquhart. And to you also, Miss Carmichael. Are you feeling well today?' she asked Ailsa.

'Much better, thank you, my dear.' Ailsa looked up with inquisitive eyes at Maud. 'I'm afraid I've been rather a poor hostess. I hope you have managed to entertain yourself in my absence.'

'You need not fear on my account, Miss Carmichael. I have not lacked for things to do.'

Ailsa smiled. 'That's good. I hear you have even had an outing or two with Hamish.' Her smile faded. 'How is your friend, Miss Cameron? I'm so very sorry about what has happened to her. I expect the police will arrive today and sort it all out.'

'Yes,' Maud's voice was sober. She walked to the sideboard, and Andrew lifted the lid on the first silver dish. Sausages.

Maud looked at them and her stomach churned. She couldn't face anything that would sit heavily inside her this morning. She shook her head at the footman, and he replaced the lid. 'I will have just toast, thank you.'

She took a slice from the toast rack and placed it on a plate. 'Are you also feeling better today, Andrew?'

He gave her a startled glance. 'Er, yes, miss.'

Maud continued to stand there. 'I heard that you had a stomach upset yesterday evening?'

His face flushed. 'Yes, miss, but it's passed now.'

'I'm pleased to hear it.' If Andrew was going to be arrested today for spying, then she wouldn't want him to be suffering unnecessarily at the same time.

'Now the weather has improved,' Ailsa went on, as Maud took a seat at the table, 'I intend to go for a walk. I feel the need to stretch my legs.' She was dressed in her usual tweed jacket and skirt. 'I'm hoping my brother will leave his room and join me.'

'Indeed,' Maud murmured. She also hoped Magnus would be out of the castle this morning. She turned to Lord Urquhart. 'And you, my lord? What are your plans?'

'I thought I might go riding.'

'Horse or bicycle?' Maud asked, glancing with a straight face at his striped blazer.

Ailsa laughed. 'We do have two bicycles, should you wish to join Hamish. You will find them in one of the outbuildings.' She must have remembered Sergeant McNeish's corpse, for she added quickly, 'The room to the side of the larger building.'

'Would you care to join me on a short cycle ride, Miss McIntyre?' Lord Urquhart asked.

'I would.' To have his lordship to herself for a while would be perfect for her purpose. Because time was running out for Daisy, and Maud wanted answers.

TWENTY-SIX

Maud returned to her room, donned her jacket, hat and gloves, and went downstairs where Lord Urquhart was waiting.

Together they made their way round to the outbuilding. He opened the door and once again they gazed in at the Aladdin's cave. Ranged along shelves and piled on the floor stood old farming implements and rusty garden tools, tins of paint and broken flowerpots, coils of rope and wooden chests open and overflowing with objects their practical use Maud could not even guess at.

'I see the bicycles.' Lord Urquhart pulled the lady's cycle out from behind the reel lawn mower and wheeled it to where she stood in the doorway. With his thumb and forefinger, he pressed each tyre in turn. 'They're firm.'

Holding the handlebars, he ran the cycle forward, squeezed both brake levers and nodded his satisfaction when the pads met the rims of each wheel and the bicycle came to a sudden halt. He grinned and passed the cycle over to Maud. 'Try it for size.'

She sat on the saddle, slipped her right booted foot onto the pedal, keeping the other on the ground and taking care to ensure her skirt wasn't entangled in the pedals. Maud was confident on a bicycle now, as the M. McIntyre Agency had bought a machine each for her and Daisy to get about in Edinburgh on their return from solving the choir murders. They were proving to be an efficient time-saver for day-to-day investigations in the city.

As Maud waited for Lord Urquhart to bring out the gentleman's cycle and test it, an image flashed into her head of the grounds of the castle in Fort William, and of her plunging from her sabotaged bicycle into a vast rhododendron. Lord Urquhart had seen her disappearing into the shrubbery and had come to her rescue. He'd pushed his way into the greenery and murmured *I have you safe*, his arms tight about her waist. Somehow they had toppled over and as they'd lain on the earth, his body pressed against hers, she had regained her sense. Now, as then, her heart leaped into a gallop. She flushed as he looked at her, an amused smile on his lips. Oh, he remembered! she thought.

He stood astride his machine. 'Where shall we go?'

'We need to go somewhere to talk in private. I've got something to tell you and I need you to tell me everything. I need to see if there is anything to this whole mess that can be put to use to free Daisy.'

'I know just the place.' He mounted his bicycle, secured the panama more firmly on his head and raised an eyebrow. 'Are you ready?'

More than ready, she thought. She nodded and pushed off ahead of him.

A rush of air by her shoulder and Lord Urquhart passed her on the driveway. 'Do try to keep up,' he called with a laugh over his shoulder.

Maud pedalled for all she was worth. They flew along the lanes, tendrils of her hair escaping from its bun, and before long reached the little bay she had spotted earlier.

The sea was no longer turbulent, but the coastline remained beautiful and wild. Leaving their bicycles propped against a stone wall, they crossed a stretch of marram grass, walked onto the soft sand of the deserted beach and found a sheltered place to sit, their backs against a rock. Maud briefly tipped her face towards the sun, feeling its slight warmth, and breathed in the tangy sea air.

'That was exhausting, but rather thrilling.'

'I can see it in your face.' He smiled.

'Lord Urquhart, this is no time for flirting,' she said, her annoyance with him plain. 'Daisy's life hangs in the balance and it is up to me – to us – to save her. Now, forget the man-about-town façade and tell me all you know, no matter how irrelevant it may seem.'

Narrowing his eyes, he stared out to sea. 'It's not easy to know where to start.'

'Start with the statuette.'

'Very well. As I've told you, I'm here on behalf of SIS. Suspicion was already on Andrew, with his German parentage and, more compelling, his known German sympathies—'

'He hasn't tried to hide them,' Maud agreed. 'Below-stairs know of his political ideologies, if no one else does.'

'He is fool enough to voice them to the other servants?'

'He is. Quite fervently, by all accounts.'

'And how do they feel about him spreading the German doctrine?'

'I think they don't take much notice of him. The older servants think he'll grow out of it and the younger ones aren't interested.'

'I see.' Lord Urquhart straightened his long legs and stared out to sea. He took a deep breath and began his report. 'I've been keeping Andrew under surveillance since I arrived at the castle. At first, I saw nothing.

'Then, one afternoon I spotted Andrew apparently examining the statuette on the table of the great hall. It's not the job of a footman to dust, and I could think of no reason why he should have the object in his hands. To my surprise, I saw him slip a folded piece of paper behind the metal plate at the base of the statuette.'

Maud frowned. 'It must have been a very small piece of paper.'

'As soon as Andrew left the hall, I examined the bronze for myself and found a cavity behind the metal plate.'

'What did the paper have on it?' she asked eagerly.

'I wasn't able to read it at that point; Ailsa appeared and was talking about what a wonderful piece it was. Magnus had told her he might be persuaded to sell it to me, and she wanted it to go to someone who would really appreciate it. Then she drew me away for afternoon tea and the next thing we knew, it was missing. From that moment, I was under suspicion, so I wrote to you and Daisy to engage your assistance in its recovery. But since you and Daisy returned the bronze to the great hall, I've had a chance to look inside and I discovered a message written in code. I hastily made a copy and would have sent it to the experts in Edinburgh by now if the storm hadn't struck.'

'And it really was secret information?' What else could it be, she thought, written in code?

'Without a doubt. The paper contained a diagram showing Royal Navy positions off the coast of Scotland. This confirms SIS fears of a plan by Germany to destroy our Navy and invade Britain via Scotland.'

Maud could hardly believe Clachan Castle was involved in a spy ring. 'So now you had your German spy and his method of passing on information.'

'I still needed to find out whose job it was to retrieve the note from the dead letter box.'

'I think I see where this is going,' Maud murmured. 'Your skulking in the great hall in the early hours of Sunday morning?'

'Indeed.'

'Well, do tell me! Did anyone appear that night – apart from me, that is?'

'I did get a bit of a shock when you appeared,' he admitted. 'I didn't know who would come and I was afraid your being there might bring you into danger.'

Maud watched a black and white oystercatcher, searching in the sand with its long red bill for cockles, as she waited for Lord Urquhart to explain himself.

'I continued to wait in the great hall. Then something strange happened.'

Maud stared at him. 'Stranger than what you have already told me?'

'Perhaps. Like you, I couldn't sleep that night. My room faces the back of the castle and I was standing at the window, watching the storm, when I saw a light glimmering through the trees. Curious, I continued to watch, wondering where it was coming from on such a night, when I realised the light was intermittent. And then it occurred to me it was signalling in code.'

'Morse code?' The high-pitched piping of the oystercatcher and the roar of the sea breaking on the beach faded into the background as he went on.

'Correct, Miss McIntyre. So I stayed where I was in the hope that I'd see more and I did. After a pause, the message started again from the beginning. Dot-dash-dot. That's r. Then a single dot for e. Dash-dot-dash-dot represents c—'

'R-E-C...'

'And so on, until it spelled the word—'

'Received?'

'Yes, exactly. I was witnessing an exchange of Morse code. It appeared that our friend Andrew was signalling from his room in the attic to whoever hid amongst the trees. I assumed Andrew's communication informed the next person in the chain that the note was ready to be collected and now the other person was acknowledging his message.'

'It must have caused them some trepidation given the wildness of the storm that night.' This was even more exciting than the mystery stories she read. 'Have you discovered who was the person sending the reply?'

'Ah, so now we are coming to it. None other than a short, elderly lady in a mackintosh and waterproof hat.'

'Good heavens!' The memory of the conversation Daisy had reported with the gardener's boy came back to Maud. 'So not a bogle, after all.'

'I'm sorry?'

'Peddie told Daisy that twice he's seen the ghost of an old lady in the grounds of the castle.'

'Who is Peddie?'

'The gardener's boy.'

'Well, if he'd had a good look at her, he'd have seen her waterproof clothing. She was still wearing the hat and coat when she came into the great hall. I watched her walk over to the statuette on the table and remove the note from its hiding place.'

'Did you follow her?'

'I was in my night attire, not for trailing the woman through trees in my dressing gown and slippers in the middle of a storm.'

'I think a spy must forego propriety. Do you know the identity of the elderly lady?' A suspicion was growing in Maud's mind.

'It has to be someone who lives close enough to see and return a signal.'

'And one who knows Morse code. Did you see anything that could identify her?'

'Nothing, it was dark.'

Maud sighed.

'Oh, I remember, she was wearing something bright around her neck.'

'Could it have been a scarf?'

'It could have.'

'What colour was it?'

'Possibly gold.'

'Or yellow?' Maud fixed him with her steady gaze.

'Do you know who it is?'

Maud smiled, now certain. 'Shieling Beag!'

'I beg your pardon?'

'It's a cottage near the end of the castle drive. That's where Peddie's Grey Lady lives. Finlay told me that Ailsa's retired lady's maid lives in the grounds in a cottage known as Shieling Beag.'

'You seem to know a lot, Miss McIntyre.'

'Below-stairs are always a fount of information. And I've met our Grey Lady. Daisy and I almost ran into her yesterday morning.'

'Daisy was out of the castle?'

'She's Daisy, what do you expect?'

Lord Urquhart seemed stunned for a second. He shook his head. 'You're right. I should expect no less from Miss Cameron. Perhaps I should recruit her to do my job.'

'As to how the Grey Lady was able to enter the castle, you will have to ask Ailsa. Possibly Lizzie – that's her name, by the way – has a key to the back door. Now, why might an elderly lady know Morse code?'

'Perhaps her father or grandfather was in the Royal Navy. That will be easy enough for the SIS to ascertain.'

Maud looked at Lord Urquhart. 'There now, I have solved your case for you. It's your turn to help me solve mine.'

A thought struck Maud. 'Why did you not confront Lizzie that night?'

'I didn't want to disturb the household and, in the process, frighten off Andrew. The information she took is safe. No one has been able to leave the island and I will inform the police when they arrive today.'

A gull shrieked overhead. Suddenly chilled, Maud rubbed her arms through her woollen jacket to bring back some warmth.

'You are cold,' Lord Urquhart said. 'We should return to the castle.'

She shook her head. 'Not yet.' She needed to think matters through and the fresh air was helping.

'Here.' He shrugged off his blazer. 'This will help,' he said, his voice oddly hoarse as he wrapped his large jacket around her shoulders.

She caught the warm smell of him, felt his broad chest against her back, his breath on her neck.

'Thank you.' She forced herself to focus on the investigation. The end was so close now. The spy in the castle was fascinating, but she must not be distracted by it. The killer was Dr Munro, Maud would stake her life on it.

She must bring the murder cases to a swift conclusion. But how had the doctor accomplished the deaths? Not just entry and exit, but also the implement he'd used. Think, Maud, think, she urged herself. The man's bag had been searched and it contained nothing suitable, nothing sharp enough.

Now she thought of it, there was nothing sharp at all in the bag, which was suspicious. Surely a doctor usually routinely carried a scalpel or a hypodermic syringe...

A syringe! Such an implement would be capable of inflicting the type of wound both victims had suffered. No such item had been found in the bag... Suddenly, the idea of how Dr Munro had managed that trick came to her. And a fine trick it was!

Maud jumped to her feet. 'We need to return to the castle!'

. . .

'Daisy, open up! I believe I have it!' Daisy flung open her door and dragged Maud inside. 'He used a *trick bag*!'

Daisy hastily removed her luncheon tray, the food half-eaten, from the armchair opposite her and put it on the writing table. 'Sit down and tell me everything.'

'The doctor.' Maud sank into the chair and pulled off her gloves. Her hat came after it and she dropped them on to the floor. 'Dr Munro murdered both men using a hypodermic syringe.'

'That would make a pin-prick hole in the body, right enough.' Daisy drew her brows together. 'But he was searched and there was nae syringe in his bag or his pocket.'

'That's what I'm telling you. He used a trick bag. The kind used by conjurers.'

Realisation dawned on Daisy's face and she gasped. 'With a false bottom!'

'Exactly!' Maud leaned forward, the better to explain her theory. 'A conjurer's bag looks very similar to a medical bag. You remember how Mr Mutrie demonstrated one to us in his theatrical shop a few months ago?'

'Aye.' Daisy's eyes shone. 'He put it over a wee box on the table and the bag snapped it up. You think that's what Dr Munro did: put his bag – a conjuror's one – over his syringe on Neil's nightstand?'

'I do. He knew Tremain would be at the dinner that night and was determined to take his revenge. I'm sure if we asked Mr Mutrie, he would tell us that a trick bag had been requested by mail order from an address in Tobermory. The doctor came with this bag when he stabbed Tremain. He realised the possibility of being searched and couldn't risk carrying it in his genuine doctor's bag.'

'I wonder why Neil didna wake and cry out?'

'Do you?' Maud settled back in the chair and waited for Daisy to work it out. It took her only a second or two.

'Maybe,' Daisy exclaimed as it came to her, 'it wasna bicarbonate of soda the doctor had given him the previous evening.'

'That would certainly explain things. Isobel said she'd handed the drum of powder to Dr Munro but hadn't seen him *actually* mix it.'

'Wouldna Neil have noticed if the doctor had given him a different powder?'

'Not if he were lying in bed and in some pain from the heartburn.'

'What about Andrew, then? Wouldna he have noticed if the doctor had changed the powder?'

'Not necessarily. Andrew said that he was in Tremain's bedroom when Dr Munro made up the mixture – not that he actually saw the man do it. A valet would be too busy about the bedchamber: tidying up, brushing clothes and putting them away. And besides, we now know from Lord Urquhart that Andrew would have had other things on his mind. It probably wouldn't have been too difficult for the doctor to use sleight of hand to replace the bicarbonate of soda with something much stronger.'

'Strong enough to knock Neil out so that he didna wake in the morning when Dr Munro broke into the room and did the deed.'

'That's exactly it, Daisy.'

Even as she spoke, Maud fell back in the chair, ice-cold with shock. Her head felt light as she stared at Daisy.

Dear God, then that must mean...

TWENTY-SEVEN

Daisy started forward from her chair. 'What is it, Maud? You've gone white.'

'You remember when the doctor first pulled the bed sheet over Tremain's head?' Maud's mouth was dry. 'You said you thought you'd seen it move a little?'

'Aye.'

'And I said perhaps there was a draught from a secret panel?'

Daisy nodded. 'And we went looking for it, found a secret cupboard and the bronze lion.' She was watching Maud's face carefully.

'Yes. And in our delight at finding it, we forgot about the significance of the draught...'

Daisy's face became as pale as Maud's; she gave a little choke. 'Are you saying you think when I saw the sheet move, Neil Tremain was in a drugged state and still alive?'

Maud swallowed. 'I think when the doctor was supposedly examining a dead Tremain, he was in fact *killing* him.'

'Using a hypodermic needle.' Daisy put a hand on her chest.

'Oh Daisy, how could we not have realised what was happening before our very eyes?'

'He covered what he was doing with his own body.' Daisy's eyes grew large. 'Murdering a man with people watching takes a lot of nerve. How are we going to prove it?'

'There will be a post-mortem on both men and no doubt the one on Tremain will show the presence of whatever substance Dr Munro used on him. It must have been something powerful, for Tremain still to be drugged so heavily the next morning. And there's the murder of Sergeant McNeish.'

Shock jogged Daisy's memory. 'You ken, Maud, I'm pretty sure the doctor was the last one out of the sergeant's room that afternoon.'

Maud studied Daisy's face. Was this sudden recollection on Daisy's part just wishful thinking, the desire to prove Dr Munro's guilt? Maud's wasn't sure, but she felt certain she, too, could picture Dr Munro ushering everyone out of the room.

'I believe you're right, Daisy. It would have taken him no time at all to puncture the officer's heart with the syringe. It was an opportunistic attack. I don't think he initially planned to kill Sergeant McNeish, but the policeman's comment in his room shortly before he was murdered, that he was seriously considering another suspect, put the wind up Munro. The syringe had proved to be such an efficient weapon in his attack on Tremain, the doctor must have put it in his pocket as a safety measure.'

'And Sandy McNeish wouldna have been expecting it. He'd have put up no resistance, the puir man.'

'Dr Munro couldn't have known you would return to retrieve your notebook. He'd had only a little time to carry out his murderous task, which explains why his second murder wasn't as clean as his first. If he'd stayed in the room any longer, his absence would have been noticed and suspicion would naturally fall on him.'

'But instead it fell on me.'

'I'm afraid so, my friend. No doubt he could hardly believe his luck. Almost the perfect crime. If you can't make a body disappear, get someone else to take the blame.'

'But would he do that? Let me go to the gallows, him being a doctor and all?'

'Who knows the working of a mind that saves with one hand and murders with the other.' A thought came to Maud. 'Do you remember the dinner conversation that first night, when Dr Munro wanted to talk about the criminal mind?'

'And Tremain asked if it was possible for a person to kill and otherwise be a decent person?' Daisy slowly nodded. 'Each man was thinking about their own hand in another's death.'

'So,' she said after a little while, 'we ken how the doctor killed the two men, and why Neil Tremain didna wake when the bedroom door burst open, but nae how the door could have been locked the night before, since he was already heavily drugged.'

'We must think hard, Daisy. Let's run through the series of events again.'

'I dinna need my notebook for this. I've thought about it so often that I could recite it in my sleep. Andrew couldna get a reply to his knocking on Neil's door, and it was the same when Magnus appeared and banged on the door and shouted loud enough to bring the rest of us from our rooms to see what the stushie was about. The doctor arrived a few minutes later.'

'When he heard what all the noise was about,' said Maud, picking up the story, 'he suggested Tremain was asleep. Do you remember, Daisy, Munro looked relieved?'

Daisy nodded fervently.

'Then he knocked on the door and still there was no response. So he tried the handle and found the door was locked, as he'd been told it was.'

'Something else about the doctor, Maud. You mind he

peered through the keyhole and said he couldna seeing anything because it was covered by the door curtain?'

'I remember.'

'Do you nae think that was a strange thing to say? I mean, why would he immediately think the curtain had been pulled across the door and nae it was the key in the lock blocking it?'

Maud felt excitement build within her as she realised what Daisy was suggesting. 'The doctor said that because he *knew* the door curtain had been drawn across! Which means—'

'He also knew the key wasna in the lock!' Daisy looked justifiably pleased with herself. 'Who suggested the door should be broken down?'

'It was Lord Urquhart.' Maud remembered that distinctly. 'He offered to do it, but the doctor didn't give him the opportunity – he stepped forward and forced the door himself. It was a crucial part of his plan that he was the one to open the door.'

'And nae one but the doctor touched him. Neil was lying on his bed under the sheet and Dr Munro went into the darkened room with Andrew behind him. The doctor put his bag on the floor and spoke to Neil. He touched his shoulder, but Neil didna move.'

'Then,' continued Maud, 'he asked Andrew to open the shutter for some light and he bent over Tremain. When Andrew was too shocked to do as he'd been bid, Lord Urquhart stepped into the room and unlatched the shutters. It must have been during this time that Dr Munro removed the syringe from his pocket and punctured Tremain's heart. Then he put the needle on the nightstand and covered it with the trick bag.'

'Aye. The doctor finished his so-called examination of his patient and said, "I'm afraid Tremain is dead." *Pleased*, more like.'

'It was when he straightened up that I saw the patch of blood on Tremain's nightshirt. And then he quickly pulled the bed sheet up and over his victim's head.'

'Which is when I saw the cover move a wee bit. Dr Munro had done that so that the puir man's final gasp of breath wasna seen by anyone.'

'Except that you did spot it, Daisy.' Maud smiled at her friend.

'But I didna speak out,' Daisy replied sadly.

'Even if you had done so immediately, it couldn't have saved Tremain. His blood was already leaking into his heart cavity.'

'But it might have saved Sandy.'

They both fell silent. Maud was the first to speak again. 'The important thing now,' she said, the need to console her friend in the forefront of her mind, 'is that we have solved the case and Dr Munro can be brought to justice.'

Daisy nodded. 'You're right. So, now we get everyone together in the great hall, including the killer himself?'

'Yes. Munro will be here for luncheon at one o'clock.' Maud glanced up at the clock on the mantle over the fire. 'It's almost time; everyone will be gathered.' Maud stood up from her chair. 'Put on your cobalt-blue linen dress, Daisy. We will go down together. You've been in this room for long enough.'

TWENTY-EIGHT

Maud and Daisy went down the stairs and into the great hall. Magnus, Ailsa, Lord Urquhart, Jane and Dr Munro were all there, standing about and talking. One by one, they turned to the detective duo.

The ladies of the M. McIntyre Agency bestowed gracious smiles on everyone. Magnus frowned at Daisy and opened his mouth to speak.

But before he could do so, Maud said, 'Mr Carmichael, could you please ask the servants to come up here? I'm sure they need to hear what Miss Cameron and I have to say as much as anyone else.'

Magnus spluttered but said nothing. He stomped over to the door leading down into the kitchens, flung it open and bellowed down the stairs, 'Finlay!'

A clatter was heard from below and Magnus's man came running up the stairs and into the great hall, kilt flapping about his legs. He drew to a halt and straightened his sporran.

'Tell Mrs Baillie to delay luncheon and get everyone up here,' Magnus growled.

'Sir?' Finlay's startled eyes travelled from Magnus's thunderous expression, around the bemused features of the others in the silent room and came to rest on Maud.

She smiled encouragingly at him. 'I feel sure the household servants would also like to know who murdered Mr Tremain and Sergeant McNeish.'

'What are you saying?' Magnus took a few quick steps towards Maud, before Lord Urquhart blocked his way.

'Just that, Mr Carmichael,' she replied. 'Miss Cameron and I have solved the case.'

Magnus snorted.

'Bring them up, Finlay.' Ailsa's usually clear voice shook.

Finlay shot from the room, and Maud spoke again. 'Now, if you could all bear with us for a moment, we're going to start with everyone's position on the morning Mr Tremain's body was found.'

Maud took care not to say *on the morning he was murdered*, for that would immediately alert Dr Munro. If luck was with them, their revelation of Munro's guilt would come at the exact moment the police arrived to arrest the doctor.

She turned to a very pale Jane Tremain and suddenly felt sorry for the silly girl. 'I hope this won't be too distressing for you, Miss Tremain?'

'I want to know who the murderer is.'

Maud put a comforting arm around Jane's trembling shoulders to steady her.

Daisy waved towards the oblong side table standing against the wall. 'If you gentlemen could bring that forward, please. Take care not to damage the statuette; it also has a part to play.' She gave her instructions in a loud, clear voice as if she were directing a couple of footmen, which Lord Urquhart and Dr Munro followed without complaint.

When the table had been moved away from the wall, she added, 'Lord Urquhart, would you mind moving one of those high-backed chairs to the other side of this table? Not too close, maybe six feet away.'

He did so, while the others looked on. He stood back. 'Like so?'

'Perfect, thank you.' Daisy smiled graciously and went on. 'The table represents Neil Tremain's bedroom door. It's not ideal, but it will have to do. If Mr Carmichael could stand by this pretend door where he had been knocking and getting no reply. And Lord Urquhart, perhaps you could stand close by.'

Oh, well done, Daisy, Maud thought, impressed with her partner's professionalism.

The two men had just assumed their positions when the servants almost tumbled into the great hall, their faces alight with a mixture of nervousness and expectation.

'We are recreating the events of Saturday morning,' Maud told them by way of greeting. 'The table is standing in for Mr Tremain's bedroom door.'

'Now,' continued Daisy, 'we need Miss Carmichael and Jane to stand by, not too far from the gentlemen; and Andrew and Finlay, a little further back as if in the passage.'

When they were in place, Maud added, 'Can everyone else who came upstairs that morning stand behind them, as if further down the corridor, please.'

There were murmurings and shuffling as the servants took their places. Dr Munro, standing by the hearth, removed the tobacco tin from his pocket, took out a cigarette and placed it between his lips. Lifting a spill from the mantelpiece, he held it in the flames and lit his cigarette.

'Can you remember what you did at this point, Mr Carmichael?' Maud asked.

'I called through the door something like "Are you all right?" and then "Open up".'

'Then Miss Cameron and I approached and asked Finlay what the trouble was and you, Finlay, told us...?'

'That Andrew had brought up Mr Tremain's can of hot water, found the door locked and he couldn't get a reply. And that Andrew had left the gentleman for a further twenty minutes or so, thinking him still asleep, but when he returned he still couldn't get a reply. Which is when I thought the laird should be informed.'

Maud turned towards Dr Munro. 'I see you have brought your medical bag,' she said, glancing at where he had set it beside the armchair by the fire. 'That will fit in nicely with our reconstruction.'

He smiled. 'I never go anywhere without it. A doctor is always on call, you know.'

'Indeed. Can you tell us where you were at this point?'

He drew on his cigarette and stepped forward. 'Having let myself in to the castle, I came up the stairs and along the second-floor corridor, following the sounds of a commotion, and asked if Mr Tremain had been taken ill again.'

'What did you do next?' Maud asked.

The doctor appeared to think. 'I seem to remember being told he wasn't responding to the calls and knocks on the door, so I called out and tried the handle, to no avail.' He thought some more. 'I tried to look through the keyhole, but it was covered by the door curtain.'

Maud resisted the strong temptation to send a significant glance towards Daisy.

'Not by the key being in the lock?' her assistant asked in an innocent voice.

'Well, of course, it could have been that,' he replied. 'I just assumed it was the curtain blocking the view.'

Was his face flushed? He had been standing by the roaring fire, but Maud thought it was more than that.

'Then I offered to force the door,' put in Lord Urquhart.

Maud raised an enquiring eyebrow at Dr Munro. 'But I think you were the one to do it, doctor?'

'Yes. It took me a couple of attempts, but then the door flew open.'

'I stepped forward into the doorway and saw a motionless figure in the bed,' said Maud.

'I called out "Papa!"' added Jane in a low voice. She wiped her eyes with a handkerchief.

'Do we have to continue this?' Dr Munro demanded. 'It was distressing enough at the time for Miss Tremain, without her having to go over it again.'

'No, I want to continue.' Jane's voice was firmer.

'Very well.' Dr Munro walked back towards the hearth and flicked his cigarette into the fire. 'I then entered the room' – he indicated towards Andrew – 'with the valet immediately behind me. Tremain didn't move as I approached the bed...'

Maud gestured for him to move to the chair representing the bed and to continue his account.

'He also didn't respond when I touched his shoulder,' the doctor reached out a hand towards the chair, then snatched it away, 'or when I turned him to lie on his back. It was already too late for him.'

Too late *for him*. It was clear to Maud that Munro had made up his mind long ago that Tremain must die.

Dr Munro gave a loud sigh.

Maud fixed him with steely eyes. 'Please, carry on.'

'Is this really necessary?'

All eyes in the room flitted from the doctor to her and back.

He gave a slight shrug. 'I told the valet to open the shutters as I needed more light to examine the patient, to be certain he was dead.'

Yes, you wanted to ensure he had died, she thought darkly.

'I had to repeat my request to open the shutters as the valet seemed unable to move.'

'Andrew was in a state of shock,' put in Lord Urquhart, 'so I performed the task.'

The embarrassed Andrew sent Lord Urquhart a grateful look.

The doctor shuddered as he stared down at the empty makeshift bed. 'When Lord Urquhart opened the window, I checked for signs of life. I felt no breath from his mouth or pulse behind his ear, so I pronounced him dead.'

'And the blood on his nightshirt?'

'It did not immediately concern me. There was so little of it, I thought it a splash from a shaving cut.' The doctor turned away.

'Just a moment, Dr Munro,' Daisy said. 'You've forgotten something. Your medical bag. Where was it when all this was happening?'

He blinked at her. 'What an extraordinary question, young lady.'

'Nonetheless,' Magnus said tersely, 'please answer the young woman, so we can get this charade over.'

'Let me try to remember the exact sequence, since you seem to think it so important... I put my bag on the nightstand, then ordered the shutters be opened and drew back the sheet ready to carry out my examination.'

'I don't think that's quite right, doctor,' Maud said.

Now the doctor did flush. 'Really, I cannot think that it matters.'

'Miss McIntyre and I like to get our facts in order,' Daisy chipped in. 'I mind that you put your bag on the floor by the bed. Then you'd pulled back the sheet and *then* moved your medical bag onto the nightstand and told Andrew to open the shutters.'

'You could well be right, but I don't see what diff—'

'She is correct, Roderick. I remember thinking that it was a sensible thing to do since you might trip over it while you were tending to Neil,' Magnus said. 'I have gone over many times in my mind the sequence of events from that morning.'

Silence fell. Maud examined her memory, as no doubt did everyone else who'd had a view of the goings-on in Neil Tremain's room. Then the doctor finally spoke.

'As I said earlier, after I was satisfied he was no long breathing, I pronounced him dead. That's all there is to say.'

'Not quite,' Daisy went on. 'After you drew the sheet back up over Neil Tremain's face, I saw it move a wee bit. At first, I thought there must be a draught from a secret panel—'

The doctor gave an unpleasant laugh. 'You ladies have such active imaginations.'

'It was only later,' Daisy continued, ignoring his comment, 'that Miss McIntyre and I realised exactly what that flutter of the sheet meant.'

All this time Jane had remained in her position next to Ailsa, but now she stepped forward, her body visibly shaking. 'What are you saying, Miss Cameron?'

'Do you want to tell us yourself, Dr Munro?' Daisy suggested.

'I need to sit down for a moment,' he said, his voice faint. 'I don't feel too well.' He lowered himself into the chair representing Tremain's deathbed, before realising what he had done. Instantly, he was back up as if the chair had propelled him out of the seat. Everyone watched the doctor move to the fire and sit in one of the great armchairs.

'I don't believe it's him,' muttered the cook.

Kirsty snorted. 'Why not? Because he's a doctor?'

'While Dr Munro is considering his response,' Maud said, 'Miss Cameron and I will recount how we came to our conclusion.'

'You haven't told us your conclusion yet,' put in Kirsty.

'I think I'll leave it to Dr Munro to provide that.' In the absence of the police, Maud wanted the man to confess and in front of witnesses.

'Meanwhile,' Daisy said, 'we'll take you back to Friday

night, when Neil Tremain suffered from an attack of heartburn. It was sheer bad luck for him, and good luck for Dr Munro, that the doctor had been invited to dinner that night. Dr Munro was already in Tremain's room when Isobel brought up a glass of water and the bicarbonate of soda—'

'It *was* bicarbonate, miss!' blurted the maid, on the verge of tears. 'It said so on the label.'

'No one doubts that, Isobel,' Maud said. 'Please, don't distress yourself.'

'Here, Isobel,' murmured the cook, pulling a handkerchief from a pocket under her apron and handing it to her daughter.

'While Andrew was busy going about his valeting duties,' Daisy went on, 'the killer changed the harmless powder for something else – likely an opiate. We'll know which when the post-mortem is done on Neil Tremain's body.'

'I'll be doing the post-mortem tomorrow.' Dr Munro seemed to be recovering his poise.

Maud picked up the story. 'Mr Tremain had told Andrew he would lock his bedroom door when the valet had left, but the opiate sent Tremain almost immediately into a drugged sleep.'

'Are you saying the door was never locked?' Magnus's tone made it clear he didn't believe her. 'I tried the handle a number of times and I can assure you that it was.'

'Oh yes, it was locked, but not by Mr Tremain. Had he been able to stir himself sufficiently to lock the bedroom door, he would have found the key was not in the lock. It had been secretly taken by the killer. He – the killer – came back later to check on his handiwork, lock the door and draw the door curtain across on his way out of the room.'

'I don't understand.' Ailsa said what everyone else was thinking, judging by the expressions on their faces.

'I am saying that later that evening, when the killer returned to Tremain's room, he locked it from the *outside*.'

Magnus frowned. 'And left him alive? Why not stab him there and then?'

Jane gasped and Ailsa helped her to a chair, making sure it was not close to the doctor who remained seated by the hearth.

Magnus went on, 'I mean, why wait until the following morning?'

'To provide an alibi for himself,' Daisy said. 'Which is where our story started.'

Dr Munro's name had not been mentioned, but now every pair of eyes in the room was staring at him.

'The killer returned that morning as promised, and broke into the locked room, which everyone assumed to be secured from the inside.' The enormity of Maud's words was becoming clear to the gathering. 'He made sure he was the first person into Mr Tremain's room in the morning. His next job was to deal appropriately with the key, so he dropped it onto the rug on his way in. This made it appear that the door had been locked from the inside and the key had fallen out when the door burst open.'

'That's clever,' said Magnus, unable to keep a touch of admiration out of his voice, 'although reprehensible,' he added quickly.

'A clever plan indeed,' Maud had to admit. 'But the killer had not counted on an investigation by the M. McIntyre Agency.' She drew a breath and continued. 'Andrew saw what he expected to see – a dead body – and, shocked, naturally hung back. As the murderer supposedly examined a dead man, he murdered a sleeping one by plunging a hypodermic needle into his victim's heart.'

Dr Munro looked up, a glimmer of hope in his features. 'That's impossible. No opiate or syringe was found in his bag or in his pockets when searched by the police officer.'

How extraordinary, Maud thought; the doctor was talking about himself in the third person. 'No, they were not, Dr

Munro, and that should have struck me earlier as strange – a doctor would usually carry such items, would he not? And yet there weren't any in your bag.'

In the silence that followed, a motor horn sounded thrice, coming nearer and nearer.

'That must be the Procurator Fiscal,' Magnus said. 'He's the only person in Tobermory who owns a motor car. See to the door, Finlay.'

Everyone's eyes followed Finlay as he headed to the lobby. No one moved as the sound of tyres rolling to a stop on the gravel drifted up from the open front door. The slam of a car door held the gathering spellbound; all except Maud and Daisy who kept their attention firmly on the sweating Dr Munro. The loud knocking on the heavy castle door was too much for the doctor's taut nerves.

He sprang to his feet.

TWENTY-NINE

Maud snatched the doctor's bag from the floor; she must act now. She turned to stand before the gathering.

'This is a trick bag.' She spoke quickly, her voice ringing loud and clear in the great room. 'In the semi-darkness of Mr Tremain's room, Dr Munro took the hypodermic syringe from his pocket and with breathtaking audacity stabbed Mr Tremain as some of us looked on. He then ordered the shutters to be opened, and while this was being done, he put the syringe on the nightstand and placed this bag on top of it. It's a method employed by magicians: engage your audience with one hand while the other is working the trick.'

As she spoke, she turned the bag over and pressed the handle to reveal the bottom of the bag snapping open. 'The base is equipped with a spring-grip device, which snaps up into the bag the item it is placed on.' She glanced at the doctor, who was glaring at her, breathing heavily.

'After he had confirmed Tremain's demise to us all,' Maud went on, 'he picked up his bag and with it took the evidence of his guilt. No doubt the opiate container used the previous evening was disposed of in the same way.'

Dr Munro pulled a small metal tin from his pocket and flipped open the lid. He wrenched out the syringe nestling inside and waved it round the great hall.

The smell of bitter almonds reached Maud's nostrils. '*Cyanide!*'

'Yes, Miss McIntyre. Cyanide. This has been most entertaining, but I'm afraid I must leave now.' He began to edge away from the hearth and out of the room, towards the door leading down to the servants' floor and unrestricted access to the outside. 'If anyone tries to stop me, I will inject them.' He scanned the gathering in the great hall. 'Just so you know, cyanide is a fast-acting chemical that interferes with the body's ability to use oxygen. I have ensured there is sufficient poison in here for it to be immediately fatal.'

Lord Urquhart took a step towards him.

'*Hamish!*' Maud screamed. '*Don't!*'

Footsteps pounded up the stairs from the front of the castle. Still facing the gathering, Dr Munro felt behind him. The door opened, he gave a final flourish of the cyanide-filled syringe and backed out of the hall, slamming the door behind him. There was a scraping noise as he wedged something under the door to hold it fast.

Lord Urquhart darted forward and turned the handle. He put his shoulder to the door and pushed. The wedge seemed to give a little.

'I'll do that, Hamish.' Magnus rushed forward as if his youth had suddenly returned to him. 'That blighter called me friend and ate at my table.'

'No, let me, Magnus. I have more body weight.'

Two police officers burst into the great hall, followed by the Procurator Fiscal and Finlay.

The senior officer touched his helmet at Magnus. 'What exactly is happening here?'

'The killer is Dr Munro, officer, and he has just escaped that way.' Maud pointed to where Lord Urquhart was trying to force open the door.

The policeman looked doubtful.

'For goodness' sake, *hurry!*' Magnus shouted. 'He's going to get out through the rear door.'

'Off you go, men,' bellowed the Fiscal, 'around the back. Don't let him get away.'

'Sir.' The senior policeman touched his helmet to William Greig and both officers dashed back towards the lobby and out of the great hall.

Maud flew in the other direction towards Lord Urquhart. She put a hand on his arm as she heard footsteps running back up the stairs. 'Listen, he's going *up* stairs, not down. He must have realised the police are going to the back of the castle and fears being caught there.'

'It's madness to think he can escape from the roof,' exclaimed Lord Urquhart, slamming himself into the door once more. The wedged door finally gave way and it scraped open.

'This way!' Daisy darted past them and sped up the stone stairs.

Maud followed, with Lord Urquhart at her heels, round and round as the staircase wound upwards, to the sound of doors being thrown open on the attic floor above.

'Hurry, Maud!' Daisy called.

Maud and Lord Urquhart emerged onto the dusty attic corridor and saw a short, narrow flight of stairs. At the top a low door hung open where Daisy stood agitated, looking out.

'He's on the roof!' she shrieked. 'I'm going after him. Go and get one of your Indian clubs, Maud. You can fling it at him.'

Before Maud or Lord Urquhart could stop her, Daisy had disappeared through the door.

'I'm coming too!' Maud cried.

'It's too dangerous.' Lord Urquhart put a hand on her arm. 'I will go.'

Maud shook him off. 'I must. Daisy is my *friend*.'

'And you are more than that to me!'

But Maud was already running up the wooden stairs, dashing cobwebs from her hair. She emerged through the low doorway to stand on a flat, leaded section of the roof. Here was the flagpole she had seen from the ground on the day of their arrival, the Carmichael colours now hanging limply in the still air. The pungent smell of damp slates hit her nostrils.

Beyond the level section where Maud stood, the roof rose huge and sprawling, ridged with slates, tower and great chimneys soaring into the watery afternoon sky. Daisy's petite frame scrambled confidently across the rooftop, following Dr Munro's more uncertain progress.

'*Munro!*' Lord Urquhart called by Maud's side. 'Stop! You can't escape and will only kill yourself.'

An unpleasant laugh was the doctor's only response. The two figures continued across the sloping roof.

'He must be making for the maintenance ladder.' Maud set out after them. She knew she had a good sense of balance from her ballet routines, but yellow lichen blossomed across the slates and one booted foot slipped out from under her. 'Oh!'

'I have you.' Lord Urquhart's arm slid round her waist and kept her upright.

'Thank you,' she gasped, her heart thudding in her chest. She glanced down from the rooftop and wished she had not. Between herself and the ground was close to one hundred feet of air.

Take care, she told herself, and make haste. *And please God, look after Daisy and Hamish.*

Ahead of them the doctor was going more slowly now; she suspected exhaustion was making itself felt. He crawled down a slated incline towards the leaded gutters at the edge of the roof and halted when he reached the maintenance ladder.

Daisy continued moving towards him, talking to him. As

Maud and Lord Urquhart drew closer, scrambling over the slates, they heard what she was saying.

'Give yourself up, doctor,' she coaxed.

He climbed to his feet and stood unsteadily, one hand on a chimney stack. 'To be hanged? I don't think so.'

'The court might show mercy. You're a good doctor—'

He gave that grating laugh again. '*Primum non nocere.*'

'First do no harm,' Maud murmured, as she and Hamish reached Daisy.

Dr Munro gave Maud a sour glance. 'Exactly. A doctor takes the Hippocratic oath, promising not only to refrain from causing harm but also to live an exemplary life. What is the chance of the court showing clemency in my case?'

'You never know,' Daisy said. 'I'm sure a lot of people will speak to your good name.'

Dr Munro glanced down at the long drop below him. 'Then instead of hanging, I'd be sentenced to penal servitude. Years of breaking rocks in the quarry at Peterhead Prison. No, thank you, that's not for me.'

Tears came to his eyes. 'Tremain killed my daughter, you know. He knocked her down in his motor car and my poor beautiful little girl died. She was only four years old. I've been told she ran out in front of him, but he should have taken greater care driving that thing through the streets of Glasgow. When my dear wife could no longer bear her thoughts of self-recrimination she took her own life. He killed my entire family.'

The tears now flowed down his face. 'I moved from Glasgow to Mull to get away from the memories of all I'd lost, but the overwhelming pain of loss followed me. And then one day I learned Tremain was a friend of Magnus's and that he was to visit the castle. I was invited to dine with them and I started to make my plans.'

Revenge, thought Maud, was supposed to be a dish best

served cold, but in her experience it was best not partaken of at all.

'It was easy that night to pretend to use the bicarbonate of soda.' The doctor laughed, a wild, sobbing sound. 'Instead, I administered a strong opiate while the valet busied himself about the room. I was relying on Tremain not recognising me at dinner and the self-centred fool had no idea. It hadn't been easy to puncture Tremain's heart the following morning with people around, but just as you said, I bent over him in the gloom with my back to all of you looking on from the doorway. The fluttering you saw, Miss Cameron, was something I'd hoped to hide: Tremain's last exhalation.' He pulled out his handkerchief, wiped his cheeks and blew his nose. 'The plan was flawless. What I hadn't bargained on was two female detectives in our midst.'

'And Sergeant McNeish?' Maud prompted gently. 'Why did you have to kill him? He had done you no harm.'

'He had to go because I guessed it was only a matter of time before he linked Tremain with the death of my family and realised I was the killer. I left his room with the rest of you, but I made sure I was the last out and stabbed him in the heart too. I don't regret killing Tremain, but I am sorry about McNeish.'

The doctor's eyes strayed towards the maintenance ladder. Maud's gaze followed. From what she could see, the metal had rusted badly. 'It's not safe,' she told him.

'I have nothing left to live for but the hangman's noose. No, my death will be at my own hands.' He attempted a smile. 'I've always wondered how it would be to fly.'

The doctor let go of the chimney and stepped closer to the edge.

Lord Urquhart's hand shot out to grab him. The doctor jerked away, plunging his hand into his pocket to retrieve the hypodermic syringe. Daisy kicked his arm, her boot making contact with his elbow. As he gasped, Maud knocked the syringe from his hand. It went skittering down the slates and came to rest in the lead gutter. Hamish took a firm hold of the doctor's arm.

'Too late, my lord,' Dr Munro said wryly. 'The needle went into my hand.' He held out his open palm to show a tiny spot of welling blood. 'I have only a few seconds before the first symptoms begin: headache, dizziness, my heart rate increasing, nausea, shortness of breath...' Already he was showing signs of difficulty in breathing. 'Then my heart rate will slow, my blood pressure drop, I will lose consciousness and suffer cardiac arrest.'

'We must get you to a doctor quickly.' Daisy went to take hold of his other arm, before realising the irony of what she had said.

He slowly shook his head. 'I'm going nowhere. I just need to sit. It won't take long.' As he sank to his knees, he fell against the chimney stack and a dark glossy swallow, on its way to Africa for the winter, flew chattering out of a crevice. It took to the sky, its long tail streaming behind, as the doctor crumpled to the slates.

Dr Munro's eyes followed the bird's flight as his life slipped quietly away.

THIRTY

'Well,' said Daisy softly, 'he didna get to fly, but maybe his soul went with that bird.'

Maud put her arm around Daisy. 'That's a lovely thought, my brave friend.'

Lord Urquhart removed his blazer and covered the dead man's face. 'I heard what you said to him, Miss Cameron, and you are correct. He was a good man, turned bad by sad events in his life.'

'Come on,' said Daisy. 'We'd best return to the great hall and tell everyone what has happened up here.'

Lord Urquhart followed Maud and Daisy back over the slates, and they all made their way through the low door and down the short wooden staircase.

'I must say, that was an impressive kick, Daisy,' Maud observed as they crossed the attic corridor and descended the stairs.

'Och, that! It was naething.' Daisy blushed and beamed, giving the lie to her words. 'I've been following Miss Domleo's drill lessons. I found her book, *The Syllabus of Physical Exercises for Public Elementary Schools*, in Edinburgh library.'

Maud was surprised. 'I know how you loath exercise. What do these exercises involve?'

'Marching on the spot, arm swinging, skipping, balancing and so on, and with nae danger of hitting yourself with a wooden club. They've been awfa useful to help keep up my strength when I was under room arrest.'

'Useful for balance when we were on the roof just now,' Maud added thoughtfully.

'Aye, I felt a bit shoogly, but I managed.'

'You didn't look at all unsteady.' Maud smiled. 'So the exercises were the reason for the thumps I've heard on occasion coming from your room.'

Lord Urquhart laughed. 'You are a very resourceful young lady, Miss Cameron. As are you, Miss McIntyre.' He smiled at them both.

Was the smile he gave Maud a little wider than that he'd given Daisy? Maud thought so.

They entered the warm, bright hall, to be greeted by a babble of voices all asking questions.

Maud held up a hand. 'One at a time, please.'

The gathering fell silent to allow Magnus as laird and their host to ask the first question. 'Did you find him?'

From the hubbub that erupted again, this seemed to be the question all wanted answering, including the two police officers and the Fiscal.

'Everyone, please!' ordered Lord Urquhart. 'Give the ladies – these *detectives* – an opportunity to reply.' He stepped back.

'Thank you, my lord.' Maud looked round the room.

The fire burned comfortingly in the large hearth. Over the mantel, looking almost alive in the dancing light of the flames, was the portrait of a male ancestor of the Carmichaels. Ailsa sat calmly in a high-backed armchair, but everyone else in the room – host and guests, servants and officers – had turned expectant faces towards Maud and Daisy. The pair stood side by side on the large rug in front of the hearth and faced the assembly.

'Daisy,' Maud said suddenly, 'would you like to tell the story?'

Daisy sent her an *are you sure* look, but then didn't hesitate. 'I'll keep it short: there's a dead man on the roof.'

Once again voices filled the high-vaulted hall. Daisy certainly knew how to start a story, Maud thought with a small smile.

Daisy raised her voice and continued. 'The dead man, Dr Munro, is the murderer of Neil Tremain and Sergeant McNeish.' The gathering fell silent and Daisy went on with her tale. 'Ten years ago, Mr Tremain ran over and killed wee Clementina, the Munros' bairn.'

'For shame!' some of the servants called out. Everyone else stayed quiet, frozen in shock.

'It was an accident,' Daisy said, raising her voice, 'but that made little difference to the grieving parents. Mrs Munro took her own life.'

Jane paled. 'Oh, I had no idea.'

Isobel began to weep, lifting the corner of her apron to wipe her eyes. Mrs Baillie put a protective arm round her daughter.

Daisy looked to Maud, who signalled for her to continue.

'Dr Munro moved away from Glasgow, up here to Mull, where he hoped to forget such dreadful memories, but of course that wasn't really possible. When he learned Neil Tremain was to stay at the castle, he came up with his plan for revenge and put it into action.' Daisy turned to Maud. 'Your turn, Maud.'

Maud now addressed the assembly. 'Before he died, Dr Munro confirmed to the three of us that instead of the indigestion remedy, he administered an opiate to Mr Tremain. Mr Tremain had stated his intention to Andrew to lock his bedroom door that night, perhaps because he'd finally recognised the doctor and was afraid Munro might remember him and return.

But the drug began to take effect too quickly for him to be able to do that. Dr Munro returned later the same evening, removed the key from inside the room, locked the door from the outside and took the key away.

'The following morning, when there was no reply from Mr Tremain's room, the doctor forced open the door. He surreptitiously dropped the key on to the rug, so that it looked as though it had fallen to the floor when he burst open the door. It was easy to conceal that task as everyone's attention was taken by the unexpected drama in the room. He was able to puncture the heart of the drugged Mr Tremain under cover of making an initial assessment of the patient and asking for the shutters to be opened to let in the light.'

Andrew made a strangled cry in his throat. 'He used me!'

'In more ways than one,' Maud said, 'as the last person to see Neil Tremain alive would come immediately under suspicion. And the fact that you followed so closely on the doctor's heels in entering the bedroom was the perfect alibi for Munro. Finally, the doctor was able to delay the call for the police by making notes and ensure the body had time to cool a little.'

'Dr Munro, a killer,' Andrew said. 'Who would have thought that of a doctor?'

'There have been other doctors who were killers,' Maud pointed out. 'In the last fifty or so years, Britain has produced Drs Palmer, Pritchard, Lamson and Cream.'

'And Dr Crippen,' put in Mrs Baillie. 'Everyone's heard of him. He's famous. Murdered his wife, fled England on a ship with his mistress disguised as a boy and both of them caught with the help of wireless telegraphy.' She nodded with satisfaction. 'Hanged two years ago.'

'He is an interesting case,' agreed Maud, 'but I'm discounting Crippen because he was an American and he wasn't a qualified doctor.'

'You've told us how Dr Munro killed Mr Tremain,' called out Finlay, 'but what about poor Sandy McNeish?'

'Sandy was a spur-of-the-moment attack,' said Daisy. 'Dr Munro hadn't planned to do anything to him. But while Lord Urquhart, Maud, the doctor and myself were all in his room discussing the case, the sergeant said something about having a suspect in mind. Dr Munro panicked. He made sure he was the last one of the four of us to leave that room and stabbed the officer within seconds of our leaving.'

'And did Sandy know who the killer was?'

Maud cut in. 'I don't think he had proof, but he would have reached the right answer eventually, I'm sure.'

'And you say the doctor's body is on the roof?' put in Mr Greig.

'Aye,' said Daisy. 'He injected himself by accident with cyanide.'

The junior policeman frowned. 'What was he doing with that?'

Magnus found his voice again. 'Roderick Munro threatened us all with the poison, before escaping from the room shortly before you arrived.'

'He'd managed to go out through the wee door and onto the roof,' put in Daisy, 'which is where it happened.'

'In addition to the doctor on the roof, you will find the sergeant laid out in the barn,' Maud said, turning to the Procurator Fiscal. 'The puncture wound can be seen on his chest.'

The Fiscal cleared his throat. 'It seems we have to thank you two ladies.'

'Private detectives,' corrected Daisy.

Lord Urquhart strode over to the Fiscal and spoke softly in his ear. Mr Greig looked over to where Andrew stood with the rest of the servants. Their eyes met and the footman gave a nervous start before he darted towards the lobby door. Thank goodness *he* didn't intend to scale the rooftop, Maud thought with relief.

'Oh, no, you don't.' The senior policeman was after Andrew in a flash and grabbed him. 'Is this the culprit, your lordship?' he asked, restraining the struggling footman.

'Yes, Sergeant. It seems the SIS are looking for him.'

'SIS?' The policeman's eyes grew round. 'Secret Intelligence Service!' He pulled Andrew back to his feet and clipped handcuffs on his wrists.

Lord Urquhart eyed the footman. 'It would go better for you, Andrew, if you gave the names of your contacts. Have a think about it on your journey to the mainland.' He turned to the Procurator Fiscal. 'I will accompany you to the main door, Mr Greig.'

Lord Urquhart, Mr Greig and the two police officers, with their charge handcuffed between them, left the great hall. As soon as they had left, the room again erupted into loud chatter.

Magnus clapped his hands for attention. 'Luncheon served in fifteen minutes.'

As the servants hastened off to the kitchens, Magnus turned to Maud and Daisy. 'I'm sure you ladies would first like to wash and change into clean clothes. Hamish, too, when he returns. And then we can eat.'

'That would be braw.' Daisy beamed. 'All that exercise has fairly given me an appetite.'

No one really wanted any luncheon, apart from Daisy, but it had been prepared and Ailsa insisted they ate it, so Maud, Daisy and Lord Urquhart had returned to their respective rooms to wash and change. Maud had slipped out of her dirty and dishevelled pink blouse with its black and white striped tie into a white and blue linen dress and now felt clean and presentable as she sat next to Lord Urquhart at the dining table.

Maud fiddled nervously with her blue and white striped belt, the bow pointing forward; then she smiled and in a moment of mischievousness slid the bow at her waist round to face him.

He looked handsome in an ivory linen suit with waistcoat and a blue cravat. Daisy had exchanged her bedraggled outfit for a purple blouse and cream skirt with a row of purple buttons down the front, and she now sat across the table from them. Ailsa was seated in the chair at the end of the table, while the laird's chair waited for him to fill it.

Jane Tremain had left the castle to journey back to Edinburgh with the police officers, clearly in a hurry to be back in the bosom of her friends. Maud honestly hoped the young woman would find the rich man she wished for and that they would be happy together.

The sound of bagpipes droned from below, growing louder.

'Glory be,' Daisy murmured. 'Are we going to have that all through the meal?'

The door was thrown open and Finlay entered playing the pipes, with Magnus striding into the hall after him.

Ailsa smiled. '"Carmichael's Triumphant Return to Clachan Castle",' she told them fondly.

'I didna ken he'd been away,' Daisy muttered.

Maud raised an amused eyebrow at Daisy. 'I think it's the triumphant bit he wants to emphasise.'

Daisy lifted a quizzical eyebrow in return and mouthed *He's triumphant? I thought we'd solved the case.*

Finlay did one tour of the table with Magnus marching behind, then took the pipes and the tune with him out of the hall and back down the stairs to the kitchen.

The laird sat in his seat at the head of the table and gave a satisfied smile. 'All's well that ends well, I think.'

'We have Miss McIntyre and Miss Cameron to thank for that, brother,' Ailsa said.

'Indeed we have. Credit where credit's due, eh?' He beamed at Maud and Daisy. 'Of course, I never believed it was Miss Cameron who was the killer. It was a good ruse to put the real murderer off the scent, don't you think?'

'Aye, it worked really well,' Daisy muttered dryly.

Relieved of the pipes, Finlay, along with Isobel, appeared with mahogany trays piled with plates and dishes of foie gras terrine, toasted bread and apple chutney.

'We're a footman short at present, laird,' Finlay said, as he placed the food on the serving table standing against the wall, 'so I've got Isobel to help me for now.'

'We'll need to see about a replacement for Andrew.' Magnus opened his napkin and tucked the end into his collar. 'And Tobermory needs a new doctor.'

'Poor, dear Roderick,' said Ailsa. 'I knew he'd lost his wife and child, but nothing more. He didn't wish to speak of it and naturally I didn't press him.'

'At least he has been saved a public trial and the hangman's noose,' Maud pointed out.

'Yes, for that we must be grateful on his behalf.' Ailsa sighed.

'May I ask you a question, Miss Carmichael?' Maud said.

'Of course.'

'Why did you dislike Neil Tremain? I had thought that perhaps you knew, or guessed, at something in his past, but it seems not.'

Ailsa gave a rueful laugh. 'I disliked the man because he was impolite, bad-tempered and a complete bore. It was as simple as that.' She took a sip of wine. 'What made you first suspect the doctor, Miss McIntyre?'

'I confess it took us a while to realise the main suspect was Dr Munro. He had cleverly confused us all by stating that Mr Tremain had been dead for at least an hour or two. This was not strictly a lie, but it led to everyone assuming the murder had taken place before the doctor had arrived at the castle that morning. I finally realised the killer was Dr Munro thanks to something Miss Cameron had noticed.'

Maud looked at Daisy to elaborate.

'Aye, well, neither of us realised the importance of it at the time, but after Dr Munro had covered the face of Neil Tremain's dead body, I saw the bed sheet move a wee bit.'

Magnus lowered his piece of toast loaded with foie gras and chutney. 'To think that Neil was still breathing at that point.' He shook his head. 'My God.'

They fell silent, each with their own thoughts.

Maud glanced at Magnus seated at the end of the table. The light from the blaze in the hearth caught his face and she was struck by the resemblance to the portrait over the mantelpiece. The same beak-like nose, the same high forehead, even the same shock of white hair and long beard. Her glance moved to Ailsa at the other end of the table. Brother and sister, looking so alike and not just a little forlorn at how life had turned out for them. Neither had married or had children. It was the end of their line.

So sad, thought Maud, as she gazed up at the vaulted ceiling. A soft light shone through the high narrow windows of stained glass, sending a myriad of colours onto the stone walls.

'You're looking very thoughtful,' Lord Urquhart murmured.

'I was just thinking how life must go on.'

'No Sherlock Holmes quote?' He smiled.

Her lips twitched in response. 'Not at present, no.'

After a moment or two, he spoke again in a low voice. 'Miss McIntyre, I wonder if you would like to walk in the garden with me when luncheon is finished?'

For one awful moment, Maud thought Lord Urquhart was going to recite the opening lines of Tennyson's poem 'Maud', inviting her to come into the garden where he, the narrator, waits alone. Past suitors had thought it amusing or romantic to quote the beginning of that work to her. If they had bothered to read the entire poem, they would have found it a tale of suicide, murder and insanity. She had expected better of Lord Urquhart. Not that he was a suitor...

Her heart gave a small but unmistakable lurch. His suggestion sounded more like Lady Catherine de Bourgh's request to Elizabeth Bennet to take a turn in the garden with her... shortly before she warned Miss Bennet to keep away from her nephew, Mr Darcy. Was Lord Urquhart going to tell her she had assumed too much in addressing him by his Christian name? Surely he knew she'd simply spoken in the heat of the moment, afraid for his life?

But there was nothing *simple* about it. She was in love with Lord Urquhart. She had feared for his life more than her own. The fear that he might have died made her cast aside her self-deception. She gazed at his perfect profile. Perhaps it was not perfect, but to her it was. It was more than his profile that she found attractive; there was a clever mind there too.

He turned towards her and she realised she was still staring. Neither had she replied to his question.

'So, will you take a turn with me in the garden?'

'Why not?' she heard herself say. 'The weather seems to be improving.'

THIRTY-ONE

Maud and Lord Urquhart followed the long path that led away from the house and down towards the loch. The afternoon air was warm and scented. Pigeons cooed on the battlements.

'It seems a long time since we spent those pleasant few days together at Duddingston House,' he began softly.

He didn't look as self-assured as usual, Maud thought. His head was bare and his dark hair slightly tousled. 'Was the stay pleasant? I thought Daisy and I had a thief and murderer to catch.'

'Well, yes, there was that.'

They strolled on.

After a while, he spoke again. 'I must congratulate you on solving the Mull castle case – and not just the one I brought you here for.'

'Thank you. There is only one thing that still puzzles me. It's not important, but I am curious.'

'What is that?'

'On Saturday afternoon, not long before Sergeant McNeish was killed, Daisy and I were aware that someone was listening outside my room.'

He smiled. 'Was it when Miss Smart and Miss Graham were writing a crime novel?'

Maud flushed. 'It was you!'

'I'm sorry, but the story was so entertaining that I couldn't resist it. Will you forgive me?'

She felt she ought to be cross, but she wasn't. 'I will.' She smiled.

Lord Urquhart cleared his throat. 'Do you think you will ever have had enough of intrigue and danger to consider settling down?'

'I cannot say. What about you with your work with the SIS? Will *you* have ever had enough of intrigue and danger and wish to settle down?'

'Have you read *Spies of the Kaiser* by William Le Queux?'

She shook her head. 'No, but I have heard of it.'

'One of the stories in the book features German agents who obtain secret details of the dockyard at Rosyth. As it's a real installation on which work has only just started, the story is a little too close for comfort. The British government is concerned about Germany's naval power and is producing improved ships. You may have heard of the first of our new warships, HMS *Dreadnought*, with its superior speed and firepower? She was built in England, but the Admiralty has placed contracts for new warships with a number of Clyde shipyards. I fear a shadow is rolling over Europe, Miss McIntyre.'

Maud shivered. He was right – a shadow was approaching. She had read enough world news to know it for herself.

'Why are you telling me this?' she asked. 'I mean, I understand its importance to this country and to Europe, but not to the conversation we are having.'

'Only that I will continue my work for as long as the organisation wishes me to do so.'

'I see.'

'What do you see?'

'That we are both dedicated to doing the right thing, no matter the cost. You catching your villains, and I mine. Whatever Germany has in store, I will continue my work for as long as the agency needs me.'

They walked in silence again. She was only vaguely aware of the neat lawn and flowers around them, the shimmering water ahead. They were on the brink of something, but she was unsure what. 'Since a possible war is coming, aren't you glad you're not the marrying kind of man?' she found herself saying.

He looked surprised. 'What makes you say that?'

'Two reasons. The possibility of a war, of course, and the number of cases I have investigated that involved some sort of *trouble* in love.'

'If there is to be a war, then love and marriage are all the more important. As to your cases, what do you mean?'

She shrugged. 'The missing fiancée in Edinburgh, a kirk elder and his barmaid in Fort William, the death of Dr Munro's daughter and wife...' She hesitated for only a moment. 'Your indiscreet letters.'

He drew in a breath. 'And on the basis of the indiscreet letters, you think that I am not the marrying type?'

'It makes me think you don't much care about women and are too comfortable in your life to feel the need of a wife.'

After a while, he said, 'I am hard to please. So hard that I am willing to wait quite a long time for the wife I really want.'

Oh, thought Maud, he is talking about a real person. Perhaps, after all, it is Jane he wants. 'Suppose she wouldn't have you after all the waiting?'

'Then I shall have to remain unmarried.'

She gazed at him, trying to read his expression in the sunlight as it flickered between the trees. 'Who is it?' she asked in a small voice.

'Who is what?'

'Who is the lucky lady?'

He stopped, caught hold of her hand and turned her to face him. 'You don't know? The great detective and you don't know who has caught my heart?'

'Don't tease me. I know all too well that I'm still learning how to do the job.'

'Me tease you? How so, when you know that I'm going to ask you to marry me.'

Maud stepped back, her heart in her mouth. 'I do *not*. Why should I be expected to know?'

'Women are supposed to know these things, aren't they?' He stepped towards her and caught her hand again. His voice was throaty and a little shaky. 'Will you marry me, Miss Maud McIntyre?'

A strange dancing started in her heart. 'I don't know. Hamish, what are you doing?'

He had taken her in his arms and was looking at her soberly.

'Now,' she said, 'I suppose you will try to kiss me.'

He gave a slow smile. 'Would you like me to?'

He was so close that she could smell the clean soap on his skin. She met his gaze. Would she like him to? Even the birds held their breath in the gentle warmth of the afternoon.

At once she wanted him to kiss her. Her eyes lingered on his lips. 'I think I would.'

Slowly, he lowered his mouth to hers. His warm, tender lips were on hers and a flame burst within her. Her heart raced, her legs trembled. When they separated, the kiss left her wanting more. She slipped her hands to his face and drank in the light in his eyes.

He smiled down at her, laughter lines around his eyes suddenly deep in his handsome face. 'At last, my love. You have either scowled at me or—'

Maud blushed deeply – she, the founder and owner of a successful detective agency. 'Oh! But I am forgetting my position.'

'Your position?' He frowned, not understanding. 'As my wife you will be Lady Urquhart. Our children will be known as the Honourable—'

'Our children?' A delightful image came to her of small, rosy-cheeked children gathered round her knee, with Hamish looking smilingly on.

'You don't want children, Miss McIntyre? I thought an heir and a second boy and a few girls.'

'It isn't that... As far as I am aware, marriage is designed to reduce women to the status of mere chattels.'

He took her hands and drew her back to him. 'With us, it will be different, I promise.'

'It's tempting to believe that, but I have the agency to run. Daisy and I need another year or two to get the business established enough so that we can hire other staff.'

'Will this staff be exclusively women, or will you be employing a few men for when you need a strong arm or two?'

'We haven't got that far in our plans.'

'Well, you should start thinking about it. Our children will need to know their mother is safe when she's out sleuthing. You can still work if you wish to, you know, after we are married. There will be no shortage of servants, including a nanny or two for the children.'

She looked up at him. 'Nonetheless, you'd expect me to run the household and, while you're off spying for the government, your estate. Where exactly is it?'

'Strathbogle is in Inverness-shire – in Glen Urquhart, on the north side of the Great Glen.'

'That's a little far to be able to continue working at the M. McIntyre Agency. I suppose I could act as managing director,' Maud said, thinking aloud. 'And Daisy could take over its day-to-day running, if that suits her. She's shown how capable she is since we have been on Mull.'

'Good. *Now* will you marry me?'

'I feel a bit dazed...'

'You're meant to feel dazed. So do I. But you feel happy too, don't you?' He sounded anxious.

She smiled. 'Oh yes, *very* happy.' It was true. She didn't need to think about her answer. How was it possible that one person could make her heart feel lighter, positively giddy with happiness? 'I thought it was Jane that you wanted.'

'Miss Tremain? You thought that? She was never the object of my affections. You know, Maud, you have been a difficult lady to catch.' He smiled and tucked a stray lock of hair behind her ear.

'More difficult than spies?' she said teasingly. Could she really marry him? 'Hamish, I need to think this through.' An idea came to her. 'Let us go up on the roof – only on the level part, I have no desire to clamber over the slates again!'

They made their way together back into the castle, through the great hall where the log fire burned brightly, and up the stairs onto the roof. It was not late, not quite time for tea, but the sun was beginning its descent in the sky.

They stood on the battlements, seeing the lighthouse blink slowly, and across Tobermory a few houses were already lit like jewels to Maud's eye, smoke unfurling from chimneys. They could hear the roar of waves far below.

'So, Maud,' said Hamish, moving to stand behind her and sliding his arms around her waist, 'what is your answer?'

'You know perfectly well I'm going to say yes.' She couldn't hide the smile in her voice.

'I do not. Why should I be expected to know?' The laughter was clear in his voice.

She turned to face him. 'Well then, my answer is yes.'

He looked down at her. 'In my eyes you eclipse and predominate the whole of your sex.'

'Sherlock Holmes,' she exclaimed in delight. '*A Scandal in Bohemia.*'

He laughed, gathered her firmly and comfortingly in his arms and kissed her. He tasted deliciously of sunshine and mint and wine.

'I thought I'd find you two here,' said Daisy, coming up behind them. 'It's taken you both long enough.'

'We've only just come up.' Maud extricated herself from Hamish.

'I'm nae meaning that. I'm meaning the two of you have been dancing around each other since you first met. The wonder is it's taken you so long to realise you love each other, when it's been obvious to me for a wee while. When are you planning to get married, or is it too soon to mention that?'

'Daisy!'

'It's not too soon for me,' said Hamish.

'Well, the wedding won't be for a year or two.' Maud felt compelled to be sensible. 'The business is in its infancy and our name is yet to be made.'

'I dinna mind running the agency. In fact, I'd be awfa happy to.'

'I'm happy for you to take over, Daisy, but you'll be on your own if I leave.'

'I can think of a lass or two that I could train up. Take that Kirsty downstairs, for example. She's not suited to being a kitchen maid; too many brains for that job. She's plucky and quick-witted and maybe she'd jump at moving to Edinburgh and giving it a go. You don't need to hold back your nuptials for years just because of the agency.'

'Good.' Hamish's smile widened.

'You and I can get a likely lass trained up afore you wed, Maud. Maybe have two or three of them eventually.'

'Thank you, Daisy. I know the agency will be in safe hands.' Maud gave her friend a hug. 'I'll be available if you have a question or want help of any kind. Some places in Inverness now have telephones, and Hamish and I will have one installed as soon as the system reaches north of Loch Ness. Until then, you can write to me and come to stay—'

'Maud! Dinna worry.' Daisy held Maud back a little so that she could look at her. 'You will hear from me, and you will see me.'

'And I'm not planning to give up work entirely.'

'She's promised that she'll employ a couple of burly men' – Hamish winked at Daisy – 'to be there for both of you when I'm not.' He slipped an arm around Maud's waist.

Maud gave a slight frown. 'I didn't promise that.'

Daisy laughed. 'He's joking, Maud. He kens it would cramp our style. But then again, it might be useful to have a lad or two. Someone like that cheeky loon Mackenzie. I wonder if he'd be interested in coming to work for the agency?'

'The footman at Duddingston House?' asked Maud.

'Aye, the very same.' Daisy grinned.

Maud raised an eyebrow. 'Is this about hiring an employee or are you planning more for him, Daisy? He did seem to take a liking to you.'

'Michty me, Maud, I dinna ken. Only time will tell.'

A LETTER FROM LYDIA

Thank you so much for reading *Death in a Scottish Castle* and for keeping me company while Maud and Daisy investigated their cases throughout this series. I am sad that the adventures of The Scottish Ladies' Detective Agency may have come to an end. If you would like to keep up-to-date with my next cosy crime series, please sign up at the following link. Your email address will never be shared and you can unsubscribe at any time.

www.bookouture.com/lydia-travers

I appreciate the kindness of those who take the time to let me know they have enjoyed the pair's escapades. I would be very grateful if you could leave a short review to help other readers to discover my books.

Thank you for reading.

Love,

Lydia x

facebook.com/LindaTylerAuthorScotland

x.com/LindaTyler100

instagram.com/lindatylerauthorScotland

ACKNOWLEDGEMENTS

I am very grateful to all the readers and reviewers who have taken an interest in Maud and Daisy and their investigations.

Huge thanks to Julie Perkins, the very best writing buddy a person could wish for. And to Joan Cameron for keeping me supplied with ideas and marmalade.

I am also grateful to the following friends for their expert advice on various matters: Margaret Owen, Kirsty Ross, Sheila Gray, Deb Goodman, Vicki Singleton and Mary Atkinson.

A vote of admiration to David Bracegirdle, the real hero of the stag episode.

A vote of thanks to Helen McAlpine for making such a good job of narrating the audiobooks.

Thanks also go to the team at Bookouture.

Last, but not least, thank you to my local library for cheerfully providing me with books – and for being there.

Other influences on my writing have been the work of comic genius PG Wodehouse and of course the various detective stories beloved by Maud.

Some liberties may have been taken with travel to Mull in 1912. Today, there are a few ferry routes from the Scottish mainland to the island, but they do not include Lochaline to Tobermory, or Oban to Tobermory.

Any mistakes are my own.

PUBLISHING TEAM

Turning a manuscript into a book requires the efforts of many people. The publishing team at Bookouture would like to acknowledge everyone who contributed to this publication.

Audio
Alba Proko
Sinead O'Connor
Melissa Tran

Commercial
Lauren Morrissette
Hannah Richmond
Imogen Allport

Cover design
Debbie Clement

Data and analysis
Mark Alder
Mohamed Bussuri

Editorial
Jess Whitlum-Cooper
Imogen Allport

Made in the USA
Las Vegas, NV
09 August 2024

93518374R00177